SEEKERS OF THE UNKNOWN

M.A.T. REESON

*To the McLaughlin Family,
Thank you for all your kindness & support! Wishing you all the best,*

Black Rose Writing | Texas

© 2018 by M.A.T. Reeson
All rights reserved. No part of this book may be reproduced, stored in a retrieval system or transmitted in any form or by any means without the prior written permission of the publishers, except by a reviewer who may quote brief passages in a review to be printed in a newspaper, magazine or journal.

The final approval for this literary material is granted by the author.

First printing

This is a work of fiction. Names, characters, businesses, places, events and incidents are either the products of the author's imagination or used in a fictitious manner. Any resemblance to actual persons, living or dead, or actual events is purely coincidental.

ISBN: 978-1-68433-166-6
PUBLISHED BY BLACK ROSE WRITING
www.blackrosewriting.com

Printed in the United States of America
Suggested Retail Price (SRP) $19.95

Seekers of the Unknown is printed in Palatino Linotype

Dedicated to:

*Mom, Dad, and Peter, for all your endless support;
and to Mr. Hackel, for telling me to never stop writing.*

SEEKERS OF THE UNKNOWN

"If you cry because the sun has gone out of your life, your tears will prevent you from seeing the stars."

~Rabindranath Tagore

Prologue

Trepidation consumed Abeo. Standing atop a mighty cliff, he peered into the nebulous fog below. The prospect of descending into the unknown churned his gut. Looking up, he saw the night sky glimmering majestically. Swiftly moving wisps of clouds would intermittently obscure his vision, but the tranquility of the stars was enough to calm his nerves. He reached for the rope tied around his lean waist and checked the knot to confirm its vigour.

"I can go last, Tenax!" Abeo yelled through the blustering wind.

"I'm sure you can! Now get going before we're caught in this storm!" Tenax hollered back. Piles of blowing snow accumulated on his thick brow while icicles hung idly on his beard.

"You know he should be doing this," Abeo fumed, moving closer so Tenax could hear.

"I'm the most experienced climber. The captain was just delegating," Tenax replied.

"You're too easy on him, you know? He's much more selfish than you think."

"Don't be so cynical, Abeo. It's unbecoming of you," Tenax said with a grin. "Now get going!"

Abeo trudged towards the cliff's edge and lowered himself down the rocky face. Pushing off gently, he felt the chilling sensation of free falling twist his stomach in a knot. Suddenly, the rope became taut, and the feeling passed. He landed his feet again against the stone wall and continued his descent into the chilling depths. Below him, an orange figure began to materialize. He could see the bottom, so he anxiously hastened his pace. With one last push, he landed on the icy ground and felt a strong grasp catch him as he clumsily slipped.

"Not so bad, right?" a charming voice echoed in his ear.

"I hate that part," Abeo responded.

Foedus patted him on the shoulder and smiled back. "Storm's building. We need to find some shelter pretty quick. The others went ahead to find a spot."

"Big surprise, Christoph was too impatient to wait for his men," Abeo scoffed.

"Now, now, Abeo." Foedus scolded condescendingly.

"You know I just hate it when he-" Abeo's rant was suddenly interrupted by a violent gust of wind that was followed by a deafening sound. Tumbling down towards them, giant rocks fell clumsily from high peaks above. Among the clouds of snow, the plummeting rocks rained relentlessly on the rocky ridges.

"Run!" Foedus yelled as he grabbed Abeo's arm and jerked him away from the wall. Both men sprinted vigorously from the collapsing mound.

As they ran, Abeo looked back frantically and watched in horror as an orange figure fell helplessly among the mountainous debris. Tenax's flailing body quickly disappeared behind a pile of rubble.

"No!" Abeo yelled. He broke away from Foedus' grasp and sprinted back towards the cliff. As he swiftly climbed over a fragmented boulder, he saw Tenax lying on the rigid floor. The bone in his leg, jutting through his skin, was fragmented like a splintered tree branch. The injured man breathed rapidly and stared helplessly up towards the culprit of his affliction.

Abeo raced towards him and placed his hand under Tenax's head. "Can you hear me?" he asked.

Tenax groaned and nodded. "I'm okay; it's just my leg."

Abeo looked back at the injury and tried to hide his discomfort.

Foedus emerged from atop the rock and looked down in horror. "Goddammit. Tenax, are you alright?"

"He's okay," Abeo replied, "but we need to get ourselves into shelter. This storm is getting worse."

Abeo and Foedus picked up the wounded man and aided him as

he hobbled on one leg, grimacing in pain with every hop. Blood ran down his leg at will, pooling at his saturated sock. After much deliberation, they saw a soft red glow emanating through the fog. Like a siren, it drew them in, eventually revealing the entrance to a cavern. Inside, four men sat quietly around a crackling fire. One of the men stood up and angrily glared at them.

"Where have you been? What happened?" Christoph's right eye sporadically twitched as he yelled.

"Small avalanche. Tenax fell from the wall during his climb down," Foedus responded between breaths. He put Tenax down gently and watched as he collapsed from exhaustion.

"Abeo, get him some water," Christoph commanded. "Foedus, see what you can do about stabilizing that leg."

"Better get him some whiskey, too," Foedus whispered to Abeo.

Abeo raced to grab some water for his friend, and then watched as Christoph struggled to pin Tenax down. Abeo could not look away as the man violently squirmed in agonizing discomfort. Foedus worked feverishly, but the pool of blood seemed to be endless. After what felt like an eternity, Tenax finally lost enough energy to struggle back. Foedus finished stabilizing his leg and let his companion get some much-needed sleep.

***

After a long stretch of hiding in shelter, the aura of the group began to dwindle. Wind and snow blew relentlessly outside the cavern, forcing them to retreat farther into the dangerous depths of the dark. The men became nervous and restless. With their supplies beginning to diminish, Christoph started pressing for the group to continue. Tenax, who was in no condition to walk, maintained he was healthy enough to travel, but Abeo was apprehensive. From experience, he knew an injured man was nothing but a cumbersome strain on an exhausted crew. Despite his concerns, Christoph decided to take advantage of a lull in the storm and proceed with the expedition. Abeo and Foedus volunteered to carry the injured man, but Tenax vehemently rejected their assistance. Unfortunately, his inability to put weight on his leg made it a necessity.

At first, the climb was pedestrian enough that bearing the massive man was simply tiresome. But as the winds began to pick up, and the incline began to grow, Tenax became a burden. The group's pace significantly slowed; the blowing snow made it nearly impossible to see.

"We need to take shelter!" Abeo yelled through the storm.

Christoph turned around and gave Abeo a malicious glare.

"We have no choice, Captain," Foedus said exasperatedly. He lowered Tenax into a seated position and rubbed his own shoulders, enjoying the temporary relief.

Christoph paused and stared angrily at Foedus, but ultimately obliged. They again found shelter in a nearby cavern and waited anxiously for the storm to pass.

"How are you feeling?" Abeo asked Tenax, passing him a can of warm beans.

"Could be worse, my friend. Thank you for all your help, I know the burden I have been."

Abeo nodded at his companion. "We're all in this together, don't forget that."

"Of course we are!" Christoph yelled with a boisterous laugh, patting Abeo aggressively on the back. "Here, Tenax, drink this. It will help you rest." He passed Tenax a cup of warm water mixed with whiskey. "Abeo, can I talk to you for a moment?" the captain asked, motioning to the back of the cavern where Foedus was already waiting.

"Of course," Abeo responded nervously and followed Christoph.

"Abeo, Foedus and I have been talking. There's no way that we can continue to go forward with Tenax in his current condition. Even if the storm subsides, the climb ahead is far too steep for anyone with one healthy leg."

"Agreed. What do you suggest?" Abeo prodded. "Should we head back?"

"No, no," Christoph chortled. "That's not an option."

"Then what?" Abeo shot back.

"Abeo," Foedus interjected, attempting to calm his friend, "what if we left Tenax here with food and supplies? We could continue and grab him on our way back. It's what's probably easiest for everyone."

"What if we can't find our way back? What if he needs assistance? His condition has not been improving; he needs proper care. I can stay back if need be."

"No. I need every one of you. We're few as is," Christoph commanded.

"We need *you* out there, Abeo. We need your skills. We have no men to spare, you know this," Foedus pleaded with his friend.

"I don't like this option. We should at least ask the others."

"Fine," Christoph replied bluntly. "When they wake up, we can discuss it with them."

Abeo was thrown back by how quickly the captain bent to his suggestion but decided to go along with it.

"Get some rest. Both of you," Christoph commanded.

Abeo retired to his bed, curled up beside the fire, and turned his head towards the depths of the cavern. The light of the flames tickled the roof of the black tunnel in front of him. He focused his mind, stared intently into the center of the darkness, and began to think about his wife. He watched as her beautiful figure illuminated in his mind. Then, peering through the darkness, he saw brimming red eyes staring back at him. The image barely lasted for a moment, but it thoroughly seared itself into his memory.

Playing it off as a hallucination, Abeo closed his eyes and attempted to sleep, but his mind would not close down. Thoughts about the impending debate vexed his psyche. He knew Christoph would not allow him to stay with Tenax, but leaving a man by himself out in the unknown was a death sentence in and of itself. His only hope was to persuade Foedus to take his side. This, he knew, was unlikely.

Eventually, his mind quieted and his thoughts dissipated. He fell into a gentle sleep, all the while still picturing the haunting red eyes.

***

Abeo awoke before the rest of the group. The cavern was eerily quiet; all that could be heard was the gentle crackle of the fire. He cranked his spine to work out the knots that riddled his back. He had endured too many restless sleeps on rocky floors.

After cogitating the issue thoroughly, he thought it best to forewarn

Tenax about Christoph's suggested plan. He crept over towards the sleeping man, but as soon as he saw his wounded friend, he knew. No warmth emanated from Tenax's body; his dark figure lay motionless. Abeo rushed over towards Tenax and placed his fingers on his neck to look for a pulse. The sensation of his cold skin was enough to know that he was gone.

"How is this possible?" Abeo whispered to himself. He pulled the blanket off Tenax and looked at the bandage around his leg. There was no sign of infection; there was no leaking pool of blood. "Everyone! Wake up!" he yelled.

The others shot up out of their improvised beds and anxiously looked up at Abeo.

"Tenax is dead," he stated coldly.

"What? How?" Foedus yelled in disbelief.

"I was hoping someone could tell me," Abeo responded.

Foedus rushed over and looked at Tenax's limp body. He frantically unwrapped the wound looking for anything that might be a clue. "I don't understand," he mumbled dejectedly. "Perhaps he lost more blood than I thought. What do we do now?" he asked, looking mournfully at Christoph.

The captain paused and stared down at his dead crewman. "Wrap the body and leave it here. If we come back this way, we'll pick it up on our return."

"You can't be serious," Abeo retorted. "We should head back. The storm still hasn't subsided, and now we're fewer in numbers than we've ever been."

"We were going on with or without him. Wrap the body and leave it here," Christoph sternly commanded. He turned his gaze and locked his opaque eyes on Abeo. "Sometimes, you know, these things just work themselves out." A malevolent grin grew underneath his thick moustache.

No one said anything, but Abeo knew the truth.

M.A.T. REESON

BOOK 1
THE MEETING

1

Foedus drew gently from his hand-crafted pipe and felt the heat of its embers. Enjoying another long drag of the combusting herb, he inhaled until his body could no longer retain the smolder. Escaping his mouth, a translucent ball of green smoke wisped about like a cloud, soaring towards the crimson horizon. As he gazed upon the tangerine sky, the one that blanketed Crepusculum—the Twilight City—he wondered if people enjoyed such pleasures in other places, not just here on the planet Unum.

Cradling the pipe in his palm, he held it away from his body and allowed his lungs to inhale fresh air. Carved in brown letters near the base of the pipe was his family insignia and motto: "Enough Is Nothing." He scorned the lasting reminder of his mother.

Attempting to distract his mind, Foedus placed the pipe on the table nearest to him, wrapped his thick hands around the railing of the balcony, and glared out at towards the eastern edge of the city. Staring at the vista, the sky's complexion melted from a collage of yellow and orange to a bold crimson. Moving his gaze west, Foedus observed golden lights flickering idyllically against a rose backdrop. The sound of clopping hooves sporadically echoed as carriages shuttled up and down the cobblestone streets, while the pleasing smell of charred wood wafted into his nose.

Stretching his muscular arms, Foedus craned his neck and stared beyond the darkening city limits. There, he saw a desolate expanse of sand, snow, and sparse grass. The Barren Plains stretched for fifty leagues towards crashing waves of rock known as the Murky

Mountains. These towering mounds of stone remained a symbol of the limits of human existence. Few had ever ventured into the lands that lay beyond; there rarely was a need to do so. Yet, deep within this rocky labyrinth, Foedus made his living.

Admiring the cityscape, Foedus observed the heart of Crepusculum. Situated downtown, a collection of ivory stone buildings cast an everlasting shadow on the subordinate markets. In the shadow of the edifices, multitudes of merchants traded and bargained whatever they could scavenge. The streets, full of filth and scum, were a blemish below the inviting sky.

Dominating his view, one structure rose above all others in both height and width. A white stone citadel acted as the base for a prodigious spire that reached so high it grazed the clouds. The Watchtower of Crepusculum was home to the Carnifex — the Imperator's secret police. Their infamy had only grown over the preceding years.

Adjacent to the Watchtower sat a crumbling building. Its worn roof sagged helplessly, and its black stone was cracked and weathered. Well-maintained and intricately designed white buildings shrouded the dark construct. Long ago, this decrepit place had been a proud building, one that could induce confidence in any man who called it his occupational home. Now, most inhabitants were embarrassed to say they were members of such an eschewed organization; the same organization that Foedus was a leading member of.

Thinking about work, Foedus reminded himself that he was to report for a meeting. The assembly enveloped him with great curiosity and concern. After the last cold season, a letter arrived at his door informing him he had been summoned for a gathering of utmost importance. Deep down, he knew it meant he was off for another expedition into the dusk. The thought brought his chestnut eyes back to the ominous mountains. *Such mystery in that ocean of stone*, he thought.

Foedus remained fixated on the dark horizon until an arousing sensation broke his stupor. He felt her as she moved towards the open door. As she did, the sweet smell of vanilla radiated from her hair and hijacked his mind. Foedus turned to find a slender brunette looking back at him with her brimming gray irises. She had told him that she was from the Interior, but her carmine skin was a dead giveaway that she was a native of Crepusculum.

"You've been out here a while," she said seductively. "Won't you return to bed? I'm cold and lonely," she whispered, blinking her long lashes.

Foedus gave her an alluring smile and then looked at her sternly. "Meretrix, darling, unfortunately, our time together must end here. I have a few pressing appointments to attend to, and it would be most unwise of me to miss them."

"We will see each other soon, won't we?" she asked.

"Undoubtedly conceivable," he replied. He smiled as he buttoned up his cerulean shirt, reached for his coat, and swung it around his broad shoulders. Foedus had grown accustomed to the chilly temperatures of Crepusculum, but a jacket seemed like the right play seeing that the warm winds had ceased for the time being; it was still technically the cold season. He placed an elegant white hat upon his head and tipped it politely. "Help yourself to anything you like, and kindly be gone upon my return."

She seemed blind to his discourtesy. "Goodbye!" she exclaimed.

Foedus rushed down the stairs and exited out the same blood-red door that everyone in the neighbourhood seemed to have. As he stepped onto the chalky cobblestone of the city streets, an empty carriage rounded the corner, and he flagged it down.

"Where to?" asked the potbellied carriage driver. The malodorous man took a sip of the rancid wine in his flask and wiped his mouth of all the residual fluid. His haggard beard and overall stench were appalling.

"Domus Imperium," Foedus replied.

The driver spat at Foedus' feet. "Government man? I charge extra for yer kind." He beamed with the five teeth he had left.

Foedus scratched his charcoal hair in hesitation but decided to oblige to the man's demands. "If you must," he agreed.

The driver nodded, and Foedus climbed into the seat beside him.

With a quick whip, the cluster of horses pulling the cart trudged forward. The massive muscular animals, covered with ragged ebony fur, were blanketed in worn leather harnesses. As they picked up speed, their heads bobbed in unison, and their heavy hooves clopped against the stony road. One gave a heavy exhale, and the steam from its mouth rose into the air like a puff of white smoke.

"So yer a government man? Don't that just make you feel sick. Most people barely make enough money to eat. Meanwhile, you and yer buddies get to live in a place like that," the meaty driver nodded his head back at Foedus' massive brick home. The construct had two separate chimneys and three private balconies. It was one of the most opulent homes in all of Eastridge. "What is it that you do there anyway? Other than steal from people?"

"I work in a small unit," Foedus calmly replied.

"Which one?" the driver asked rather aggressively.

Foedus smiled. "Where are you from, uh, I never did catch your name now did I?"

"Name's Ebrius. And you can damn well mind yer own business as to where I'm from and do me the courtesy of answering *my* questions."

"Well, Ebrius, seeing as you seem to have an apparent distaste for the Imperium, I find it in my best interest to keep that information confidential. As for your side of this equation, given your current knowledge for some of the things our government has done to traitors, and given that I may just be a member of the particular unit responsible for policing such matters, it would probably be in your best interest to keep as quiet as you possibly could so that I can enjoy the rest of this distasteful, yet mandatory, carriage ride in some relative peace. Does that sound agreeable?"

Ebrius stared blankly back at Foedus and nodded his head gently. He took another sloppy swig from his flask and steered the carriages towards their destination. After an eternity of stench and silence, Ebrius finally stopped the carriage in front of a large building. Standing before them, a daunting staircase rose steeply towards an imposing white palace; its giant columns supported an intricate roof festooned with flowers and banners. Further up, a second flight of pearl steps climbed towards two marble doors that were decorated with gleaming gold handles. The Imperium, in all its abundance, loved to spend on itself.

Generally, people roamed this area like herds of animals flocking towards the feed, but the frigid temperatures had kept Crepusculum's citizens indoors. Foedus looked to the west and saw the star Glacies lingering slightly above the peaks of the Murky Mountains. The cold season was nearly at an end.

"Here," Foedus handed Ebrius some money.

Ebrius snatched it from his hands and worriedly looked back at him. "Are you really a Carnifex?" he asked nervously.

Foedus saw the heat emanating off the man's forehead. He grinned and adjusted his hat. "No, don't sweat it." He smiled and nodded at Ebrius.

The carriage driver wiped his moist forehead and observed the layer of liquid on his open palm. "You're not a… you know? Are you?"

"Don't let that wine play tricks on you, Ebrius. It's quite chilly out here." He tipped his hat and walked down the street towards his deteriorating office.

Ebrius wiped his forehead and stared in amazement. "They do exist," he whispered to himself. For the first time in his life, he had met a real Seeker of the Unknown.

2

Walking under the apricot sky, Christoph approached his crumbling office. He removed a silver key from his pocket and inserted it into a rusty brass lock. The key resisted its insertion, forcing him to lean into it. He cranked the creaky lock and pushed open the heavy door. Gazing into the dark room ahead of him, he lit the lamp in his hand and squinted his square eyes. The familiar smell of weathered stone and burning gas induced in him a nostalgic feeling.

As he entered the building, the illumination of the lamp materialized his tall shadow on the opposite wall. He sauntered into the room and raised the light directly in front of his face. Turning his head slightly, he saw another lamp hanging on the wall. A few feet farther down were others. Christoph lit each flame in order until the entire hall showered in a dull ambient glow.

Directing his attention to the center of the room, a long wooden table, its burgundy finish chiseled and worn, stretched the length of the hall. Alone in the dingy chamber, the weathered counter stood steadily upon its sturdy legs. White chairs composed of twisting metal lined the perimeter, while an assortment of hand-crafted goblets sat orderly in front of each seat. Below each goblet, small engravings populated the table's edge; some were severely faded, others freshly sculpted. They were the names of all the Seekers who had ever sat in that hall. At the head of the table, covered in black leather, sat a large wooden throne. In front of it was where Christoph's name was etched.

Christoph, the Lord Admiral of the Seekers of the Unknown, adjusted his brown coat and brushed his fingers through his jet-black hair. He stared wistfully at the gloomy glow of the hanging lamps. In truth, despite being a Seeker for so many years, Christoph never truly felt comfortable in the dark. Being a member of the Seekers had always been a riveting experience, but lately it seemed to bring with it progressively fewer accolades. Once a highly revered position, the title of Lord Admiral had become synonymous with disappointment. Still, Christoph enjoyed his work. He considered himself a strong leader and a tenacious motivator. Now, after years of death-defying expeditions, he could finally make commands from the safety of the Imperium. He knew he would miss the thrills, but the time to settle down had arrived.

Over the preceding generations, the Seekers endured a multitude of challenges. Christoph had witnessed several of his friends retire or pass away. To make matters worse, progressively fewer Discipuli—or protégés—had emerged to replenish their dwindling ranks. Most importantly, the numerous unremarkable expeditions of late had only enhanced the Imperator's lack of patience; Christoph could feel the mounting pressure. Sure, the public still admired the Seekers, but their reverence was mainly attributed to their mysterious status—no one really knew if true Seekers even existed anymore. To Christoph, it was apparent that change sat impatiently on the horizon.

The admiral walked up a spiral staircase and approached the small office sitting on the second floor. He pushed open a dilapidated door and walked into his refuge. Christoph loved to be at the office. The thrill of success had done more for him in life than any person ever had. Truthfully, he had a morbid resentment for most people. Even those that he did like were mainly there to prevent solitary-induced insanity. He saw nothing but negative things in others, yet somehow found ways to exude an aura of confidence in those around him. Why? Because it immediately benefited him; their success was his success.

Stroking his salt and pepper moustache, he stared at the dirty mirror standing in the corner of the room. He looked on in disbelief at his leathery skin. *How had time condensed so suddenly?* he wondered. It was as though the more he scrambled to prolong the movement of time, the faster it passed him by.

Breaking away from his stupor, Christoph gazed over to his desk. Sitting on top of the table was a file as thick as his hand. He pinched the corner of the folder and teased the cover open. On top of the document was a note he had gone over a hundred times. In fine print, it read:

Seekers of the Unknown,
A large task lies ahead of you. Out of necessity of the people who reside in our beloved capital, Asticus Lux, this mission has been deemed urgent, crucial, and mandatory.
No Seeker exempt.
Sincerely,
The Office of the Imperator

The news actually excited him, and the men were in need of adventure. For them, expeditions still stimulated the same feeling that used to boil his blood and vitalize his mind. The challenge of really needing to use your skills and having to understand what your mind is interpreting for you; he could think of no greater thrill.

As he thought about the men, he wondered how long it would be until everyone arrived and in what order they would do so. Undoubtedly, Foedus would show up first. Christoph often despised how dangerously his second-in-command did things, but Foedus had always been his favourite; he was the one man Christoph could rely on no matter what the circumstances. No doubt, Cordatus and Petram would arrive together. The student and the teacher were never too far apart. More than anything, Christoph was eager to meet the two Discipuli that Turpis had recruited. The last few rookies had not worked out. There were whispers that no real Seekers even existed anymore.

Finally, there was Abeo. The first officer walked half the length of the city to get downtown when all around him carriage drivers begged for the opportunity to take his money. Christoph's renegade subservient had a propensity to make everything difficult for him. The admiral grinned, "quite the eclectic team I've got, now isn't it?" he proclaimed to himself.

His fingers pushed the letter past the threshold of being turned, and he gazed down at the what lay beneath. Observing the page, Christoph looked at a map of Solis Imperium covered in notes and drawings. On the eastern edge of the parchment, he saw the Fire Desert. Nearest to this scorching inferno was the small and proud city of Lucidus. Its clay houses baked in the relentless radiation of Stella, their beaming red sun.

To the southwest, square in the middle of the Imperium, was Lux, the capital. It was there that the Palatium Imperium—the baroque palace of the Imperator—stood. Christoph had been to this magnificent building many times, but its splendour never failed to amaze him. Surrounding Lux, an emerald lake—known as the Lake of Life—cradled the urban center. Stemming from this vast body of water, three winding rivers stretched west, south, and northwest. During the warm season, melted glacial runoff injected fresh water into the terrestrial arteries, quenching the people of the Interior. Once, Christoph had laid eyes on the fantastical frigid floes responsible for the periodic torrent. The image had seared itself deep into his memory bank. If there was one thing to be said about the expeditions, it was that they never failed to provide visual magnificence.

Continuing to study the map, Christoph noted a southward road that meandered towards the wild jungles of the Cirfa—a colony of the Imperium. There, the Imperium had found archaic people living in straw huts. These barbarians were invaluable because they were effective at extracting coveted resources buried deep within the dense jungles. Penumbra, the city nearest to Cirfa, substantially benefited from this discovery. The old town nearly tripled in size from prospectors and entrepreneurs saturating the market.

Christoph's gaze followed a particularly sinuous river and made its way to the western edge of the map. A winding road snaked along the river's boundless perimeter and followed a westward path towards Crepusculum. Colloquially known as Rebellion Road, the trail had seen prouder days. Its ferric cobblestone had faded into dirty white, cracking and crumbling under the weight of the numerous travelers who once sought refuge in the Twilight City. Crepusculum, at least to Christoph, was a dump. Sure, the sky was beautiful and the landscape picturesque, but the joy of perennial light was too much to overcome. Perhaps in time it would become more to his liking, but the more time he spent there, the worse he felt.

Continuing to flip through the file, Christoph scanned the pages. He had read through them too many times to count; still, he felt compelled to scroll through them again. Exhaling to expel any tension in his body, he stared out at the foreboding Murky Mountains. Then, the sound of the front door vibrating against the concrete floor grasped his attention. Someone had arrived.

"Who's there, dare I ask?" he yelled down.

"You would be this impolite and not even attempt to welcome me at the door; even for a regular such as myself?" a charming voice echoed within the hall. "Furthermore, you were candid enough to ask, rather rudely, for my immediate identity before any formal salutation. What kind of establishment are you running here, sir?"

Christoph grinned exclusively on one side so that his eye was squinted shut by his rising cheek. As he descended the spiral staircase, he entered the hall and saw Foedus standing in the doorway, looking as healthy as ever. "You're a predictable man, you know that?"

"Perhaps, but in such a way that it is unpredictable as to how predictable I decide to be. Making me unpredictably predictable. You see?"

"Yes," Christoph stated bluntly; in truth, he did not. "Have you seen Abeo recently?"

"A while back I stopped in to see him."

"How was he?"

"He was his old self for the most part, but at times he appeared to slip in and out of complete consciousness. He told me he was listening, and maybe he genuinely was, but his mind was not in that room. Where it was, I couldn't say."

Christoph stroked his moustache again and looked back at the suave man in front of him. "I hope you're ready for this one because it won't be easy. No, it won't."

"I just do the job that's put in front of me," Foedus said with a grin.

"As you always have," the admiral replied with a sheepish smile.

Foedus took off his hat and stared into the inside of it, contemplating the results of an internal debate. "What do they think we're going to find there? Is there some hidden treasure we don't know about?"

"There are no answers to the questions you ask. They expect us to find everything and nothing. Our task is simply to confirm their suspicions," Christoph asserted.

"Why the sudden intoxicating interest?"

The admiral looked back at the file situated in his hand and then back up at Foedus. He passed the document over to his second-in-command and allowed him to peruse through the confidential report. "There are things in that file I cannot explain," he said earnestly.

Foedus opened the front cover and flipped through the pages. As he read, his eyes widened, and his mouth hung ajar. "Was he actually right?" he asked.

"It would seem so."

3

"I don't know, Cordatus. There has to be something pretty big for Christoph to call us all in. Last time he sent us out there we almost cleared the Murky Mountains. You know, if we had attempted to cross the god-damn lake I doubt any of us are sitting here right now." Petram grabbed his glass and drew the refreshing ale to his lips. He wiped his mouth and pointed at the elderly gentleman sitting across the table. "I know you know something. You and Abeo are always conjuring up some theory. When was the last time you saw him, anyway?"

Cordatus went to open his mouth but was interrupted by a beefy gentleman wearing a thick beard. His ebony skin dripped with sweat and his breath reeked of liquor. "Abeo has lost his mind," he slurred. Running his hands through his curly hair, the giant man fixated his piercing eyes on Cordatus. "The man was always too softhearted. But after his wife died, a damn shame seeing as she was a beautiful woman, he just crumbled."

"Abeo isn't weak, you idiot. He's simply deep within his mind. It's something we all wish we could achieve more often," Petram retorted.

"Next time we're in a bind out there, ask yourself if you would really want to put your life in the hands of Abeo, Pet." The towering man spat while staring down at his shorter, yet equally broad, counterpart.

Petram hated when anyone used his abbreviated name but decided to let it slide. "You know, Turpis, when we went deep into the dark, and I mean as deep as we went last time, our senses failed us at times. All of us." Petram looked over at the elderly man, hoping he'd interject. Instead, Cordatus gently nodded, encouraging Petram to continue.

"The vulnerability is enough to make your legs give out below you," he continued. "But Abeo never seems has any problems in the dark. I mean, the man is from Crepusculum. He belongs out there. You're just jealous of his strength of mind."

Turpis grinned and wiped his forehead of the perpetual sweat raining off it. He took a swig from his glass and exhaled in ecstasy. "I'm not like you, Pet. I don't get scared and I sure as shit am not jealous of the weakest link. But hey, next time you feel 'vulnerable,' I'm sure that self-indulgent piece of trash will be right there for you. Once he's gone, we'll all be better off!" Turpis slammed his fist down on the table and aggressively leaned over Petram.

Petram's complexion transformed into an even deeper shade of red. He scratched the stubble on his neck, smirked, calmly took a sip of his drink, and then looked back up at Turpis. In a flash, he shot up out of his chair and situated himself in an inimical position. Moving his face closer to Turpis', he grinned antagonistically.

"Settle down now, gentlemen," Cordatus coolly suggested. He raised his arm and leisurely lowered it as if easing it into a hot bath.

Turpis backed away slowly but continued to pierce Petram with his nebulous eyes. "If we're really going that far back again," he whispered, "I hope you know that when he cries for help, it'll fall on deaf ears." He stumbled backward and returned to the table where had been sitting before the interruption.

Patiently awaiting Turpis' return, two young men sat obediently at his table and sipped on their ales. One of them confidently held his beverage while he surveyed the room, likely looking for a prospective bed-warmer. The muscles of under his dark skin were well defined, as were the veins in his hands and wrist; his thick black hair, parted perfectly to the side, exposed his prominent brow. Sitting beneath his pretentious smile was a chin that resembled the stern of a boat.

In contrast, sitting beside the confident man, was a timid adolescent. The boy was thin and tall, which made his body seem like a fair wind would blow him over, and his chestnut hair looked as if it had never been tended to before. The boy sipped on his ale and stared intently into the glass, looking both puzzled and intrigued.

"I swear he's getting harder and harder to tolerate. He wasn't this much of an ass before, was he?" Petram asked the old man.

Cordatus stroked his thick beard gently and looked back at his young friend. "There's an anger inside of Turpis that blocks his pathways. He doesn't see as well as he used to."

"What is your honest opinion of Abeo? Do you think his mind is going?"

"No, it's stronger than ever as far as I can tell. He just needs to be out there; he belongs out there. When he's here, I believe it does something to his mind. Cura used to calm him in ways that distracted his head, but since her passing, he has suffered dearly."

Petram looked over his shoulder at the table where Turpis sat. "Who're the kids?" he asked, nodding his head in their general direction.

"Discipuli. Supposedly very skilled for their age. Rare find these days. Most who have any inkling of mind wouldn't make it past Prima Mons. This one," he pointed at the muscular young man, "is from Lucidus." Cordatus noted. "He appears to share a personality with Foedus. He has that ominous charm."

"I've never heard you describe Foedus as ominous before. Sure, he's tough when he needs to be, but I'd be hard-pressed to see any malice in the man."

"I did not imply malice with my statement. I just believe Foedus' charm is masking something. It is a part of him now, but I know that charisma is an act to conceal an insecurity."

"I guess I could see it. I just couldn't guess the cause of it," Petram said while staring down at his empty glass. "I'm going to grab a refill. Maybe I'll introduce myself and get a feel for the guy. Do you want one more?"

Cordatus nodded his head and smiled.

Petram pushed himself away from the table and walked over to the others.

"Going up for a refill, everyone good?" he asked.

Turpis waved nonchalantly, indicating he heard Petram but that he was not going to give him the respect of responding. This angered

Petram, but he bit his tongue and turned to the other men at the table. "Gentlemen?" he probed.

The muscular young man smiled. He had fair skin and searing dark brown eyes; his youth was unmistakable compared the company he kept. He smiled and put up a flat hand. "I could use a refill," he replied assuredly.

"Damn right you could," Petram responded. "I'm Petram, by the way. Welcome to the club, I hear you've got quite the talent."

"You heard right," he stated proudly.

"Kid's a prodigy," Turpis grumbled. His head lazily drifted towards the table.

"What's wrong, Turpy? That rye starting to hit you?" Petram asked condescendingly.

"Nah, I'm good," he grumbled as he placed his head in his hands.

Petram laughed and turned back to the kid. "So, generally the polite thing to do when someone introduces themselves is to reciprocate."

"Sorry," he chuckled. "I'm Proditor, but call me Prod."

Petram shook his hand firmly and stared at him for what seemed like a minute. Finally, he let go and picked up Prod's empty glass. He turned to the feeble looking boy who sat adjacent to Turpis. "What about you, kid, what's your name?"

It seemed to take the young man a moment to realize that Petram was talking to him. He coughed a few times and cleared his throat. "Veritas," he replied softly.

Petram eyed the young man inquisitively. There was something odd about him, but he couldn't put his finger on it. He studied his face intently. Just then, Veritas looked up slowly. Petram gaped in awe. Veritas' eyes were dazzling purple around the outside, but soft blue towards the pupil. Orange specks intermittently sprinkled the inside of the swirling collage of colours concealed within his irises. "I've never seen eyes…like, uh, like that," he stammered.

"Oh, uh, yeah," Veritas replied embarrassed. He lowered his head and averted Petram's gawk.

Petram cleared his throat and looked back at Turpis' big head buried in his hands. "Do you need another drink, Veritas?" he asked.

"No, thanks," Veritas whispered in response, returning his gaze to the bottom of his glass.

Petram headed towards the bar and asked for three ales. He leaned against the wooden island and surveilled the room. Directly in front of him, four boisterous people attempted to make their point known above the others' by yelling as loud as possible. To their right, an inebriated man awkwardly corralled his imposing arm around the shoulders of a sufficiently annoyed young woman. Petram couldn't help but snicker at his imposing awkwardness.

He turned around to glimpse back at Turpis' table and saw the big man's face firmly planted on the sticky surface. Farther back, Petram looked to find Cordatus, only to notice that the old man was no longer there.

"What's taking so long?" a brittle voice inquired behind him. He swirled around and saw Cordatus with three glasses of ale in his hands and a sanguine smile drawn across his weathered face.

"You still have the stealth, old man," Petram praised as he took the beers from Cordatus' hands.

Cordatus smiled. "Drink quickly. We must leave for the meeting soon."

Petram tipped his glass at Cordatus and inhaled half the beer. "I wonder how upset Christoph will be when Turpis shows up to the meeting half alive?"

"I suppose we'll find out," Cordatus responded with a smirk.

They started walking back to the table before Petram stopped and turned to face the old man. "Hey, random question, but have you ever seen someone with blue eyes before?"

"Once," he said. "On the face of a child."

"Whose?" Petram probed inquisitively.

"Abeo's."

4

The courtyard was a garden of chalky stone and imposing weeds, its entire perimeter lined by a dilapidated stone wall. Encased in the wall, a white metal gate stood as the final barrier between the rocky lawn and the grassy clearing on the other side. Vines grew chaotically around the bars of the gate, suffocating the metallic grid.

Adjacent to the gate stood a paltry home. Its dark windows were covered with milky-white bars while shingles rested unsteadily upon its sodden roof. Green paint flaked like skin after a burn, and the house creaked as if to bemoan its own existence.

The only redeeming piece of the shanty was the beautiful tree that inhabited the courtyard. The tree's base ruptured through the rocky floor, extending its canopy high above the chalky landing. A collage of blue leaves eclipsed its golden trunk, while hues of lavender trickled gently from the violet flowers that poked their heads out of foliage.

Under the canopy, Abeo stared aimlessly upwards into the aphotic verdure. His somber eyes admired the tree's intricacies; he studied the complexity of the branching patterns and the shape of the individual leaves. Tasting the cold air, he rested his head on the worn wooden bench upon which he sat. His heavy eyelids slipped close, and he exhaled a deep breath. It was in times of complete silence that he could still feel her presence.

Abeo placed his hands upon the tips of his sharp knees and gazed into the back of his mind. At first, there was just darkness, but as his breathing slowed, he felt his mind activate. "Speak to me, Cura," he murmured. Then, her gentle touch was suddenly upon him. He felt compassionate fingers grazing his thin shoulders, while her soft breath showered his neck with an unmistakable warmth. The scent of oceanic breeze rained from her hair, and she softly whispered in his ear. "Where have you been, my love?"

"Studying the sky," he murmured back.

"I wish I could understand the way you do. I wish I could look at something that doesn't change and always see something different. How do you find variation in stagnation?"

"Nothing is stagnant. Motion is a property of life." Abeo stated calmly. He stared back at his wife. "The sky moves Cura, I'm sure of it."

Cura smiled and crossed her arms. "How can you tell?"

"The colours have changed along the horizon. It's subtle, but it's there."

She looked back at him with the same satisfied smirk that was permanently painted on her face. "So, is this what this meeting is about, or is this something that you've come up with on your own?"

"Good question," he said abruptly. "If I see it, then there's no way Cordatus hasn't. Even if he has, that doesn't necessarily mean he'll say anything. Plus, no one even knows what that suggests. I mean, really, how could they? Maybe my skills are weakened, I don't know. I still feel that change is there, though, I just-"

"Stop," Cura gently interrupted. She placed her ebony hand on his faded cheek and smiled. "Stop chasing your mind; you will tie your circuits in knots."

He smiled and brushed her hair behind her ears. "If we have to go back, I may be gone awhile. They wouldn't call the whole company if it wasn't important."

"I know," she lamented.

He cupped her soft cheeks in his hand. It was amazing how just her stare could infuse intimacy into his body. His gaze carried him towards the charcoal centers of her eyes until he was enveloped by total darkness. Then, with a sudden jerk, he awoke under the cherry sky. Alone.

Abeo wiped his eyes, performed a few exaggerated blinks, and walked towards the gate at the edge of the courtyard. Wrapping his hands around the metal frame, he allowed his forehead to slowly drift towards the cool metal. Resting his head for a moment, he raised it and admired the endless expanse before him. He had always enjoyed living on the western edge of Crepusculum; it was much more serene on the dark side of the city, and he wanted to be as far away from the bustle as possible. Abeo dreaded socializing with others. He hated indulging in the superficial facade—a requirement for membership in the realm of normalcy. The quiet life suited him better.

Staring across the Barren Plains, he admired the magnificent Murky Mountains and the twinkling stars that lingered above them. It reminded him of the cosmic beauty reserved for the other side. For him, and him alone, the expeditions had become increasingly therapeutic.

After another moment of solitude, Abeo paced around the courtyard. He placed his hands near the base of his spine and massaged his back in an effort to alleviate the soreness that relentlessly vexed him. Staring off to the west, he observed the fractal details on the mountains. To him, every admiring observation seemed to be met with an increased appreciation for nature's complexity. Once, all he could see were the daunting silhouettes of the rocky giants. Now, he could feel the cold stone just by looking at it.

Making his way back to the colourful tree, he put his hand on the stem and felt the energy inside. All he could think of was Cura and the purity she radiated. He reminisced about the last time that he laid eyes on her; it was the last time a meeting had been called. Out in to the darkness he had gone, not knowing he would never again get to stare into her mesmeric gaze.

Abeo sighed, walked out the back gate, and began his lengthy stroll to work. Trudging through the open plain, he eventually reached the border between nature and infrastructure. The cobblestone street was slick under his feet, and he watched as the drizzling rain streamed down the street. Thick grey clouds soared above the Twilight City, moving quickly across the crimson sky. He wiped the refreshing condensation off his forehead and swept his wet hand against the back of his pants. The humidity always seemed to affect him more than it did anyone else.

As he continued down the sodden sidewalk, he focused on the sound of moist stone cracking under his feet. Adjacent to his path, black metal cylinders speared out from the path's shoulder, demarcating the city's limits. Walking along the border had always been a ceremonial journey for Abeo. He enjoyed the fresh air and silence; they allowed him to be more within his thoughts. The announcement of a full-fledged meeting excited him. Maybe it was finally time that his questions were answered. Surely, some of the more astute Seekers had noticed the changes, too.

It then dawned on him that he had not seen the others in ages. *I would bet anything that Turpis has gotten fat*, he laughed to himself. Turpis had already been close to acquiring his own gravitational pull the last time Abeo had seen him. The two quarreled over almost everything; he had very little desire to see the man again.

The sole person he did maintain contact with was Foedus. His relationship with the captain had severely declined over the preceding seasons. He wished the opposite were true, but the passing of Cura had caused Abeo to shut himself out from his friends. Foedus had stopped by to check on him awhile back, but the confrontation was awkward at best. Abeo sighed in disappointment at how far he had let things crumble around him. The seemingly endless depression mounted like an insurmountable debt. It had lingered for so long that he had become accustomed to its pain. It was almost as if he was beginning to enjoy the hardship, the sorrow, and the darkness.

Peeking over his shoulder to ensure no carriages were flying down the street, Abeo crossed the sodden road in a hurried gait and made his way down a wide boulevard. Modest homes and shops lined the roadway. The farther Abeo voyaged down the road the larger the buildings became. Elegant trees, complete with silver and gold leaves, lined the median dividing the boulevard.

As he began to approach the Restaurant District, he noticed a familiar elderly woman sitting at a table outside a small café. Her stringy grey hair and gentle smile were unmistakable. She was shorter than average, and her skin was faded red. She sipped a steaming dark liquid out of a pearl cup and stared at him with her brimming eyes.

"A little late for you isn't it, Gene?" Abeo asked.

"Couldn't pass up an opportunity to see the legendary Abeo. So wise and so brave, spending his time fortified in his home." She smiled and took another sip of her drink.

"How did you know I would be passing by, may I ask?"

"Just so happens that your good friend Foedus stopped by here recently. He told me that there was some exceedingly important meeting that's supposed to be right around this time. So I thought to myself, an aunt can't pass up an opportunity to see her only nephew, now can she?"

"I suppose not," he smiled and gave her a warm hug. "I'm sorry I have not been around much; I've just been-"

"Don't," she interrupted, putting her finger onto his lips. "I know how it is to lose someone, too. You don't have to explain it to me. What you do need to start doing is pulling yourself together. No more of this sitting at home dwelling on the way life has poured hardship on your shoulders. You know I am sorry for your losses, but you have other, more important, things to accomplish. This meeting, I know it's not going to be for an insignificant reason. The things you said to me before, about the sky, do you think it could have to do with this?"

"Could be." Abeo wiped the fresh rain off his forehead. He stared at his endearing aunt with compassion. Gene had always been a pillar of strength in his life. Without her, he may have never been able to reach his true potential as a Seeker.

"So that's all you're going to give me, is it?" she asked, seemingly unsurprised.

"It is all I know thus far, Gene. If I felt I could tell you more, I promise you I would."

"You don't need to make promises to me, dear. You just need to take care of yourself out there. You need to make me feel that I may lay my eyes upon you again and know you're safe." She wiped a tear from the corner of her eye.

"You need to stop trying to take the world in your hands. Of course, I will do what I can to survive; it is in our nature to endure. You can't predict what may or may not happen at any one time. Whether it is out there or right here on this street, death comes to all of us, and when it does, the best thing we can do is greet it graciously."

"Of course I know that. Sometimes all a mother needs are reassurances, no matter how futile their legitimacy may be."

"You are not my mother, Genetrix."

"I am your mother's sister, and when she passed, I assumed the responsibility of taking care of you. She asked me to do it, which means that I am going to do it until I no longer can. You can accept it, or you can deny it, but either way, it is happening."

Abeo exhaled and gave her a warm smile. He placed his thin hands against her wrinkled cheek and stroked her hair behind her protruding ear. "I would be nowhere in this world without you. You have made me everything that I am and more. But at some point, you need to let go of the delusion that you can just control my destiny. Time is on a set path that can't be stopped. My future has been sealed somewhere on this planar continuum, and not you, nor the love you bear for me, can stop that."

"I will never stop trying, my boy." She cracked a smile and let a tear drop from her hazel eye. "You were meant to be out there; all of our family was. Something about the darkness draws us in. There is beauty out there, Abeo. The light that shines against the encompassing dark will always be more distinct."

Abeo wrapped his arms around the petit woman and kissed the top of her head gently. "If I do not return, thank you for your never-ending guidance and virtue. You will be the light that guides me in the dark."

Gene wiped her face on her sleeve and kissed his cheek. She patted his shoulder and stared into his eyes. "Goodbye, Abeo. Find your sanctuary."

He nodded and smiled.

Gene turned and walked back into the café, carrying the weight of time and uncertainty on her fragile shoulders.

Once she disappeared, Abeo continued to make his way down the boulevard. Not long after, he entered the Market District. Everywhere he looked, tents were set up in groups of four or five. They lined the alleys like plaque in an artery. Homeless men and women yelled at the privileged pedestrians, petitioning for charity. Advertisements for fruit, bread, cheese, wine, blankets, coats, and shoes echoed throughout the streets. People stumbled around in haggard clothing, begging for food and money. Abeo kept his head towards the ground and continued to make his way into the Government District.

Down the road, he saw the large pillars of Domus Imperium. Its white marble steps encompassed the entire block. Despite its faults, the Imperium knew how to design masterful edifices. The lavish palace was captivatingly beautiful.

Abeo diverged into an alley just a block away from Domus Imperium. He crept down the dark path, careful not to wake those who slept on their makeshift beds. Many of the homeless had animals sleeping by their side; the smell of excrement lingered throughout the entire backstreet.

Finally, Abeo arrived at a small black building. Its stone was cracked in a hundred different places. He wrapped his bleached hands around the brass handle and slowly forced the creaking door open. Inside, tangerine lamps spread their light against the rocky enclosure. His eyes adjusted immediately to the glowing room in front of him. Everyone was already seated, anxiously awaiting his arrival.

"Well, it's about time, now isn't it?" Christoph's boisterous voice announced from the head of the table. "If you're all done contemplating the existence of life on your casual stroll to the office, it would be nice to get this show on the road," he said snidely.

The others all sat at their assigned spots at the weathered table. Abeo looked at Foedus sitting to the right of Christoph and nodded at his friend.

"Shall we begin?" the admiral asked, more aggressively this time.

"Sure, Christophorus. Let's get going."

5

The orange hue radiating from the lamps illuminated the blue brick wall upon which they hung. It reminded Petram of home. He had grown up in Lux, a place where Stella's light, scattered by the sky, bathed the city in blue. The red star beamed unforgivingly in the warm summer months, gradually shrinking in size during the periodic and refreshing chill of winter. The City of Light was perpetually inundated by Stella's rays. Over a million residents, housed in a battery of glass domes, called Lux their home. The greatest minds, the most notorious artists, the richest families, and the most powerful individuals all congregated in the Imperium's cultural hub.

Petram glanced over at Cordatus. A thick horseshoe of salt and pepper hair reinforced his glossy forehead. His thin silver eyes stared back at Petram, and he smiled softly, instilling a calmness in him.

To Cordatus' left, sitting broad shouldered and perfectly upright, was the captain. Foedus, acting as if he had more pressing issues than attending a meeting, nonchalantly sipped his wine. Silver-spoon from birth, Foedus perfectly fit the mould for entitlement. Yet, despite his social advantage, the captain always adhered to his place among the ranks. Unfortunately, the only person with real power over Foedus was Christoph, and he loved the captain as one loves a loyal dog.

On the other side of Cordatus, Turpis' bulky body spilled over the side of his chair. Petram tolerated the boisterous man, but he did not like him. Turpis' breath smelled of rye as often as the sky was red in Crepusculum. His dark beard wrapped around his swollen cheeks, and a corpulent nose perched menacingly above his sinister lips. Trying to maintain his focus on the admiral, Turpis forcibly squinted and wiped the sweat from his face. Every once in a while, he would glance over at Abeo.

In truth, Abeo looked more frail than Petram had ever seen him. His patchy beard and haggard hair made him look twice his age. Abeo sat exceptionally still and let his eyes wander.

Petram took a sip of the silver goblet in front of him. Before each Seeker was a uniquely decorated chalice. Petram's was decorated with a lion standing on its hind-legs reaching towards Stella. The animal's sharp white teeth fanged from its open mouth as if growling at the heavens. Inside the cup, the aroma of a bold red wine ascended into his nose. Enticed by the smell, Petram took a small sip and felt a gentle bite on his tongue.

"Good wine, isn't it?" Christoph asked with his arrogant smirk.

"Such an excellent vintage, indeed. I would be inclined to assume that there is some special occasion that warrants such wine?" Petram probed.

"Indeed there is," the admiral replied quietly. He stared down at the pile of papers in front of him and looked back at the seven men. "Indeed there is," he repeated as he cleared his throat. "But I believe we have some catching up to do first if it's all the same to Petram?"

"By all means," Petram responded, opening his hand and inviting Christoph to continue.

"Abeo," Christoph said unexpectedly, "what have you been up to since the last time I saw you? I hope that shanty over on the west end is still standing. It is, isn't it?"

"It is," Abeo responded calmly.

"Well, what a bundle of joy you've been. Thank you, Abeo." Christoph smiled with his lips but glared with his eyes.

An audacious voice suddenly broke the moment of silence. "I'm assuming we're going to have loads of time to get to know each other. Why don't we just get to the contents of that file that's sitting under your fist," Prod blurted out.

The entire room went silent. Christoph squinted his right eye and glared into Prod's soul with the other. The veins on his temples vigorously pulsated as he clenched his hands.

"And who exactly are you, may I ask?" Christoph questioned the young man.

Turpis went to answer on the zealous man's behalf, but Prod was too quick for him. "My name is Prod, er, Proditor, sir."

"Ah, indeed it is," Christoph noted. "Well, since this is your first meeting, I'm inclined to give you a pass. But hear me now, boy, next time you interrupt me or question me in any way, I will pull your fingernails out one by one until you learn your place amongst men. Does that sound alright with you?"

Prod tried to hang on to his self-assured grin, but the corners of his mouth were pulled down my invisible fishhooks. He nodded firmly and averted his eyes.

Eagerly reaching for his goblet, Petram took another sip of wine, and tried to suppress his laughter.

Christoph sat back on his throne, folded his hands together, and allowed a manufactured smile to emerge under his moustache. "Well, gentlemen, shall we begin?"

Everyone nodded synchronously. Prod more voraciously than anyone else.

The admiral placed the pads of his fingertips on the top of the file and arched his wrist upwards. "In this file," he started, "is critical information. Information that is hard to comprehend. I will get into the details right away, but first I need to know," he gazed around the room and observed of the faces of the men around him, "I need to know if all of you are prepared to do more than we've ever asked of you. If there is anyone here who thinks himself unable to do an expedition longer and more challenging than ever before, he should leave now and turn in his pin."

Petram anxiously glanced over at Cordatus. He loved the old man, and he wanted to have him by his side no matter where he went. That being said, the last expedition had pushed Cordatus to his limits, and that was seasons ago. Petram focused on the old man's arm, hoping to see it move. No such thing occurred.

Christoph leaned back in his chair and shared another pretentious grin. "Good, because I'm going to need all of you."

Petram rolled his eyes inconspicuously. He resented how Christoph always claimed, "he needed everyone," as if they were there to protect him against some great danger. The so-called "Lord Admiral" had not joined in an expedition since Petram himself was a Discipulus. Christoph was more than happy to sit back and send them to all the places he was too afraid to set foot.

The admiral looked at Prod and smiled. "That means you too, rookie."

Prod nodded with a masking confidence.

"What about this one?" Turpis questioned, pointing his imposing finger at Veritas.

Christoph leaned to his right to take a look at the young man hidden behind Petram and grinned. "Ah yes, I almost forgot about this one. What do you think, boy? Are you ready to go on a big bad adventure?" Christoph grinned and leaned forward to await his answer.

Veritas blinked and stoically stared back at his new superior. "Absolutely," he stated calmly.

Christoph's face went from emotionless to exuberant. "Excellent!" he exclaimed. "So, here are the answers to all the questions you want to ask: Will you be gone long? Yes. What are you looking for? The same thing as every time. Why now? We'll get to that. Finally, am I coming with you? No. It is important for me to be here and make the important decisions close to the Imperium. Now, is there anything I missed?"

Foedus grabbed his wine and took an auditory sip. His goblet, engraved with his father's coat of arms, was covered by a crest centered by a pentagonal shield decorated with blue and gold stripes. Above the insignia was a silver helmet decorated with a white stallion. Foedus' loud drinking drew Christoph's attention.

"I know you have something to say, so you might as well say it," he spat.

"I have nothing to say. You just seem to have developed a habit of opting out of our increasingly perilous expeditions. Convenient for you, isn't it?"

Christoph glared back at Foedus intently, and the captain

reciprocated. Foedus had hit a nerve. Petram was ready to eject from his chair he was so convinced some sort of melee was going to ensue.

Instead, Christoph burst out laughing and tapped Foedus' shoulder. "Can I never escape your ongoing judgment, old friend?"

"Unlikely, it would seem," Foedus replied with a charming smile.

Christoph perched his lips together to hide his smile and effectively replaced it with his business face. "Any more questions, or shall I continue?"

"How far are we going?" Abeo asked. Everyone looked up astonishingly, surprised to hear him speak.

The admiral stared back and grinned. "Of course it would be you to ask, wouldn't it?"

Abeo's face did not change. He seemed frozen in the moment, unable to be unlocked from time until he received an answer.

Christoph looked back at Abeo. He placed his palm over his mouth and stroked his thick moustache vertically downward. Looking down, he finally turned back and whispered: "farther than you've ever gone before; farther than we even know about. You will go through the Murky Mountains and into whatever lies beyond that."

Abeo's eyes widened. He opened his mouth to say something, but nothing came out. Instead, he quietly returned his gaze to his lap.

Christoph surveyed the room with his squinted eye. He shot them all a smile, revealing his yellow-stained teeth. "Gentlemen, it's time to make history."

6

Foedus stared at Christoph in disbelief. "You want us to go past the Murky Mountains? For what purpose?"

The admiral was too busy monitoring Abeo, looking for some astonished reaction, but Abeo did not oblige to his desires.

"Is this a joke?" Turpis shouted. "We are the fewest this group has ever been, and you expect us to be able to take on some ridiculous mission?"

"You will do what I ask to do because it is your duty to do so," Christoph replied with a sinister stare. "Am I out of line in assuming this should be your mindset, as well?"

Turpis bit his lower lip and gave a reassuring nod.

"Good," Christoph said calmly. He surveyed the room and saw seven pairs of inquisitive eyes peering right back at him. Flipping through the pages of the file, he scanned over the collection of maps, cleared his throat, and adjusted his moustache. "As most of you know, the Seekers of the Unknown were established by our ancestors to search out those lands foreign to us in the west. For centuries now, we have been given the task of going to the dark places that no others dare to explore. Our unique skills allow us to survive in such places. Initially, the role of the Seekers was simply to discover that which we did not know. It was our job to find the hidden paths within the mountains in order to develop a better understanding of what lay within those dark alcoves. Pioneers, like Avos and his team of fifty, discovered valuable resources—the iron mines of the Northern Quarter—almost two centuries ago. This changed everything."

Foedus rolled his eyes as he listened to the same story he had heard a million times. He looked around the table and observed the others. Abeo maintained his introspective position, while Cordatus stroked his beard and looked impatiently back at Christoph. As always, the old man anxiously interrupted the admiral to correct any historical fact he may have besmirched. Petram, too, looked surprisingly interested, as if he had never heard the story before. Cordatus' Discipulus desperately wanted to follow his footsteps of wisdom.

"As the role of the Seekers expanded," Christoph continued, "we began to study the dispersion of life throughout Unum. We knew little of the dark lands then—I suppose there was some hope other creatures lived in the darkness—but this notion soon disappeared; the lack of vegetation made it impossible for anything to exist in such a hostile climate. Without a primary food source, life just cannot survive. There are, of course, those creatures that still reside in the mountains, feeding on the smaller animals of the Barren Plains. They, like us, depend on deeper senses than the animals that inhabit the Interior. An important reminder: there are beasts that live in the dark, so always keep yourself on high alert." Christoph paused and took a sip from his goblet. He looked at Veritas who was busy examining the movement of his own wrist. Christoph clenched his teeth. "You'd be better off knowing this, boy," he said calmly.

Veritas looked up surprised and shot back a coy smile. Its effect on Christoph was null.

"Now, where was I?" The admiral flipped to a map of the Imperium. A series of curved vertical lines covered the page. Foedus noticed a dark black demarcation traced across Lux. Adjacent to this line was a collection of red bands that exponentially increased their distance from each other.

The admiral smoothed out the page, although no crease existed, and looked over at Cordatus. "A while back, the old man here noticed something significant. I'll let him explain what he found."

Cordatus took a sip of his wine and stood up slowly from his chair. He cleared his throat and took the map from Christoph's hand, turning it for everyone to see. "At first the changes were subtle and hard to recognize. I initially realized it when one of my trees died. For as long as I have lived in my home, that tree had never struggled to survive. Last year, it started to shed its leaves; they changed colour as it happened. I had no answers to this riddle, no idea what had happened, until I saw that the plant no longer basked in the light of Stella. Every year that red ball continuously showered her light over the leaves of my beautiful tree. Now, the house casts a shadow on it. It was at this moment I realized the true gravity of what was happening." He looked back down at the map. "For the past three seasons, I have been studying the movement of the horizon and the gradual changes it has undergone. For reasons I do not know, our light moves west. The light of Lux will soon become too great to handle. Temperatures are rising at an elevated pace. This is having a detrimental effect on agriculture in particular. Small increases in temperatures have driven major droughts, wildfires, and species extinction. Now, before anyone panics or thinks that the world is ending, allow me to expand. The rate at which the light is moving is still a manageable one. There is a good chance our capital may be uninhabitable in the future, but that future is, for now, not immediate. We believe we have the benefit of time, but the sooner we move, the greater chance we give ourselves with dealing with this problem."

Foedus studied the entire table and stared astonishingly back at Cordatus. The others looked abhorred. Abeo often mentioned to him how he felt that the sky was shifting towards them, but Foedus had figured he was probably reading too deep into things. The captain took a sip from his cup and attempted to maintain his composure, acting as if he had known all along.

"I don't understand what this means," Petram queried. "What exactly are you expecting us to do about it? We're Seekers, not gods."

Christoph acknowledged the validity of the question. "The Imperium has seen fit to send the remaining Seekers as far as they can go to study as much as they possibly can. Your task's difficulty lies in both its arduousness and its ambiguity. There is nothing that you are looking for, in particular. We need to find out what lies beyond the mountains. We need to know if, when the time comes, our people can settle and live in these lands."

"How long are we supposed to go for?" Turpis inquired.

"That has not yet been decided. You will be sent with owls to use for correspondence. Petram, I would encourage you to bring Sucirevam with you, as well. The old bird still has some journeys left in her I would imagine?"

Petram nodded. He seemed to have a deep connection with his winged animal. Even in the darkest places, she always seemed to find him. Foedus remembered Petram's first expedition. He had brought his owl with him, and everyone had laughed. They told him there was no way an amateur-trained owl was going to make it through the Murky Mountains. By the end of the expedition, she was the only one that had managed to find her way back.

"When do we leave?" Foedus asked, interrupting the silence.

"Soon. Take tonight to say goodbye to those close to you. For the rookies, find a way to wake up with a woman in your bed. It'll be the last time you do for a very long time. I'm sure Foedus can find a way to accommodate you through his infinite connections," Christoph said, smiling at the captain.

Turpis licked his lips and patted Prod hard on the back. "We'll go have some fun tonight, kid."

"Absolutely!" the young man responded.

"What about you?" Turpis prodded at Veritas.

The young man looked back at him disinterested. "I think I'll just get some rest, I want to be fresh for the beginning of the expedition," he replied gently.

Turpis laughed boisterously

Foedus looked across at Abeo. "I know you're in, don't even pretend that you're not," the captain professed loud enough so everyone could hear.

Abeo nodded appreciatively at Foedus, but shook his head. "No thanks," he said coldly.

Foedus frowned dejectedly. "What are we getting for supplies?" he asked Christoph. "Am I going to have to bring my own whiskey?"

"The necessary food requirements will be rationed off when you all return here for your equipment," Christoph responded. "There will be enough for a lengthy journey. If you end up staying out there longer, you better hope to discover some alternative food source." The room got very quiet, and each face became increasingly austere. "This journey, men, will change the world. What you discover will shape the future. The very soil that you find could one day be the home of your grandchildren. There will be no guarantee of return, as there never is, but you can rest assured that the glory is already yours. This group is full of strong leadership and young talent. Stick together, do your jobs, and you will once again be able to return to this beautiful place you call home. Now, you go to discover a new world."

Book 2
The Journey

7

Solitude is a respite from the societal prison. The thought permeated through Christoph's mind as he strutted around his empty chamber; the same one that the seven remaining Seekers of the Unknown had just vacated. Christoph stroked his thick moustache and released a relieving sigh. He enjoyed his time alone more than anything else; the silence promoted his mind to be more insightful. There were no distractions, there was no need to artificially act excited to see someone. He hated pretending to be enthralled by minutia. His own company was sufficient.

Walking back to his office, Christoph looked at the file sitting atop his desk. Flipping the corners of the pages along his thumb, he felt cool air escape from the scarlet folder. Sitting down at his desk, he grabbed a piece of parchment and attempted to start his letter, but a stack of black folders caught his eye and broke his focus—reports from every expedition that had taken place during his tenure. One report, barely held together by a worn piece of string, was three times thicker than any of the others. Christoph fixated for a moment on the black folder, but eventually returned his mind to the task at hand. He grabbed a feather from its ink bath and began to scribble his message:

For the eyes of the Imperator,

Tonight, on the fourth quadrant of the season of Vesper, the seven remaining Seekers of the Unknown departed on their expedition across the Barren Plains and into the Lower Pass of the Murky Mountains. They have been informed of the circumstances; there were no objections.

Each Seeker was equipped with a weapon of choice, as well as our standard issued rifle, accompanied by stocks of powder and ammunition. The two Discipuli were given weapons from the Seeker storehouse. One falchion was bequeathed to the one named **Veritas**, *and a broad sword to the more physically-capable young man named* **Proditor**.

Christoph thought back to when he had handed the two boys their weapons. Prod seemed excited to wrap his hands around the massive sword. The young man had admired how the lustrous steel reflected the glow of the hall's lanterns. Veritas, on the other hand, seemed unenthused when given his blade. Christoph had witnessed the weapon's former owner, Fortis, slay the beasts of the dark long ago. He had been a true warrior. To see that sword go into the weak grip of a boy felt unjust.

Christoph dipped his feather back in the pool of red ink and raised it above the skin of liquid, allowing the excess to drip back into the cup. He continued to scribble:

The Seekers were also given three mules to aid in the transport of their supplies. If used sparingly, they have been equipped with food stocks for a lengthy journey. As is protocol, water supplies are minimal, so they will need to rely on old reservoirs to maintain their course.

I have given the Seekers an owl, as well as encouraged one of them to bring his own. They will be corresponding with me throughout the journey as often as they can. Anything of paramount importance will be immediately brought to your attention.
Sincerely,
Christophorus
Lord Admiral of the Seekers of the Unknown

Christoph rolled the parchment into a tight cylinder, tied it with a black and gold string, and rose from his desk. He walked towards the spiral staircase in the corner of the room, climbed the stairs until he reached a rotting wooden door, and walked out onto the roof of the building. Once upon a time, he could see the entire city from the rooftop. Now, the imposing white edifices blocked almost any view to the east. He looked towards the west and saw the Murky Mountains looming in the distance. Above them, a small light hovered in the violet sky. Vesper, the most luminous star, had descended behind the towers of stone. Christoph could not understand why the stars moved. *Mysteries of the dark,* he supposed.

As he walked over to the caged area where the owls were kept, he watched his favourite, Onucitra, hop up and sit observant on her perch. Her feathers, a vibrant collage of lavender and sapphire, surrounded her radiant gold beak. She turned her head independent of her body and flapped her protracted wings in excitement, knowing that she was going to go out on a mission. Christoph believed that an animal's simplicity allowed it to be more genuine and less devious. He trusted animals more than people because he found them easier to manipulate.

"Alright, settle down now. It's okay." Christoph gave the owl some food and opened the door of her cage. She hopped out and perched herself on his forearm. "You have a long journey ahead of you, Onucitra. You better eat up before you go."

He tied the letter to the owl's scaly ankle, just above her clawed feet, and gave her one more stroke from head to tail before thrusting his arm upward. Christoph watched as the cold coloured creature swiftly took off towards the burning sky.

8

A fire crackled loudly in the center of the camp; its flames writhed towards the crimson sky as if to return to their fiery home. Above it, Cordatus stirred a metal pot filled with bubbling stew. The tantalizing smell drew in the gaze of six pairs of hungry eyes; only Abeo was not bewitched by the prospect of food.

Around the perimeter of the fire were four tents, each illuminated by the soft glow of the lamps inhabiting their interior. Behind them, the mules paced with vexation; their heavy hooves clapped against the hard ground. Abeo walked towards them and brushed the long snout of Airam. She had traveled many journeys with the Seekers. Like him, she seemed to find comfort in the darkness. The other two mules, Anin and Atnip, munched on the sparse brown grass that poked out from the ground.

"The food ready yet or what?" Turpis asked abrasively.

"Just about," Cordatus responded calmly while stirring the pot counterclockwise. The old man threw in a few herbs and mixed it one more time. "That should just about do it," he said with a smile.

Each man brought their steel cup to the pot and allowed Cordatus to pour in their slew of stewed meat, potatoes, and vegetables. They sipped and slurped at it cautiously; one could not afford to let the food chill with the temperatures slowly falling.

"Abeo, have some," Cordatus requested, waving him over.

Abeo obliged. He grabbed his share and then retreated into isolation. Brittle grass crunched under his feet, and the cool breeze nipped at his exposed face. He gazed up at the sky and soaked in all of its beauty. To the east, he could still see the vibrant lights of

Crepusculum. An inferno of yellow and orange domed over the last remaining vestige of the Imperium. His green eyes soared across the horizon and followed the darkening sky. Starting from the bright lights of the Twilight City, the roof of the planet became a collage of violet and emerald. Then, his eyes met the foreboding wall of rock to the west. Lingering above the high peaks, small specks of light flickered on and off. The stars had always instilled endless wonder in Abeo. In his mind, nothing compared to being smothered by the cosmic blanket. *Such beauty in such foreboding darkness*, he thought.

Behind him, he heard the whispers of the others. Undoubtedly, they were perplexed by his behaviour, but he was not worried. To him, the solidarity of his mind was not in question. A strong hand grabbed his shoulder and broke his attention away from the mountains.

"What's on your mind?" Foedus inquired.

Abeo turned and looked at his friend. "I don't know," he responded quietly.

The captain wasn't prepared to let him off easy, so he probed Abeo to carry on.

"There's something different about this time," Abeo continued. "Remember the last expedition? I couldn't explain it, but I felt something. I saw it in my mind. It felt real, and it had substance to it." He paused. "It was like the air around me radiated life. I haven't been able to stop thinking about it since. It's like a whirlwind inside of my head that sucks all my other thoughts in—a vortex of consciousness."

Foedus looked back at him concernedly. "Does Cordatus have an explanation? I would assume the answer to most of your questions are buried in some book, and, since he's read them all, he might just be the man to ask."

"I remember asking him at the time, but he had no solutions," Abeo sighed. He cranked his head backward and looked at the swirl of crimson and cobalt. "I'm staying out here, no matter what we do or don't find."

Foedus' eyes popped open, and his thick eyebrows ascended to the top of his forehead. "What the hell do you mean?"

"There's nothing left for me back there. It's a heaving wasteland of urban filth, a landfill of sloth and greed. I belong out here; I always have." His eyes scanned Foedus' face for a moment. "This will be our last expedition. There won't be much need for us anymore. We're just the human shield, the front line, storming towards a ceremonial suicide."

"If you get any more morbid the darkness might just come to us. It'll save us some travel time I suppose," Foedus laughed, but Abeo did not reciprocate. "Look, you're not staying out in the unknown. Even you wouldn't survive. You can't live off hunting the few animals that find shelter in the dark. In case your memory left with your personality, try to remember that they are better adapted to their environment than you are."

"There's more out there. It doesn't make sense. Why are there so many out here? What do they eat?"

"Cordatus claims that they migrate south into the Blood Mountains to feed on what they can. They find their way back to the dark to hide and sleep."

"The Blood Mountains were miles away from where we were last time, and still we ran into bears, panthers, and falcons. Seems like an arduous journey for predators that large just to find shelter," Abeo replied.

"You may still be right. I suppose we're on the right track to answering your inquiries, Abeo. Just remember, we need you to make this work. Your mind will, as always, prove invaluable."

Abeo nodded but did not change his stoic expression. "I will do what I can."

"That's all I wanted to hear," Foedus smile. He tapped Abeo on the shoulder and walked away. Then, he stopped and turned. "Oh, by the way, I've paired you with the kid, the one with blue eyes. You haven't had a Discipulus yet. Plus, he seems like he'd be a good fit for you."

Abeo knew that any rookie Seeker was always to be paired with a mentor, or Praeceptoris, to build trust and communication—two vital components in the dark. His Praeceptoris had been a complex man named Aerugo who had taught Abeo how to control his mind and focus on the inner thoughts. It was something he had trouble with at first, but after the experience of one expedition, he had come to hold a whole new arsenal of talents.

"Where's he from?" Abeo inquired.

"Opus Dorum," Foedus responded, raising his eyebrows, expecting Abeo to be intrigued by the response.

"Interesting," Abeo replied.

Once, Abeo visited Opus Dorum—or OD, as it was colloquially known—and once was more than enough. OD was a small mining town that lay to north of Crepusculum. It was built after a group of Seekers had discovered important resources in the Murky Mountains. In particular, OD had abundance of ignasaxum—readily combustible black rocks. Any living person could maintain a steady fire with just one rock, which made ignasaxum a "hot" commodity. Years later, gold and silver were found deeper in the mines, causing a greater influx of workers. The old Upper Pass that had been used by the Seekers for centuries was transformed into an industrial road. OD was full of poor workers who struggled to feed themselves or their families because they spent most of what they made at the local bars, or indulging in exotic herbs and drugs imported from Lux. The rates of violence, rape, and belligerence were unimaginable, but no one in the Imperium ever noticed. As long as the tenants of the Interior were raking in resources, all was well in the eyes of the Capital. Abeo knew how rare it was to find someone from OD who wasn't mentally damaged in one way or another. Veritas seemed to be the diamond in the rough.

"Kind of looks like him, doesn't he?" Foedus probed tepidly.

"He does," Abeo managed to croak quietly.

Foedus smiled empathically and put his hand on Abeo's shoulder. "Get some rest."

The captain walked across to the other side of the dwindling fire and into his tent; Abeo did the same. Everyone was resting, even the fire was slowly sizzling to sleep. As he went inside his tent, he looked at Veritas huddled underneath a thick green blanket. The young man opened his blue eyes. Abeo unrolled his bed set and took a drink of water. He looked back again at Veritas, uncomfortably scratched the back of his head, and cleared his throat. Before he could say anything,

Veritas spoke.

"What do you see out there?" he asked.

"Why do you ask?" Abeo replied defensively.

"Do you see a never ending tunnel with bright lights that tease you when you try to reach for them?"

Abeo made no response. He continued to listen and nodded for Veritas to continue.

"Sometimes I see red eyes peering inside my mind, or voices that act like a siren calling me in. I've seen it before in my deepest dreams, but it always fades as the light returns and I awaken. But now, now it's like I'm at that state right after waking up. I can see it so vividly if I just close my eyes. It changes from time to time, but it's become something tangible. I want to understand, I just…" he stopped himself, realizing that the increased speed in which he was telling the story. "I'm sorry, I just thought maybe someone could explain it to me. Everyone else would probably just think I'm weak or that my mind is cloudy. At least, that's what Turpis said."

Abeo peered back into the boy's blue eyes. They washed over him like a cool wave, the impending tide throwing him back in time. He remembered the smile and laugh of his son, and he remembered when he found out he would never see his son again.

"Turpis is right," he retorted coldly. "You're better off keeping it to yourself." He blew out the lamp, wrapped himself in his blankets, and closed his eyes. As he drifted off into sleep, two scarlet eyes emerged behind his eyelids and peered right back at him.

9

The only thing that Petram could hear was the clopping of Anin's hooves. As he walked, his sagging head bobbed in unison with the mule's saunter. He and Cordatus lagged behind of the rest of the group. They had briefly stopped so that he could take a rest; a varicose ulcer persistently plagued the old man. In his prime, Cordatus could've endured any expedition in full, but time does not discriminate.

When it came to his Praeceptoris, Petram was always willing to help. He often reminisced on the moment the two had met. He remembered being instantly entranced by Cordatus' breadth of knowledge. Petram owed much to the old man; Cordatus' wisdom had helped shape him into the man he thought he'd never be able to become. Even if it meant temporary separation from the group, it never bothered him to stop for a rest and let his mentor regain his strength.

Drawing his gaze towards the darkening sky, Petram watched as red fingers clawed over the horizon. Obscuring his view, a monstrous mountain stretched towards the violet sky. Clusters of snow precariously clung to steep cliffs while craggy stone splintered out of the mountain's spine. Its jagged peaks were a caution to those who wished to explore beyond. From experience, Petram knew that behind Prima Mons—the First Mountain—was a labyrinth of ridges and gorges. Its presence instilled nothing but anxious feelings.

"I know I've been here three times," he paused, "but it still chills my bones and makes me sick every time I look at it. I know I'm not afraid, but I feel overwhelmed with fear. I can't explain why," Petram bemoaned.

Cordatus cleared his throat. "I read a theory once. It proclaimed that there is a moment in every human life when we come to realize our own existence. We all lived in a time where we knew nothing but the natural instincts around us. We ate because we were hungry; we slept because we were tired; we wept because we were upset. Eventually, our brains evolved abstract thinking. None of us remember this moment because it occurred in our childhood, but it happened. This moment, when we finally became aware of our own existence, became the centerpiece for all of our fear. We realized that we were not immortal. When we see something that reminds us of finality, it can cause us to feel physically ill. This, I believe, is the sensation you are feeling."

Petram's raised his eyebrows in disbelief. "You know, it's okay to let rhetorical questions go. Just because you always have an answer doesn't mean you have to give it," he laughed.

"What good are questions if they aren't answered?"

"I didn't ask you anything, old man," Petram boasted.

"Didn't you?" Cordatus responded satisfactorily.

Petram looked ahead and saw the lights of the camp. Foedus had stopped near the entrance to the Lower Pass. Tonight would be their last sleep under sunlight.

Cordatus had once told Petram about how the old Seekers had taken their original route via the Upper Pass. The old man himself had been part of the last group to use the antiquated trail. "To get to the entrance," he would say, "one had to climb up steep slippery rocks and crawl through dark alcoves. It seemed like a man fell to his death once every couple of expeditions. I lost many friends to the void," he would somberly say before pushing to change the subject.

Petram knew that the older Seekers were hardier than he was. They were rugged pioneers naïve to the comforts he took for granted. It wasn't until recently that the Seekers had effectively mastered the Lower Pass—a significantly safer route. Petram wondered what privileges future Seekers, shoulder they exist, would have.

"What do you think of Abeo? Honest opinion," Petram asked, attempting to distract his mind. "He seems so far away, but I still can't believe he's lost anything."

"You're right, he's lost nothing. It's what he's gained that's changed him."

"What do you mean?"

"He has gained much grief, and grief is chained to thoughts of depression. It infects the mind with morbid ideas that force it to focus on the negative aspects of life. Then, the negativity redirects proper pathways towards anguish, and anguish carries with it the desperate desire for answers. It is how the dogma of afterlife takes hold—the endless quest for a universal solution demands an outcome. Abeo must find a way to distract his mind away from its desire to ruminate. I have no doubt he will find his way. How he does so, I cannot say."

Petram took a swig from his canteen and felt the cold water fall into his stomach. His lips cracked from the dry air, and he struggled to keep them moist. The orange light of the camp was close. The prospect of a warm tent and bed enticed him more than anything else.

"Are you ready? How do you feel?" Cordatus asked concernedly.

"I believe so. I mean, you can never really know until you're out there, right? So far, nothing has felt different. If anything, I feel more aware, and more tapped into my higher mind."

"Good. Because there may be a time where I will not be there to guide you," Cordatus suggested delicately.

"Corda-" Petram started, but the old man would not entertain any interjection.

"It may be soon, or it may be in a while," Cordatus continued. "Either way, you need to be prepared for that inevitability. I don't want you to forget the things I've taught you."

"I know," Petram mumbled.

"I know you do," his mentored reassured.

"Let's not dwell on that right now."

"I suppose that is a perfect time for us to stop," Cordatus said with a smile.

Petram looked up and saw that they had reached the camp.

***

"You ready to go?" Petram heard Foedus ask, while he tightened the straps around his wrist. The captain was not looking at him, he was addressing Abeo.

"Your question implies that I need to shut myself down and attempt to recharge my batteries. Or that I need some kind of ritual to prepare myself for something that I do as second nature," Abeo calmly replied.

Foedus smiled. "So, you're ready then?"

Abeo felt the question unwarranted and refused to give another answer.

Meanwhile, the rest of the group prepared themselves for the impending journey. They packed away their tents and gathered up their gear. Turpis ordered Prod around, commanding him to ready the mules. Prod attempted to tighten Airam's harness, but the mule shuffled away from the young man, seemingly aware of his discomfort with the animal. Prod attempted to pet her snout, but she quickly shifted her head away from his hand.

Petram switched his gaze over to his captain and watched as Foedus unsheathed a curved sword from his holster. The scattered light of the sky brilliantly reflected off the shiny metal; the sword emitted a scintillating blue-green near its base and dark red off its tip.

"Make sure it's sharp. I'll feel better knowing that your weapon is in pristine condition," Petram jabbed.

"It doesn't need to be sharp for it to be effective. It simply needs to be in my hand, Petram," Foedus replied confidently.

"Hopefully you won't need it at all," Cordatus croaked. The old man was busy inventorying food and rearranging rations into separate bags. Each bag was marked with a coloured ribbon to denote the time frame for which it was to last.

"Keep focused on your task, old man. When the time comes, I will do the same. For that, you will be thankful."

Cordatus shot Foedus a dissatisfied look and returned to his organizing.

"Hey, where's your Discipulus?" Foedus asked Abeo.

Abeo paused and swirled his head around.

"You lost him already?" the captain exclaimed in disbelief.

"You can't lose something that you never had," Abeo shot back.

Foedus gave his friend an annoyed look. "We're leaving shortly, kindly find him. Petram, go help him."

Abeo gave Foedus a blank stare and then walked away into the darkness. Everyone knew that Foedus was the senior among them, and they respected his rank. What they hated was when he acted like an arrogant tyrant, as if spawned from Christoph's narcissistic womb. Abeo, never a fan of authority to begin with, resented the captain's pretentions more than anyone else.

Jogging to catch up to Abeo, Petram stumbled across the stony floor. He felt his way through the maze of jagged rock. The area around the Lower Pass was full of randomness. All around them, steep rocks enclosed their camp. Up above, black stones leaned ominously, grazing the lavish firmament.

Petram closed his eyes, relaxed his body, and focused his mind. As he opened his eyes, the cool blue hue of the rock revealed itself. Petram swiveled his head slowly and surveyed the landscape. Finally, his eyes found what they were looking for—a red and orange splotch. Veritas sitting under a boulder, had his head buried in his tucked-in legs. Emerging from the darkness, another illuminated blob appeared. It was Abeo. As he made his way towards Veritas, the young man continued to sit solitarily, completely entrenched in the stony nook.

"If the darkness is affecting you already, you might as well turn back," Abeo stated condescendingly.

Veritas paid no attention to his remark. He remained motionless and hugged his folded legs against his chest.

Petram stared at the orange glow emanating from under his skin. He watched the blood moving through his veins and the periodic inflation of his lungs. Veritas' breathing was abnormally slow; his body was totally rigid, as if he were fusing with his rocky surroundings.

"It's time to go," Abeo prodded.

Veritas didn't move. His lungs pumped out air at a steady pace, but his muscles remained motionless.

Petram sighed. "We'd be lying if we told you not to be scared. I get it. That being said, all of us here have made it through a number of different expeditions. You're in experienced hands."

Finally, Veritas lifted his head and looked back at both of them. His blue eyes pierced through the darkness. "You think I'm scared?" he whispered. "I am not scared. Fear is simply a state of mind. Once understood, it can be overcome."

Abeo scratched the back of his neck. "Care to explain the whole head-buried-in-your-knees-while-sitting-in-an-obscure-dark-corner then?"

"Simple meditation," the frail adolescent replied. "I need to be in a place of quiet to fully focus my mind on our impending journey. I overhead Turpis telling Prod that many dangers lay in the dark tunnel. I don't wish to hold anyone back."

"Impressive," Petram nodded, taken aback by the young man's premature maturity

"Although," Abeo interjected, "natural skill doesn't require tricking the mind. It is simply there whenever one chooses to use it."

Veritas stared blankly back at Abeo. "Perhaps you are underutilizing your minds' potential," he calmly rebutted.

Petram let out a quick chuckle, enjoying the Discipulus' unanticipated sense-of-humor.

Abeo, however, was not impressed. He peered back at Veritas, then reached behind his neck and used his crossed hands to pull out two small swords. Casually, he twirled one in his hand and looked back at Veritas' unchanged face. Abeo ran his finger along the sharp edge of the blade and admired the radiant beauty of the steel.

"I hope your meditation worked because I won't be holding your hand out there. I didn't want you; I was assigned you. You can follow me if you want, but I won't be responsible for your fate."

"Nor will I yours," Veritas responded coldly. He stood up and walked away, brushing up against Abeo as he passed. The young man walked back towards the camp, his heart beating at the same steady frequency.

10

The entourage of men approached magnificent mountainous walls that continued to grow the closer they came. Craning his neck as far as he could, Foedus looked up at the altitudinous peak of Prima Mons. Reaching this landmark indicated they had officially cleared the Barren Plains. As the grassland ended, the trail turned into a steep path of sedimentary stone. Heavy breathing and clopping hooves were the only audible sounds, and a cool breeze swept across their course, biting softly against any exposed skin. They continued up the path until they reached a small opening; it was the entrance to the Lower Pass. The opening was obscured by both the complex folding of the mountainous facade and the scarcity of light. Buried deep within the darkness, the Lower Pass was a remarkable find.

Foedus looked back to make sure the entire group was with him. Most had managed to follow closely, but three Seekers—Cordatus, Petram, and Abeo—lagged. It frustrated him when the others could not keep pace.

"Pass me that lamp, would you Prod?" the captain requested of the confident young man. Prod grabbed a lamp from the Airam's harness and handed it over to his captain.

"Turpis, you take a lamp as well. We'll need to stay close, especially near the end," Foedus dictated.

The others nodded in agreement.

The cavern that lay in their wait was a circuitous labyrinth that winded underneath Prima Mons. Diverging into a multiplicity of different paths, the rocky web preyed on inexperienced travelers. Through much trial and error, the Seekers had found a particular route to the other side of the mountain. There, narrow ridges winded their way through stretches of rock, eventually opening up into an immense valley. Foedus knew all too well the dangers of caverns and the beasts that resided within them.

Once the lagging company had caught up, Foedus initiated the next phase of the journey. He made his way through the opening and was immediately enveloped by darkness. Taking a match from his pocket, he struck it against the wall and lit the lamp in his hand. Orange light showered the black and blue stone, illuminating a narrow corridor. A thin layer of water and ice covered the stony floor, making their footing precarious at best. Foedus led the way, securely testing every step before exerting his full weight onto it.

"So, I hear you're from Lucidus, is that right, Prod?" Foedus probed.

"That's right," Prod responded proudly.

"'City of Champions,'" Turpis chimed in.

Foedus knew that Lucidus was known for its elite athletes. Some of the Imperium's greatest champions and warriors were bred in the inferno of the proud urban center. Most of the locals Foedus had ever been acquainted with were of athletic stature, Turpis notwithstanding.

"It is a beautiful city," Foedus replied, attempting to maintain the conversation.

"A lot better than out here," Prod jabbed.

Although Foedus did not disagree that the pale lights of Crepusculum were no match for the shine of the Interior, he also knew about the beauty of the night sky and the surprise in store for the young man.

"How long does this cavern extend?" Prod asked, breathing heavier than before. The deeper they descended into the tunnel, the denser the air became.

"We have quite a way to go, but it widens up ahead. Then, we follow the creek until we reach the fork, take a left, then a right, squeeze through a tight crevice, and then we'll be on the other side." Foedus had done the trip so many times, he was convinced that he could navigate with his eyes closed.

Seekers of the Unknown

As they walked, minor conversations started and stopped like the cyclical rising and falling of a boat on choppy water. Foedus continued to lead the way, occasionally losing his focus to contemplative thought. His breathing became heavy, and a small bead of sweat began to form on his thick brow. *I really need to stop smoking*, he thought to himself. At this reflection, he felt his breast pocket to make sure he had brought his pipe. Feeling its hard exterior pressed against his chest induced immediate relief. Then, his thoughts veered to his mother.

He was seven when she left. Nodum, his father, was a well-respected advisor to the Imperator. His job, similar to Foedus, was to probe undiscovered lands for resources and riches, but Foedus' father didn't have the same skill set as his son did. In fact, growing up Foedus knew very little about what the Seekers were or what they did. He had heard the name in passing, but the people of Lux paid little attention to the problems of the West.

Nodum himself had experienced a rough childhood. The youngest of ten children, he had very little growing up. Relying on his own perseverance and hard work, he eventually ended up employed by the Royal Family. Nodum owed everything he had to his relentless work ethic. Unfortunately, the demands of his job drew him away from home more than was acceptable for some.

Foedus' mother, Solvitis, was the daughter of one of Lux's richest families. She was an untamed young soul who fell in love with a handsome gentleman; a gentleman who represented everything she wasn't—honourable. Solvitis was not fit to be a mother. Foedus recalled when she would remind him how she wished he had never been born. She told him time and time again the many ways in which he had ruined her life. To her, Foedus had been nothing more than a cumbersome anchor on her boundless ship. A woman eternally unsatisfied, her family motto, "Enough Is Nothing," fittingly encapsulated her character. For Solvitis, marriage and a child were just another check on her bucket list.

One day, Foedus returned home to see his father quietly drinking whiskey in the kitchen. His hair was a mess, and his eyes were bloodshot. In his sweaty palm, he clutched a goodbye letter from his wife. Solvitis left Foedus and his father in order to expand her horizons. To her husband, she left a small sum of money—sand compared to her island of inheritance; to her son, she left a wooden-pipe that had been in her family for centuries. That was all, nothing more.

After her departure, Nodum buried himself in work. His life became dependent on his duty to the Imperium. Initially, Foedus blamed his father for his occupational obsession. To him, only Nodum's negligence could rationally explain his mother's departure. Then, he blamed himself. Despite all the rationale before him, Foedus could not help but assume that her leaving had more to do with her distaste for him than it had with her own unresolved demons.

Over time, as the two of them grew to depend on each other for support, Foedus came to love and respect his father. He saw how Nodum's loyalty and dedication had, at the very least, rewarded him with love from his son. Not some manufactured form love, like the kind his mother liberally handed out; this love was genuine and enduring. For the first time in his life, Foedus understood the sacrifice his father had made for him. He came to see how the act of parenting is one of the most selfless endeavours an individual can pursue. It requires constant time and energy, yet its rewards are often sparse. Foedus liked to think that, during those moments they did spend together, his father felt his sacrifices had been worth it.

After his mother left, Foedus went to boarding school where he learned the proper etiquette required to be a gentleman. He learned how to dress, how to speak, how to eat, and how to hunt. Most importantly, he learned the value of loyalty, obedience, and order. Yet, despite his attempts to suppress her from his thoughts, Solvitis' eyes remained entrenched into Foedus' face. Every time he looked in the mirror, he saw her. He remembered the days when even his reflection was too much to bear. In an attempt to avoid his own image, he would routinely lay out his clothes and belongings in a familiar place before indulging in a hot shower. Then, he would extinguish the lamp and let the steaming water run over his scalp has he meditated in the dark. For a time, he was able to evade his reflection, until one day, even in the dark, he could see himself. At the time, he thought his mind was just playing tricks on him, but as he continued to practice his introspection, his ability to see in the dark only improved. His mother's final parting gift, an advantageous mutation, would come to define who he was.

The captain's nostalgic journey was suddenly interrupted by a familiar landmark. He had reached an opening in the tunnel. Through the other side, the cavern bubbled outwards to reveal a shallow pool of emerald water. A trickling stream meandered its way through the eroded stone and gently replenished the rocky bowl.

"Let's take a break here," he said to the group. Then, he noticed, he was completely alone. In his deep reminiscence, he had bolted ahead of the others. Baffled by his own mental lapse, he sat down on a small ledge and awaited the rest of the group. Once again, the captain sat solitarily.

11

All Petram could feel was cold rock rippling across his open palm. He sensed the roof of the cave above his crouched head. The tunnel was barely wide enough for two men to walk side-by-side. The floor, a perfect blend of moist stone and ice, made it nearly impossible to follow the path without the assistance of the rigid walls. In front of him, Petram saw the magenta glow of Foedus; the captain's head bobbed dangerously close to the roof of the cave.

"It gets tight up here," Foedus yelled back, "we'll have to go one at a time."

Single file they wriggled their way through a small gap in the wall. When it was Petram's turn, he sucked in his stomach and tightly rubbed up against the stony fissure. As he maneuvered through, he felt the back of his head scrape against a sharp rock. He grunted in pain.

"You alright?" Cordatus asked behind him.

"I think I cut the back of my head," Petram bemoaned.

"Just keep going, we'll deal with it on the other side," Cordatus suggested.

Petram continued shuffling his straightened legs and felt the alcove start to widen. The sensation of warm liquid running down his head continuously grabbed his attention. He was unsure whether it was real or just his imagination. Finally, a pocket formed in the crevice, giving him enough room to feel the back of his head. Blood and sweat amalgamated underneath his bushy hair.

"Great, I'm bleeding," he griped.

"Let me see," Foedus demanded. "Veritas, grab me a cloth out of that bag." The captain took the cloth from Veritas and brought it towards Petram's head.

"Here, I'll do it," Prod interjected.

Foedus gave him a surprised look.

"I used to work in a hospital, I've picked up a thing or two," the young man explained.

The captain looked at Petram skeptically.

"It's fine," Petram asserted.

Prod wrapped the cloth around the back of Petram's head and tied it off to the side. "That okay?" he inquired.

"Good, thanks," Petram replied.

"Let's move," Abeo croaked coldly.

Petram looked at Cordatus' red face. Juxtaposed against the blue tinge of the walls, it looked ever more apparent. "Can't wait more than one minute for anyone, can he?" he jabbed sarcastically.

"If you feel like resting in this cave instead of in the open air at the end of it, then be my guest, Petram. Otherwise, we should get going," Abeo stated, as he continued to make his way down the dark cave. A dim fluorescent ball of gold surrounded his silhouette. The lamps were a godsend in the caverns, but they risked drawing unwanted attention.

As the group continued to descend the narrow tunnel, light from the lamps danced excitedly on the walls of the cave. Abeo and Foedus traded turns leading as each man casually attempted to stay one step ahead of the other, forcing the rest of the group to walk at taxing pace. Petram's legs ached, and his head throbbed. His lips were desiccated from the dry air, and he licked them in an attempt to relieve the dehydration, but they swiftly returned to their parched state.

"How are you holding up?" Petram asked Prod.

"So far so good. I don't understand what the big deal is, it's just walking in a little bit of dark. Nothing the lamps can't fix. Hell, we don't even need to use our skills," Prod said confidently.

Petram scoffed. "Do you really think those lamps are going to last forever? If we kept them on the whole time, the fuel would burn out. Even if we did have some limitless fuel, we could never keep the lights on out there—it would draw too much attention. We just use them to help acclimate. By the time we're out of this tunnel, you better be ready to tap into your mind. There are beasts that live in the caves and down in the valley."

"What do they eat?" Prod queried.

"They travel inland to hunt in the Barren Plains and then retreat to the mountains to hibernate and escape poachers."

"Seems like a long journey just to get some rest."

"Which means they'll be damn hungry when they feast their eyes on you. Have you ever even used that thing?" Petram asked, nodding at the thick sword sheathed in its rust-coloured holster.

"Not this particular one, but I know how to wield a sword, don't you worry," he replied with conviction.

Petram smirked, but his elation was interrupted by a sudden overwhelming darkness.

"Where did the lights go?" Prod yelled.

"Hush!" Turpis spat somewhere in front of him.

Everything became eerily silent. The only sound that emanated was the soft splat of water droplets falling from the cave roof to the floor. Then they heard it. A deep growl echoed through the rocky tomb. Petram felt Prod shift uncomfortably beside him.

"Can you see me?" Abeo whispered.

"Not yet," Petram responded.

"Concentrate," Cordatus murmured.

Petram closed his eyes and tried to focus. As he slowed his breathing, his muscles loosened, and his heart rate abated. Fuzzy images materialized in front of him. Gradually, they manifested into a collage of colours as each man appeared as a fusion of red and aureate light. The group huddled together in front of him. Cordatus stared intently, while Prod waved his hands vigorously in front of his face. Veritas stood stoically next to Abeo; his piecing blue eyes were unmistakable.

"What's happening? Why'd we stop?" Petram whispered.

"Cave lion," Abeo replied.

"Are you sure?" Cordatus questioned.

"Absolutely. We're close to the end of the tunnel. We need to keep going. Keep all lamps off," Abeo ordered.

Turpis irritably grunted. "I'm hearing this from him, am I hearing this from you," he asked the captain.

Foedus looked at Abeo sternly and then turned to Turpis. "You are. Keep your wits about you and keep your weapons ready. We'll be lucky if it hasn't already picked up our scent."

Each man grabbed his weapon and began to follow the captain. Petram vaguely made out the outline of the cave around him. The rocks were painted blue and green, but their colour faded the farther down the cave he looked.

Another loud growl radiated through the cave.

As they trudged down the dark tunnel, the walls of the cave began to expand. Petram smelled fresh air. They were close.

Then, right in front of him, Veritas made an ill step and slipped on a patch of icy rock. As he did, he jerked backward and flailed his arms in the air. Petram reached out to catch him. As the young man's light body landed awkwardly in his arms, his falchion flew out of its holster. Ricocheting loudly against the rigid floor, the sword's clanging echoed loudly throughout the cavern. Everyone stopped moving and ceased breathing. A deep growl resonated again in the hollow chamber.

Petram looked at Abeo whose head was on a loose swivel. His eyes became locked on the back portion of the cave. "Run," he spat. "Now!"

Everything became an instant panic. The group scrambled frantically down the dark corridor. Behind him, Petram heard an intense bellow. He craned his neck and saw, sprinting towards him, a massive four-legged creature. The beast had a thick mane around its head and four gigantic dagger-like teeth. He had never seen a cave lion before; its sheer size overwhelmed his body and caused his legs to quit. Stumbling forward, Petram slipped on a patch of ice. His entire arm reverberated with intense pain as his elbow smacked the stone. Turning onto his back, Petram watched as the beast walked slowly towards him. It opened its mouth and expelled a murderous roar, causing his body to become paralyzed with dread. His desire to survive did not outweigh his fear of being eaten alive. Closing his eyes, he tried to steady his trembling breath. As the beast inched closer, he felt warm steam emanating from its nostrils. This was it; this is how he died.

Suddenly, the boom of a rifle resonated inside the cave, and a whizzing sound echoed above his head. His eyes burst open, and he watched as a bullet struck the lion in its right shoulder, causing it to shriek in pain. In pure anger, the beast violently swiped its paw at Petram's face. As if through muscle memory, he managed to unsheathe his sword and block the attack with the flat part of the blade. The sword nearly escaped his grip, but he hung on to the weapon, grasping the hilt with every ounce of strength he had. The lion came back for another attack, but this time Petram blocked it with the side of the blade, and gashed the bottom of the lion's gigantic paw. Dark red fluid flowed out of the wound and trickled towards the cobalt floor.

Another loud bang echoed, followed by another whizzing bullet, his time hitting the beast directly in its eye. The cave lion stumbled backward and wept in defeat, finally retreating into the darkness from which it came.

Petram dropped his sword, let his head fall back against the cold stone. He looked straight up at the roof of the cave and saw the glow of small winged creatures clinging to the rocks above.

"Are you hurt?" Cordatus asked. He put his hand on Petram's shoulder and looked down at the young man with concern.

"Relatively unscathed, all things considered," Petram replied weakly.

"Good, then let's get out of this place."

Prod helped carry Petram out of the dark corridor. Not long after, the air in the cave became cool and fresh. A soft breeze brushed against Petram's hairy face. They climbed up a gentle incline of jagged rock and ducked under a low hanging ledge. On the other side of the overhang, towering mountain walls formed a deep trench. Petram jerked his head backward and looked straight up. White and yellow lights populated the violet sky, decorated with ribbons of green and blue that wavered aimlessly across the firmament. No experience could top the first time he had laid his eyes on the stars, but observing the cosmic blanket still sent a ripple of enchantment through his body.

As they trekked, the walls of the trench began to subside. Walking on a gentle slope gave the illusion that the walls were falling downwards. Not long after, the group reached a plateau at the end of the canal and stopped to set up camp. All around them, tall cliffs surveilled their every move.

"Turpis, build us a fire," Foedus ordered.

"Prod, build us a fire," Turpis relayed. "Prod? Prod!"

Prod sat on a boulder and stared in wonder at the sky. Turpis yelled at him a few more times until he finally regained his attention. Prod apologized and started to build a fire, but his gaze continued to be bewitched by the first night sky he had ever seen.

12

A fierce wind forced Foedus' tent to rattle. The strings holding up the tent pulled taught as the cloth roof rippled all around him. He lay awake for the second straight rest; his body had yet to adjust to the darkness. Grabbing his wool coat, he wrapped it around his shoulders and stepped outside. The others, quietly resting, had remained silent since the incident in the cave. Petram was unusually reticent; the episode had clearly overwhelmed his mind. The model he had abstracted for the world no longer existed as it once was; it needed restoration. Foedus knew such trauma would inevitably induce irrevocable change. Yet, even in detritus, there still exists life.

    A cold wind ripped through rocky channel, forcing the other tents to ruffle in the breeze. Their camp was set underneath a small overhanging cliff. The rocky wall underneath had eroded to form a protective basin, making it the perfect spot for shelter.

    Foedus contemplated what was still to come. From experience, he knew that path ahead was full of steep inclines. Their journey would eventually lead them to a deep canyon carved out by a frigid river. The Paradise Valley, a place befitting of its name, was an ocular nirvana buried within the unknown. The Seekers often used the stream as a reservoir. With their water supplies beginning to dwindle, it would be essential they reach the valley soon.

    As the captain stared at the sparking sky, he focused and relaxed his mind. Foedus was a talented Seeker, but he still relied on Abeo's skill in the depths of the void. The captain gazed up at the sea of lights above him and watched the stars flicker on and off. It was as if they reached out towards him, only to pull away as they got near. Foedus fought against his heavy eyelids and continued to bask in the swirls of colours that illuminated the sky.

"It never ceases to amaze, does it?" a weak voice asked.

Foedus turned around and looked at Cordatus slowly walking towards him, bundled in a thick brown coat.

"I always hear the others say that it loses its wonder," the captain responded. "For me, the more I see it, the more I appreciate it. I can often recreate the images in my head, but I can never truly experience it the way it is out here. Sometimes I think we were meant to look upon this brilliance. Maybe it would answer some of those questions your God refuses to."

"My God doesn't refuse to answer questions," Cordatus shot back. "He simply has no need to do so; it is upon us to find the answers within ourselves. He has set the stage, but you must act the play. Besides, he is *my* God. He isn't meant to be yours. You must find your own."

Foedus snickered. "You always have an answer, old man. I've always respected that. I assure you, your ability to conjure justifications never goes unappreciated."

"Neither does your charm, my friend."

Foedus laughed. "It's no secret you've never really liked me, Cordatus, but do you think maybe at some point you could explain to me why?"

Cordatus remained quiet and stared up at the sky.

"So I don't even deserve an answer?"

"It is not that I do not like you, Foedus. It is that I have no need to give you my praises. You have used that threshold on yourself, you see? I do not worry about your capacity for self-assurance."

"It doesn't help anyone to be weak and insecure. Confidence is what paves the way for true courage."

"A real leader, aren't you?"

"I am a man who does what needs to be done and does it the best that he can."

"Indeed you are. And when it comes down to it, will that be enough?"

"Nothing is enough," Foedus mumbled back at Cordatus. He paused and ran his hands through his thick ebony hair. "The journey is the job; don't you see? We venture toward nothing in the hopes of finding something. We always move and yet we never reach a destination."

"Maybe we do not wish to reach this destination. Maybe it is the perilous expedition and the wonder of where it concludes that defines the destination itself."

"I do. I want to find where it ends. I want to know where I stand. I'm tired of the endless chase, the constant quest for satisfaction and recognition. And where is Christoph in all this? Undoubtedly sitting back in his comfortable office, basking in the warmth of Crepusculum."

"That would likely be the first time anyone has ever referred to Crepusculum as warm," Cordatus chuckled.

Foedus smiled. "Where does this end, old man? What are we even doing out here? What are we supposed to find?"

Cordatus sat down on a small boulder. His legs shook, and he grunted as he sat. "Maybe nothing. Not all things are supposed to make sense; not all journeys have to end in heroism or a purpose."

"For me, I think it does."

"Desire for ubiquitous understanding is a dangerous one. I've seen it drive men into insanity because they couldn't answer the questions they felt were necessary to define their own existence. My father once told me that at the end of understanding is the desire for annihilation."

"So what are you saying? That there isn't necessarily an answer for everything, or that all answers lead to the inevitable fate of life?"

"Perhaps both."

"How can you claim that?" Foedus asked.

"Why can I not?"

"Because every time you're faced with a quandary, you simply retreat into the solace of omnipotence. You actually believe that some unexplained force is the answer to anything that your books cannot explain. Your God simply fills the gaps that your mind cannot"

Cordatus stroked his beard and stretched out his vibrating legs. "The idea of God is an obscure concept. I believe that there is an explanation; we just can't comprehend what it is. My God is an abstract idea rather than an actual being. It represents that which I cannot fathom."

"Sounds like a convenient option to have. Something can't be answered? That's okay, God understands it."

"It's called faith. It is an unquestioning belief."

"It's called willful ignorance."

"Call it what you will, but faith is there to discover, not to conjure. I am at peace with my beliefs, and that is all that matters to me," the old man said, rather smugly.

"Perhaps your primitive mind is playing tricks on you, finding a way to convince yourself that what you want to believe is true. You always find a way to explain things in your own clever way, Cordatus," Foedus shot him his infamous smile, "but the days are coming when you will no longer be able to justify your claims. Soon enough, a new generation of thinkers will be ushered in. You are a dying member of an endangered breed."

Cordatus smirked and twirled the hairs of his beard around his index finger. "I believe I should return to my quarters to get as much rest as I can. We do have the beginning of an arduous climb ahead of us."

"Indeed we do. The steep descent to paradise," Foedus mumbled back, returning his gaze to the sky.

"Goodnight, Captain," Cordatus asserted. He returned to his tent.

Foedus remained by the fire and stared into its depths. He recalled the times he went camping with his father. The two of them had always made a fire to cook food, not to keep warm. It was much different making a fire for warmth and light as was necessary on the expeditions. He had always enjoyed those camping trips. Out in the wilderness, and away from civilization, he rediscovered his primitive side and basked in the tranquility of nature. Being a Seeker had made him excited about being out in the wild again—just as he had on those recreational retreats eons ago. It didn't take long, however, for elation to turn into trepidation. The cold and the dark took its toll on everyone. The captain closed his eyes and tried to enjoy the warmth that he was so accustomed to. As he did, he slowly fell into a dream where he was smoking his pipe and drinking a bold red wine. Here, in his dreams, he enjoyed the comforts of home and embraced the place to which he belonged.

13

Abeo's thoughts wandered aimlessly through his mind. Flashing out of nowhere, images and sentences would demand his attention. He walked by himself, far ahead of the group. The others had stayed behind to take care of Prod; the Discipulus had become suddenly ill, supposedly tormented by spouts of nausea and dizziness. Cordatus mentioned he had seen a similar affliction before in rookie Seekers, diagnosing it as an overreaction to the darkness. It frequently slipped Abeo's mind that they had two first-timers in their company. Veritas seemed so in his element, he often forgot the young man was an amateur.

Walking alone, he savoured the moment and indulged in his reveries. Abeo knew that Foedus had purposefully delegated the task of scouting the impending path to him. His friend knew it was a job that he thoroughly enjoyed.

As he walked, he thought about the men who had first discovered the passage upon which he travelled. Few knew their names; they were minor details in ancient tales that had fallen into the mythical realm. Like the fading of a distant coastline on a cruising ship, their memory became less significant the more time passed.

After another few minutes of walking, the pass became narrow, and Abeo was forced to orient himself sideways to slide through. As he squirmed through the channel, he felt a sharp rock brush up against the base of his spine. A thin layer of skin scraped off the bottom of his back, and he cringed from the resultant sting. Nonetheless, he continued on, constantly changing his breathing patterns to conform to the contours of the crevice.

Eventually, the rock opened up and rose upwards towards a small plateau. As Abeo approached the landing, a dark valley exposed itself in the distance, infinitely expanding towards the horizon. He looked upon the landscape in awe. Up above, a sea of stars lay submerged in the nebulous fabric lining the firmament. Ribbons of emerald whimsically danced in wavering lines, making the vista evermore enchanting. The view from the top of the Paradise Valley was always his favourite part of the journey. The climb down was always his least.

For all of his strengths and mental courage, Abeo genuinely feared heights. The thought of falling to a gruesome death had lingered in his mind every time he had been forced to attempt the plunge. Dwelling on the descent, he thought about Tenax and the fall that ultimately led to his demise. Abeo couldn't imagine the conscious state that occurred during a fall. *What was the feeling of affirmed and impending death? Was it met with delirium or acceptance?* he wondered.

Taking a deep breath, he tried to savour the view until the others arrived. The natural beauty reminded him of Cura. Abeo had always tried to explain the scenery to her, but she could never really understand. The only comparison he was ever able to give her was the beauty of her smile. Although she adamantly refused to accept the compliment, she was always flattered.

He thought back to the last time he saw her. At the time, the Princep—the Imperator's son and representative in Crepusculum—was Soleil. In an attempt to make a name for himself, he made the bold decision to renovate the entire downtown district. The Twilight City was the oldest urban center in the entire Imperium. The buildings were disintegrated and in dire need of upgrade. Soleil wanted to bring Crepusculum into the modern age of infrastructure.

At first, the people of the city praised him for the facelift. But it didn't take long for the commoners to turn on the nobility. Soleil's lavish plans became too opulent for the realm to afford. Government buildings were built far beyond cost and were open exclusively to the monarchy. The commoners were left with no money to spend and no food to eat. To make matters worse, conflict in Cirfa forced fiscal allocation towards military conquests, flying under the propagandistic banner: "For the Betterment of the Imperium."

Seekers of the Unknown

The tipping point came when Soleil organized a banquet for the newly renovated Domus Imperium. Distinguished guests were exclusive invitees to the grand opening. As the Imperium's elite, dolled up in their lavish garbs, entered the palace, they were aggressively ambushed by peasant men and women begging for scraps of food. The poor desperately clawed at the nobility, begging for simple humanity. One of the men managed to reach a dignitary's wife and ripped the jewel-encrusted collar off her neck. As she fell to the ground, the man frantically ran off into the streets, claiming there would be vengeance for the Soleil's injustices. Indeed, vengeance would be had. Soon after, the commoner's limp body was found hanging from the pillars of the city center—a reminder to those who dared challenge the order.

From this point on, small attacks on the wealthy began to occur. Notable people started to go missing or were involved in "tragic accidents." Word spread that a full-scale revolution was on the horizon. Attacks continued to escalate, so the government responded with the Carnifex—an elite group of soldiers designed to find those responsible for any revolutionary fervor and publicly make an example of them. Beheadings and hangings became daily occurrences. Those who had once been deemed trustworthy were no longer considered so.

Cura was quickly wrapped up in the hysteria, claiming to have been influenced by Abeo's grievances. Truthfully, they both despised the Princep for publically declaring that the Seekers were, as he put it: "an old and useless organization crawling toward its grave." For all the money he was willing to spend, the Princep refused to fund the Seekers. He declined to renovate their building, leaving it as the one blemish on his renewal project. Cura was vocal about her outrage, but Abeo knew the real motivation behind her dismay—the Imperium had sat idly as their son had died an unnecessary death.

For Abeo, problems of the Imperium became outside the realm of his concern. Initially, his revolutionary piety was unmatched. Often, he would spend hours ranting about the crumbling structure the elite had imposed on the rest of society, but the lack of change and the growing violence had left him nothing but jaded. He felt an increasing insignificance of himself. As time passed, the problems of the world became seemingly insurmountable.

Cura disagreed with his perspective. She continued to hold true, claiming he should have a greater concern for those with whom he shared a greater identity.

"But if I don't like most of the people within this false sense of cultural universality we call a nation, what's the point of having pride?" he remembered asking her. "Patriotism is just a made up concept that we've embedded into each successive generation to provide some sense of unity. It's an ambiguous idea that advantageous people in power use to drive others to do their bidding. It's a means to an end."

"You don't have to be so cynical," she retorted. "There are strengths in unity, as long as that unity is among the masses and not between the few. It's important for us to join in or else the cause loses momentum."

"Cura, it's not on you to make this change. We've seen it before, and we'll see it again. If we remove Soleil, he'll just be replaced with someone worse."

"You can't stand still forever, Abeo."

"I'm not standing still. The world constantly moves. If I'm on it, then there is no way for me to be still," he smiled.

She scoffed at him, "sometimes I wonder if you really are even on it."

By the time he had returned from his next expedition, she was gone. Soleil had died and was indeed replaced by someone even worse. The world continued to turn, but Abeo's place on it no longer existed.

Rubbing his tired eyes, he stared at the tantalizing sky and tried to soak in the view. He wanted was to absorb all of the lights so that nothing but darkness surrounded him. He yearned to accomplish and understand everything, to reach the end of the game. But every time he reopened his eyes, the lights kept beaming back, refusing to disappear. He dwelled the significance of this juncture in time, and held true to his contention that this moment was simply an event that would continuously be anew. He felt inconsequential, and his grief felt negligible. Yet, he was comforted by the thought that evidence for his existence would endure. Looking at the night sky, now, more than ever, this feeling was apparent.

14

The view from the top was immaculate. Foedus admired the infinite shining stars and the emerald lights that aimlessly danced across the sky. Buried underneath the heavens lay a colossal valley. An amalgamation of charcoal rock and chalky stone composed the canyon walls, while a torturous tributary meandered through the mountainous maze, continuously carving out a circuitous stream through the rocky range.

As the group busily packed up their belongings, Cordatus feverishly cooked a quick meal and kindly instructed the others to indulge. Most of the men refused; fear of the impending descent had sufficiently suppressed their appetites.

Foedus, eager to induce confidence in his crew, happily grabbed a bowl and began to consume his food. As he sipped at the steaming stew, he grabbed a green strip of cloth and tore it in half. Snatching a small piece of wood from his bag, he placed the stick between his legs and pointed it upwards. Removing a sharp dagger from its holster, he whittled the end of the stick so that it tapered near the top. The captain pressed his finger gently on the point and smiled in approval.

"Can you imagine trying to kill something with just one of these?" he asked Cordatus who was still stirring the stew.

"I can't imagine survival without particular knowledge or resources; yet, somehow, God devised the mechanism to do such things."

Foedus rolled his eyes. "God or ingenuity? Don't sell yourself and your species short."

"Perhaps both. Maybe God created an experiment, one that had to run on certain principles, and simply let it run its course. There was no interference, just a natural flow of events."

"So what created God? You use that word as a synonym for ignorance. The term itself is simply an answer to a question you don't know."

Cordatus grabbed Foedus' bowl and refilled it. "Eat. You will be glad you did," he demanded.

The captain realized Cordatus no longer wished to discuss the issue so decided to drop it for the time being. He loved to debate with the old man and respected his wisdom, but the two of them were never able to reconcile their fundamental differences. It was as if, in another life, they had been enemies. Foedus looked at the deep wrinkles embedded in Cordatus' face—eons of experience ingrained into his physical structure. The old man was intelligent and kind, but he was not a leader; he was never willing to pursue the responsibility that came with commanding. It was Foedus' ability to take charge in the dark, to calm the nerves of others, and to fuse a group of distinctive personalities into a cohesive unit, that had made him the ideal leader.

The captain walked to the edge of the cliff and peered down at the ominous expanse. In the distance, he heard the river moving expeditiously through the valley. He took the green cloth and wrapped it around the whittled stick. Then, using his dagger, he dug a hole and hammered the stick into the sediment and pushed several smaller rocks around the base.

"What're you doing that for?" asked Prod.

"Useful markers to retrace our steps when the time comes," the captain responded.

"If the time comes," Abeo said in passing.

Prod looked anxiously at his captain.

"Don't listen to him," Foedus reassured.

"Aye, aye, Captain," Prod responded with a confident grin.

Once they were all prepared, Foedus guided them down a gently sloping path. As they walked, rocks cracked under their heavy boots, and the trail reversed back and fourth down the wall of the mountain. Carefully, Foedus analyzed the subtle contours of the deceptively uneven trail. Minuscule ridges and valleys made the footing exceptionally difficult. Nonetheless, down the path they went, endlessly descending towards a fleeting destination. Each subsequent switchback was met with another cavity of obscurity. The amplifying sound of water swishing below was the only motivating factor. At the bottom of the trail, a steep wall stood perpendicular to a small ridge. From experience, Foedus knew that this was where the descent became especially dangerous. He had done it more times than he could count, but the task still riddled him with apprehension. He looked back to make sure the rest of the group was with him. Turpis and the two Discipuli maintained their proximity, while Cordatus and Petram lagged behind. The captain peeked over the edge and looked at what awaited them. One mistake could have fatal consequences.

"Here is how this is going to work," Foedus instructed. "Each of us is going to tie this rope around his waist and be lowered down by the men at the top. You must use your legs to push off the rock, but do not push too hard; you don't want the men lowering you to lose their grip and see you fall to your death. Communication here will be imperative."

"And how will the last few get down?" Veritas inquired.

"We have one climbing kit that contains a pair of axe picks and spiked metal shoes. The three of us," Foedus nodded to Turpis and Abeo, "will decide which one will have to make the climb. It is not for you to worry about, it is a duty of the veterans."

"And the animals?" Prod inquired.

"Once the first couple of men are down, the rest of us will lower them one at a time. Their harnesses are equipped with hooks to aid in their descent, but we will need guidance from the bottom since it is impossible to see from this vantage point."

Veritas nodded respectfully. Foedus had noticed the young man's loyalty and compliance and admired it greatly. He knew that Veritas had great talent, but what his intentions were, he still could not be sure. He had found Prod easier to read, and he did not trust what he could not control.

"Cordatus, you go first. I assume repelling has not yet left your toolkit?"

"Not yet, or anytime soon," Cordatus responded sharply.

Petram helped tighten the rope around Cordatus' plump waist. The old man had kept in relatively good shape for his age, but some proliferations could not be inhibited. Cordatus tugged on the rope and nodded at his Discipulus.

Slowly, they lowered Cordatus into an encompassing pit of darkness. Foedus supervised as the thick rope slid sluggishly through their collective grip. The rope creaked from the strain of Cordatus' weight. Veritas' feet shuffled over the loose rock as he attempted to reaffirm his footing. Then, the tension in the rope ceased, and they loosened their grip.

"Alright?" Petram yelled down the cliff.

"Good!" Cordatus' faded voice echoed from below.

"Alright pull the rope back up. Veritas, you go next," Foedus commanded.

Veritas and Prod were quick to reach the bottom. After them—much to the chagrin of the hoofed creatures—the mules were sent down one-by-one; Petram joined them at the bottom soon after. The three remaining men all looked at each other with subtle grins.

"I'll climb down last," Abeo declared casually.

Foedus shifted uncomfortably and wiped his brow of sweat. "No, I'll do it." In truth, the captain wanted someone else to make the climb, but he had an internal competition with Abeo that he refused to lose. He knew that Abeo's skill was stronger than his; it wasn't this that bothered him. It was Abeo's inability to be a member of the team that frustrated Foedus to no end. The captain had always supported his friend and asked for very little in return. At times, he felt as if he was the only one Abeo related to. At others, they were lesser than acquaintances. He didn't like being challenged by anyone, let alone his first officer. Pride suppressed his fear.

"Why don't you let me do it?" Turpis interjected. "We can't risk losing you as crew leader, and Abeo isn't nearly strong enough to make that climb anymore. Time's been rough on you, hasn't it?" Turpis grinned and smacked Abeo aggressively on the back. Abeo's face remained unchanged.

"If you're willing to do it, I think you're the best candidate for it, Turpis." Foedus agreed. "Abeo, do you have any opposition to me going first? You are the lighter of the two of us; it would leave Turpis with less of a burden."

Abeo nodded in agreement.

The captain tied the rope around his waist and dove backward into the void. He felt the jagged rock under his feet and pushed off it fearlessly. For a moment, he felt liberated, suspended in a caliginous cloud, until the tension of the rope pulled him back into reality. Trying to focus his mind, he watched as the pale shadow of the cliff suddenly became a magnificent blend of orange and blue. He analyzed the contours carefully, looking for the best place to land his feet. As he looked down, the faint crimson glow of the others began to materialize. With a great thrust, he launched off the rock and again allowed the rope to pull him back. The subsequent plunge following each push was met with the acute fear that the rope would not pull back. The gruesome outcome of his body hitting the ground seized his mind. It seemed so easy to just let go. How could his life, something he had developed for so long, just cease to exist?

Chattering voices suddenly broke Foedus from his stupor. He looked down and clearly saw the glowing bodies of the others.

"One more push, Captain," Prod yelled. Foedus thrusted off once more and felt his heels scrape along the slick rock. As he landed, his foot slipped, and he awkwardly stumbled to the ground.

"You alright?" Prod asked while trying to help support his superior.

"Good." Foedus replied defensively.

"All good?" Turpis' ragged voice echoed from above.

"Yes!" Foedus yelled back. He untied the rope from his waist and watched as it slithered its way back up the rock.

"Who's doing the climb?" Petram questioned.

"Turpis volunteered, surprisingly enough," Foedus responded.

"Odd, he's not usually one to take a challenge head on," Cordatus noted.

"Probably just trying to impress the rookies," Foedus whispered to them. The other two smiled in agreement. They cranked their heads upwards and looked for any sign of Abeo.

"Can you see him yet?" Cordatus asked. He stared intently up towards the dark heavens; the protruding cliffs blocked most of the sky's light.

"I think I see him. Right there," Veritas pointed.

"Oh yes, I see. He still has a way to go then," Cordatus responded.

Foedus reached for his canteen and unscrewed the cap. He took a swig of the cool water and felt it descend down his throat into his stomach. The sensation chilled his dark skin, but the relief was momentary. The canteen was nearly empty, and he only had one left. They needed to get to the river soon. Foedus couldn't afford any perturbations.

"Almost there, Abeo!" Petram yelled up at the repelling man.

"Is there an ideal place to land?" Abeo asked.

"Try your best to swing to your right if you can, the rock is less slippery on that side," Petram cried back.

"The right?" he called down.

"Yeah!"

Foedus watched as Abeo pushed off the wall and swung down quickly. The force of his feet against the rock caused a few rogue pieces to fall, forcing Veritas to dive out of the way to avoid being crushed.

"Everyone alright?" Abeo yelled down.

"Good!" Veritas called back.

Abeo pushed off once more, but this time the rope did not pull him back. Instead, it coiled around itself and quickly chased him down towards the ground. Waving his arms and legs, he tried desperately find something to grasp. Suddenly and violently, he met the hard ground. A loud cracking sound echoed through the valley, forcing the others to cringe. Abeo groaned as he ricocheted off the flat ground. His head and left arm hung helpless on the edge of a cliff while the rest of his body lay unsteadily on a small stretch of stone.

Petram and Foedus raced towards him, but Veritas was the first to reach the injured man. He instantly pulled Abeo back onto the solid surface. Abeo lay on his back, his eyes tightly clenched closed. He expelled a muffled groan and grinded his teeth.

"What's hurt? What happened? Can you feel anything?" Veritas questioned feverishly.

"Easy boy," Cordatus cautioned. "Let him catch his breath. Abeo, are you all right? What do you need?"

They all watched as Abeo struggled to breathe. He cringed in pain and shifted uncomfortably.

"Abeo, just tell us you're okay," Petram asserted.

Abeo took another deep breath and reached towards Prods canteen.

"Give him some water, Prod," Foedus commanded.

Prod unscrewed the cap and carefully poured the water into Abeo's half opened mouth. He thankfully drank, and then coughed when his thirst had become quenched. Then, he lowered his head on the rock, and wiped his mouth with his forearm.

"My ankle," he mumbled, "It…it's shattered." He let go of another distressing groan.

"What happened?" Foedus inquired.

Abeo grunted as he slowly shifted his weight. He wiped his forehead and looked straight at Foedus. "He let go of me on purpose."

15

The men waited anxiously while Turpis descended the face of the cliff. The sound of his steel pikes puncturing into stone clanged loudly up above, causing rocky shrapnel to rain down on the observers below. As he approached the base, his heavy breathing became increasingly noticeable.

Abeo could only watch from the callous rock upon which he sat. His ankle throbbed uncontrollably, and he felt the slow drip of warm blood sliding down the top of his foot, collecting in a growing puddle under his heel. He took another swig of cool water from Prod's canteen as he had lost his during the fall.

The rest of the group gathered around Turpis' landing point, anxious to hear what had happened. Abeo knew that Turpis wasn't fond of him; the two had often clashed. During their previous expedition, Abeo had urged Foedus to find shelter when he sensed an incoming snowstorm. Turpis, eager to finish the expedition with haste, felt there was no need for such unnecessary precautions. Get in, get out, get paid—it was all that mattered to the big man. In the end, Foedus ruled in favour of Abeo. A violent storm raged shortly after. *How many lives would have been needlessly lost because of one impetuous man*? Abeo wondered.

Before his descent, Abeo had asked Turpis if he felt confident anchoring the rope on his own. Turpis had confidently nodded and even decided to tether himself to a boulder for insurance. Despite his assurances, Abeo had been nervous the entire way down. He had never been particularly fond of heights; having his fate in the hands of a contemptuous coworker only amplified his trepidation. Nonetheless,

Abeo found it hard to believe that Turpis would dare attempt something so blatant. At the same time, he couldn't shake the feeling that the incident wasn't accidental. Abeo knew Turpis would have an excuse and Foedus would buy it. He knew his guard would have to be formidably enhanced.

"What happened?" Foedus questioned Turpis calmly. The captain stared at the massive man intently but gave no show of anger; he was afraid to entice the volatile beast.

"When?" Turpis said bewildered.

"You let go of the rope, Abeo fell at least fifteen feet. His ankle is battered, if not broken. Why did you let go of the rope?"

"Let go? I heard him yell up to me that he was good. I even called back to confirm." Turpis acted irreproachable. Abeo wasn't convinced.

"I did no such thing. No one here heard you call, unless I'm mistaken?" Abeo accused.

"Perhaps there was confusion when you were calling down, asking about the best place to land," Petram suggested. "It's possible that our voices drowned out Turpis'."

Turpis nodded and put his thick hand on the Foedus' broad shoulder. "You know I would never do something to endanger the group. I mean, look at him. We…I am going to have to lug his weak body down the steep trail, and we know that won't be easy. Why would I ever do something to put us in that situation?"

Foedus nodded in agreement. "I know that you wouldn't, Turpis. A simple misunderstanding which, unfortunately, has left us in a handicapped position. We can't linger here much longer, our water supplies are running thin, and there's still the potential of storms hitting at any moment. Cordatus, I need you to do whatever you can to solidify Abeo's ankle so that it doesn't get any worse. Each of us will have to take turns assisting him down the slope until we reach the bottom. We will set up camp there. For now, eat what you can and regain your energy."

Abeo watched as Cordatus gathered medical equipment from his bag while Prod started a fire. Foedus, frustrated with the situation, disappeared down the dark path to scout out what lay ahead. Veritas looked peculiarly at up and down the cliff and then stared over at Turpis.

"The hell do you want?" Turpis asked the young man aggressively.

"I'm just curious, when you let go of the rope, you must have noticed that there was still significant pull on it. I mean, if Abeo had actually reached the ground, wouldn't you have felt the lack of tension on the rope?"

"What are you saying?" Turpis growled.

"Nothing. I'm merely asking how a veteran Seeker, of your caliber, could be so oblivious to an incident he was directly involved with? That's all."

Turpis scoured at the young man and shoved him backward. He put his hand around the base of Veritas' neck and moved his face close to him. "Listen to me," he seethed, "you're just a kid who knows nothing. Next time you feel the need to challenge me, you better be able to back it up. I know you think you understand the way things work, but you don't. You don't know a single fucking thing!"

"Hey!" Abeo yelled. He attempted to get up but Cordatus prevented him from standing. Veritas squirmed away from Turpis' vice-like grip, and wrestled his thick forearm away from his throat. The young man gasped at the sudden inhalation of fresh air and coughed to clear his throat.

"What the hell, Turpis!" Petram rebuked.

Turpis grunted and stormed away. As he left, he kicked over Veritas' canteen, spilling its contents in the process. Then, he started down the path on his own, no doubt ensuring that the captain's opinion was sufficiently swayed in his favour. Foedus was the one man that Turpis ever seemed to be afraid to stand up to. He had occasional brush-ups with everyone else, but Foedus and Turpis had always been amicable.

Oblivious to everything, Prod sat by the pot of stew he had warmed and enjoyed a bowl of broth and meat. "Come grab it before it gets cold!" he hollered over.

Veritas looked at Abeo with his dazzling blue eyes. He put his hand on the injured man's shoulder and asked him about his ankle. Abeo responded, claiming he was fine. In truth, he didn't know how he was going to make the downhill climb. Veritas offered to grab him a bowl of food, and he obliged. Abeo had begun to take a liking to his Discipulus. Veritas' demeanour and poise had impressed him. Not just this, the respect the young man exuded was a quality he found exceedingly rare in the emerging youth. Then, he then wondered if it was actually a generational change or perhaps a deviation in his own perception. *Was he getting old and losing touch with the times?* The thought perpetually vexed his mind.

Cordatus bent down beside Abeo and began lifting his pant leg upwards to expose the injured ankle. Abeo cringed from the pain.

"It's alright," Cordatus calmed. He grabbed a loose rock and placed it under Abeo's calf to elevate his leg. The old man unraveled a roll of cloth, licked the end of it, and placed the wet end on Abeo's foot so that it stuck to his skin. Abeo surrendered a groan of pain as Cordatus lightly pushed and rotated his foot. With great speed, he weaved the cloth around his wounded ankle.

"Did you actually learn how to do all these things from books?" Abeo asked through clenched teeth.

"No, I learned how to do this when I was a medic during Primis Rebellio."

"I didn't know you took part in the First Rebellion."

"I did indeed. Back then, Crepusculum was just a small hub city on the edge of the world. Most people lived in the Interior because of the crop growth and the warmer climate. But when a massive drought hit, no one really knew how to handle the situation. The elite of the Imperium decided they would help themselves to whatever lands were prosperous. When the First Rebellion started in Lux, I decided I would do what I could to help the cause. The Imperium had left my father, an honest farmer, with barely enough to survive on. He was already a feeble man, but without the necessary nourishment, he dwindled like a flame without air to breathe." Cordatus swiftly tore the cloth and tucked in the loose end to fasten the wrapping.

"If you were involved in the First Rebellion, how did you manage to escape arrest all these years?"

"I fled to Crepusculum and disappeared until things returned to normal. After that, I found the Seekers. The Imperium had been growing tired of the Seekers for almost half a century, even before I joined. To them, we were an increasingly useless group of freaks. Me joining went completely under the radar. When the Imperium pushed back on the rebellion, the rebels migrated to Crepusculum. The city became a haven for revolutionary ideas. It's probably why the Second Rebellion happened there instead of Lux. Why do you think the Market Riot occurred in the Twilight City and not in the Capital?"

Abeo swallowed audibly and looked upwards towards the sky.

"Sorry," Cordatus whispered. "I too often forget."

"It's no matter. Is the wrapping done? We should try to get going. Let's finish this story another time?"

"Of course," Cordatus muttered.

Petram came over and helped Abeo get to his feet. He balanced on one leg and tried to put his wrapped foot on the ground. Petram situated his arm under Abeo's armpit and stabilized him as he limped towards the top of the path. Side-by-side the two men laboured into the deepening darkness.

16

The engaged effort required to make each cautious step exhausted Petram's body. He blinked to alleviate the irritable dryness plaguing his brown eyes, but the relief was always fleeting. Abeo limped alongside with his shoulder draped around Petram's neck. Despite his light weight, the first officer had become a burden on his muscles.

"Do you mind if we stop for a drink?" Abeo plead. His voice was frail; his body looked cadaverous.

"Of course," Petram obliged. He placed Abeo into a seated position against the adjacent wall. The relief on his shoulders was euphoric. He rubbed the back of his neck and felt a pool of sweat. How much of it was his, he couldn't be sure.

Abeo gulped back a quarter of the canteen and exhaled in relief. "We can't be too far from the caves," he croaked. "I'm certain we're almost there. The air has significantly thickened; I can almost taste it."

"I hope you're right because my neck is killing me."

"I'm sorry I've been so cumbersome. I can try and use the wall as a brace instead if you need a break?"

"No, that's fine. Like you said, we're almost there. Plus, if you lose your balance and aggravate the injury it's going to take more than just me to get you back home."

Abeo peered at the ground. "If I go back," he mumbled.

"What's the supposed to mean?" Petram inquired.

Abeo exhaled and gazed at the sprinkled sky. "There's nothing left for me back home. I sit alone in my house hoping that I can escape the emotional vacuum Cura left for me, but I can't. Every time I think I've eluded the sorrow, it just hauls me back in. I have always felt more myself out here. The farther we go, the more comfortable I become. I've never understood why. Even Cordatus hasn't been able to explain it, granted he has definitely tried."

Petram smiled at this comment. "The old man does love a challenge." He, too, looked up to enjoy the view, and then returned his prominent gaze to Abeo. "So, how does this work? Once we get as far as we can, you're just going to stay there and hope for the best?"

"I don't know yet. At this point, I have to trust my instincts. They're all I have left."

"And you're going to survive on what, exactly?"

"Whatever I can find. And if I can't find anything, then I will obligingly accept my death. It's going to happen soon enough; I might as well let it happen on my own terms."

"So you're just willing to wither away in the cold and the darkness? Why? Because you suffered some losses and now you don't have the will to pick yourself up? Shit, Abeo. Man up a little."

"What difference does it make to you? If I go back, I'll just spend the rest of my life doing things I don't want with people I don't even like. I've always preferred to be alone anyways. She..." he began to struggle with the words, "she was the only one I was always happy to be around. She made me comfortable and calm," he paused and cleared his throat. "She was the perfect balance of camaraderie and solitude. She understood me. And, instead of trying to change me, she embraced me."

"She was rare, Abeo. No one will ever deny that. But giving in to sorrow is not the answer."

"If it's what I deem best for myself, what difference does it make for anyone else? The communal always think they knows what's best for the individual, but how can a narrow set of norms pertain to all people in all situations—each of us, with our own unique consciousness, somehow attempting to develop rules we can all play by."

Petram chuckled, "you can derive whatever rationale you want, and I know you will, but despite your nihilistic psychobabble, you should realize that I'm simply looking out for a friend. You're one of the smartest men I've ever met, but you push people away like they're some sort of contagious virus."

"Because some of them are," Abeo said sternly. "People care more about themselves than anything else. Moral values are easy to adhere to when there's nothing to lose. When survival comes into play, the game completely changes. Selfishness controls our deeper minds. It makes us take advantage of others, and it infects the social fabric. The more I've lived, the more I've learned that the negatives involved with socialization far outweigh the positives. Keep your personal posse to a few people who actually like you. Forget the ones that don't; they just shave time off your life by pretending to care."

"Sure," Petram replied, "most acquaintances are just superficial relationships, most often existing when someone needs something, but they still provide entertainment, leisure, and relaxation. Not every social interaction has to be rooted in love. It's okay to have platonic friendships or to use others for selfish benefits. You provide this service to others, consciously or not. I've noticed that you never come out for drinks with the crew. The post-trek parties are always a good time. It's the perfect way to blow off some steam and reacquaint your mind with serenity. Surrounding yourself with others is not a negative thing, Abeo."

"Why do I need to blow off steam in the first place?" Abeo asked. "Our society pushes us to live lives of hardship that can only be maintained by the assurance that one day it will all be worth it. When the prophecy fails to come true, people, desperate to maintain their fabricated reality, drown themselves in one vice or another."

Petram acknowledged his point by nodding. "Maybe. But, without that communal, industrious endeavor, the social structure will collapse. Everyone needs to sacrifice and pitch in or else the roof caves in. If people just ate and slept, who would farm the fields? Who would build the homes and pave the roads? People want to, no need to, have purpose in their lives."

"Perhaps," Abeo conceded. "What scares me is how often that purpose comes from an ideology. Without the reassurance that there's something more after this life, the justification to perform hard labour vanishes. If divine assurance doesn't hold, then people, trying to obtain the highest quality of life, will be crushed by the insurmountable competition. An untenable number of disheartened and overqualified workers will be left to maintain the social base. Our only hope is to escape the labyrinth and find whatever shred of solitude still exists on this planet. That's what I'm going to do. Before it's all gone."

"Fair enough, Abeo," Petram said. "I'm going to accept my fortune with grace. Maybe you should, too, instead of cursing at the relatively good life you have. All that steam makes the good moments what they are. Suffering is a part of life, but the relief does not exist without the strain." Petram massaged the back of his neck and rotated his head to stretch out his cramped muscles. He exhaled one more moment of solace and looked back at the injured man sitting before him. "Shall we continue?"

Abeo moved his ankle and grimaced in pain. He tightened the wrapping and pushed himself into a standing position. "Ready when you are."

17

The ambient glow of the fire revealed the chalky stone resting underneath their camp. Foedus surveyed the group. No one had spoken for a while; the first sign of fatigue was rearing its tired head. Running alongside the camp, the mouth of the Deceptive River splashed loudly against the stony shore. Lining the cool stream was a narrow plateau lined by a towering wall of jagged stone. Illuminating the rocky trench, light from the fire stretched its long fingers and tickled the rocky citadel with soothing light.

"Veritas, pass me a bowl of that stew will you? The smell of it is tantalizing," the captain commanded. Veritas handed Foedus a steaming bowl of stew and a small loaf of semi-stale bread. He dipped the bread in the hardy gravy and took a bite. The warm broth soothed his icy throat.

"So, where do we go from here?" Prod asked hesitantly.

"Where? Not sure I can give you a straight answer, my young compatriot. Basically, we follow the water because we die without it. This part of the river eventually joins up with a bunch of other creeks and widens. From there, the water starts to freeze. Eventually, if we don't get lost, we should hit the Emerald Lake. We've never gone farther than that. So, to answer your question, I'm not entirely sure." Foedus took another bite of his bread and smiled back at Prod.

"I'm assuming we're going across this time?" Petram questioned, hoping that his intuitions were wrong.

"I'm afraid we have no other choice, it's the limit to where we've gone, and we've been asked to delve as far as we can."

"What a joke!" Turpis yelled. His broad chest heaved upwards as he aggressively inhaled. "What are we going to find on the other side of that lake? Nothing! Just more rock, ice, and snow. The whole expedition is pointless if you ask me. Christoph is just bending over for the Imperium."

"Hold your tongue," Foedus snapped at him.

Turpis perched his lips and shot his captain a loathsome look but obliged nonetheless.

"In case you forget, this is your job," Foedus continued. "This is what you signed up for, so stop pretending like you're suddenly enlightened about the dangers involved."

Cordatus raised shaking hand in the air, signaling his desire to weigh in on the matter.

"What?" Foedus demanded.

"Before we tear each other's heads off, let us remember that we need to get there first," Cordatus cautioned. "Abeo is weak and we've finally reached a safe location with water. We're also running low on ignasaxum. You know as well as I do that the only way we can start a fire is with those stones. We need to rest here for a while until Abeo's ankle begins to heal, otherwise he'll risk never improving. The Discipuli can go with Petram and learn the best places to find ignasaxum. The rest of us should look at the inventory of our supplies and begin to form a rationing plan. We may be out here longer than we had hoped."

Foedus sighed and stroked his thickening beard. "As always, your calming demeanour is equivocally useful. It's settled. Petram, you take the kids and make sure we don't freeze to death. Cordatus, leave rationing to Turpis and myself. You just make sure Abeo's ankle heals properly, I don't want him to get any worse."

"He's already a burden," Turpis scoffed.

Foedus shot him another threatening look. "I think we all just need some rest. It's been a long journey already. We will reconvene after a rejuvenating sleep."

Everybody retired to their respective tents except for Turpis. Instead, he somberly gazed into the flames. The broad man scratched his hairy arms and sighed. Foedus waited for him to say something, but the only sound that escaped was intermittent grunting.

Finally, Foedus broke the silence. "You know, Cordatus once said to me 'fire is like us—it, too, needs to breathe.' He told me about how ignasaxum release a kind of breath when you ignite them with a flame. Tiny creatures that live on the rocks, ones so small that even we can't see them, have some sort of compound that gets released when they are set on fire. That's what allows the fire to flourish."

"Sounds like a bunch of malarkey to me," Turpis spat. "The old man just spews everything he reads like it's scripture."

"Maybe you're right, but it makes you think, doesn't it?" Foedus paused. "How much of the world is out there that we can't perceive? What if, right now, there is a whole other universe living simultaneously in time with us, but just under different physical laws?"

"Would it matter?"

"Why wouldn't it?"

"We're not on this planet for very long. Once we die, that's it. It makes more sense to enjoy the present and just accept things as unexplained and not let it affect how you live. Savour the simple pleasures—a delicious meal, an amusing conversation, the architecture of Lux, the collage of colours that coalesce on the Crepusculum horizon, the taste of cool ale, or the mesmerizing touch of a woman you love."

Foedus chuckled. "Have you ever even dared to love a woman, Turpis? All you ever do is complain how hard it is to get them to leave in the morning."

"And you're any different?"

"Well, other than the fact that I'm exceedingly more successful in charming them, I suppose not." Foedus released his patented laugh as he took a swig of water from his canteen.

Turpis continued to gaze into the flickering flames. "I loved a woman once. She loved me, too, but she was too afraid to act on it. Next thing I knew, she got dragged in with some idiotic revolutionaries and I never saw her again."

Foedus took a moment to absorb the information. It was unlike Turpis to reveal any emotion other than blunt anger. The captain was dumbfounded. "Maybe she will come back. Young women tend to get wrapped up in fads pretty easily; she'll eventually tire from this one just the same."

"I don't think that will be happening anytime soon."

"And why not?"

"Because she's dead," Turpis asserted with a morbid immediacy.

"My apologies," Foedus replied with his best attempt at sympathy. "What was her name? Perhaps I knew her."

"I'm off to sleep," Turpis mumbled. He averted his eyes from the flame and glared at Foedus. "You keep what I said to yourself," he sternly warned.

"Goodnight, Turpis," Foedus calmly replied. He pondered on what Turpis had said, but eventually became distracted by the sky. At long last, he was alone around the fire. He listened to the tickling trickle of the river and the soft popping of the flame. He extinguished what remained of the dwindling fire with the contents of his canteen and listened to it sizzle to sleep. Then, he sipped what little water he had left and enjoyed the cool sensation as it descended his throat. One could not live without fire or water, yet the two entities were mutually destructive to each other. Like the dark and the light, the two opposing sides defined each other's existence.

18

The air was uncomfortably humid. Thick smoke blanketed a frantic horde of insurgents. Just as Cordatus had predicted, Crepusculum, with its heavy concentration of revolutionary minds, became the setting for the largest organized revolt the Imperium had ever faced. Men and women ran around with torches, setting ablaze to all things flammable. The chalky white stone of the imposing buildings became stained with charcoal spots.

Frenetic beings forced themselves past Abeo. Suddenly aware of his own body, he was situated in the epicenter of the chaotic crowd. Trying to flee the flames, men and women violently shoved each other, trampling those who lost their footing. Cries for "Food, Freedom, and Equality" muffled the screams of those buried and burned in the pandemonium.

Abeo remained frozen. He stood in the middle of the massive plaza that lay before Domus Imperium. Men hammered at the doors trying to tear down the building stone by stone. A haze of dense smoke lingered above, effectively blocking the beautiful sky. Abeo dazedly gazed at the madness around him. He was ensconced within a bubble of tranquility.

All of a sudden, peeking out from the dense crowd, was Cura. Her thick black hair bounced as she jogged through the throng. Her seductive green eyes were consumed by concern, yet her caramel skin still attracted the only light not impeded by the thickening haze. She looked for a way out of the crushing chaos, and raised her shaped eyebrows as soon as an opening appeared. As she attempted to squeeze between two quarrelling men, her leg caught a rut. She stumbled forward and disappeared into the crowd.

Abeo jerked forward to run towards her but was immediately forced back. He looked down and found his feet securely cemented into the cobblestone. Attempting to break free, he drove his thigh upward, but his legs refused to budge. Hurriedly, he looked back at where Cura had fallen, but she still wasn't visible. Instead, standing stoically amongst the crowd, was a man. Yet, he was like no man Abeo had ever seen before. His hair was a pale gold, and his skin was fair and white. Most noticeable of all, were his eyes—they were a striking shade of red. A thick streak of blood ran from the crown of his head, down the length of his nose, and curled into the crevices on the outside his lips. The skin on the top of his head had been cut away exposing brain and bone. The man nodded slowly and closed his eyes. Abeo looked back at his feet and then back to where the man stood, but he was no longer there.

In a panic, Abeo jerked his legs up and down. He watched in horror as they sunk deeper into the solid floor. "No!" he screamed, reaching his hand outwards. "Cura! NO! Let me go!" Harder and harder he pulled his legs, wrenching them uncontrollably. Finally, with one hard thrust, he felt the cobblestone crack, followed by an unrelenting pain in his ankle. He screamed out in agony only to open his eyes and see Veritas shaking his shoulders, trying to wake him.

"Abeo!" Veritas yelled. "Calm yourself! You're awake!"

Abeo slowed his breathing and sat up, wiping his forehead from the sweat.

"You alright?" Veritas asked.

"Uh, yeah. I think. Sorry, just such a vivid dream."

The door to the tent opened, and Foedus peered inside. He said nothing, he just looked at Abeo.

"Just a dream," Abeo whispered between breaths.

"How's the ankle?"

"I'll live."

Foedus nodded at Veritas. "Give us a moment."

Veritas obliged and climbed out of the tent.

"Petram cooked some food if you're hungry," Foedus yelled at him as he left. The captain came into the tent and sat down beside his friend.

"Cura?"

Abeo sighed and wiped his forehead again. "Do you have some water?"

Foedus pulled out his canteen and handed it over to Abeo; he gulped the cool liquid down with haste.

"She was just standing there, so close that I could just run and help her," Abeo continued. "She must have felt so helpless in all that entropy. All those people, claiming to fight for the fair treatment of everyone," he scoffed, "and at the same time allowing innocents to get burned or trampled. They laugh as their enemies writhe in pain. Ironic, isn't it? A violent rebellion fighting to end bloodshed. And for what? What did any of them die for?"

"Such is the way of civilization, I suppose," Foedus mumbled.

"The powerful give the illusion of control until the veil is torn down and their volatility is exposed. This allows a new group of leadership to fill the vacuum of control that was left behind. A new regime gains popularity through promises of change and soon realizes you can't stay powerful without a little fear and a pinch of tyranny—not to mention you need to exterminate your opponents when you're trying to win. Next thing you know, you have yourself a brand new version what you just got rid of. Nice little flat circle."

"I know you think that, but I have little problem with our world. Progress has been made, however small it may seem."

"Progress?" Abeo scoffed. "What does that even mean? A few more people are rich? The power clique pretends to care a bit more just to give some sense of stability. You're kidding yourself if you believe anything has changed."

Foedus shook his head, "watch what you say, Abeo. I know you imagine you have free reign right now, but our laws hold true, even out here."

Abeo laughed. "You're always a slave to those above you. What happens when the mighty fall, old friend? Do you go down with them, or do you climb over the cadavers and sit on that empty throne? Where does your loyalty lie?"

The captain shot his friend a wry smile, attempting to mask the offense he took to his comments. He nodded, got up, and moved to leave the tent. As he exited, he turned back and looked at his oldest companion. "I believe in doing my job and fulfilling the oaths assigned to me. My loyalty lies where it needs to be. If you question it again, you will have me and me alone to answer to. Remember your place." He paused and looked down somberly. "Get some rest; we're heading out whether or not that ankle holds up."

Abeo sat in the darkness and the silence of the tent. He leaned his body back down against the bed, still warm from before, and eased back into a comfortable position. As he slowly closed his eyes, he thought about the white-skinned man with the blood-red eyes.

19

Petram felt as if he had walked to the edge of the world and back. His legs burned, his back ached, and the bottoms of his feet refused to stop hurting. Stopping for a rest, he dipped his thick hand into the river. The water was unbearably frigid; he felt as if millions of needles simultaneous pricked his skin. Withdrawing his arm, he brought the cool water to his face and felt the refreshing sting on his dark skin.

"Let's take a rest here," Foedus yelled back at his trailing company.

Petram looked up at the sky and gazed at a brilliant yellow star twinkling in the distance. Solaris had always been the most intriguing star to him; it flickered brilliantly above, always remaining directly overhead. It was the one star that refused to change its position in the sky—a rock, eternally reliable.

"How's the ankle?" Petram asked Abeo.

"Not any worse, but it's not going to heal until I can stay off it for a while," Abeo responded.

"I don't think that will be happening anytime soon," Cordatus conceded.

"We must be close to the caverns we took shelter in last time. The river's starting to freeze up and the canyon's starting to narrow," Petram pointed out.

Cordatus agreed. "Can't be long now."

"Where will we go after that?" Petram inquired.

"Across the ice," Abeo stated gravely.

Petram had never heard of anyone attempting to cross the Emerald Lake. He reminisced about the first time he had seen it. The immense sheet of ice stretched for miles in every direction. On the other side of the lake was one of the most incredible sights he had ever seen in his life. There, a towering mound of blue-stained ice completely covered the rocky basin upon which it lay. Giant clumps of frozen water rubbed up against each other, echoing hauntingly throughout the unprotected expanse. Streams of melted water carved intricate designs into the icy block, eventually coalescing into the Deceptive River.

"What do we expect to find on the other side? I don't see it being worth the risk," Petram argued.

"The Imperium doesn't care about the Seekers," Abeo interjected. "From the very beginning they saw us as a sacrificial entity they could use for their own purposes. They just want to exploit our talents to do the bidding that they are incapable of doing. Perhaps they are threatened—or just ignorant. Nonetheless, their primary goal has been to throw us like lambs to the slaughter. All they care about is that we find something useful. Once we do, the Legion will lead its own excursions. Do you think they'd put the future of our civilization in the hands of a couple of mutants? Those who are different are never trusted. We are just pawns. The best we can hope for is to make it to the other side and possibly be rewarded as glorified soldiers."

"Sure makes you feel useful, doesn't it?" Petram laughed, but his laugh was simply a mask for the realization in the validity of what Abeo had said.

As they set up camp, Petram watched as Abeo unstrapped his backpack from around his shoulders and sat down exhaustedly.

"Go grab some food. We'll set up your tent for you," Petram offered, nodding at Cordatus.

"Obliged," Abeo responded. He struggled to his feet and hobbled over to the fire to grab something to eat.

"He's not improving much," Petram whispered to Cordatus as he unloaded the tent from Abeo's bag.

"No, I'm afraid it will not heal until he gets proper rest. Something, I fear, that likely won't happen."

"We should try and convince Foedus to take some time once we reach the lake. It would probably be best to council over whether to take the risk or not, don't you think?"

Cordatus coughed from a sudden burst of laughter. "I'm afraid that we're under strict orders to go as far as we possibly can. With Foedus at the helm, I don't imagine we'll be veering too far from Christoph's commands."

"Captain Foedus: a man of no treasons," Petram joked. They both chuckled and continued to assemble Abeo's tent.

Petram looked over at the old man. He had taught Petram so much. Not just general knowledge, but what it meant to truly live. When he had met Cordatus, ages ago, Petram was working for the Central Treasury in Lux. It was a nefarious business with little reward for those at the bottom. Petram worked hard and did his job, but the politics and corruption eventually frustrated him too much.

He had always contained the hidden Seeker talent, but never really understood what it was. His parents, afraid that he would be taken away from them, advised him to hide it as best as he could. Throughout his childhood, he had to fight the urge not to explore his inner mind. Before he met Cordatus, he thought that the Seekers were more of a myth than a legitimate organization. From everything he had heard, the magical Seekers of the Unknown seemed like they came straight out of folklore. Men who had a unique ability to see in darkness; it all seemed so absurd. Eventually, his mind struggled to contain the persevering curiosity that had become a staple of his personality. He frequently spent his spare time scouring over old books in the libraries of Lux, burying himself in a sea of knowledge. He explored the writings of Miletus—the pioneer of astronomy, geometry, mathematics—who had postulated theories as to what made the Seekers unique. Petram desperately wanted to understand why he was different; or, rather, why so few were the same. *How could an ability to see in the dark be advantageous for a world that basked in constant light?* he wondered.

It was during one of these inquisitive occasions that he ran into an elderly man scouring through the same collection of books he had recently indulged in himself. To say it was rare to see another person in that section of library would be an understatement, so he decided to introduce himself in the hopes that perhaps this enigmatic man had answers to the endless questions stored within his mind. He didn't know why, but he was thoroughly convinced that something was different about this elderly gentleman.

"I am curious," Cordatus had asked "what draws you into this particular literary setting?"

"You are curious about my curiosity?" Petram responded with a grin.

"Not necessarily," Cordatus replied with a coy smile. "My curiosity has led me to understand the world far better than I ever thought possible. Without it, I would not have cared to explore the dark mysteries of our world or even those outside this realm. It is this desire for understanding which drives us as a species to attempt to comprehend our own existence, you see. So, to answer your question, I am not curious about your curiosity, for curiosity is simply a commonality of minds. I am merely inquiring about your particular interest in this particular subject. A curious curiosity, if you will."

After that, Petram went on to describe his childhood experiences to Cordatus. He told him how he could see things in the dark that others couldn't; he talked about seeing his dreams with his eyes open and having the capacity to explore a different state of understanding. Petram kept waiting for the old man to interrupt him and enlighten him about his mental insanity. Instead, Cordatus just nodded and smiled. For the first time in his life, Petram felt someone had actually understood him.

20

Apricot tentacles slithered into and out of existence, leaving in their wake warm air and milky smoke. The fire made little sound as it quietly raged on, searing the ignasaxum so that the stones radiated bold blue. Up above, the twinkle of thousands of white, yellow, and red dots played a cosmic symphony orchestrated by the invisible atmosphere.

Abeo adjusted from one uncomfortable position to another. The cold air numbed the pain in his ankle just enough for him to rest his eyes for a few moments before it throbbed again. He heard Turpis' heavy breathing from the tent across the fire. *Did he drop me on purpose?* he wondered. The question vexed him almost as much as the physical pain. Abeo had always known Turpis had a disregard for him; from the beginning of their time together, the mammoth man had been spiteful towards Abeo.

Despite being older, Turpis was considered Abeo's junior. The Seekers had recruited Abeo at a very young age. His acutely perceptive mother had noticed his innate ability to navigate in the dark early on. In his youth, he and his cousins would often find dark tunnels to play popular games like Dark Tag, Hider and Seeker, or, his personal favourite, Night-Crawlers. His relatives, too, had a keen sense for the dark—their pedigree firmly rooted in Crepusculum—but no one was as good as Abeo. He was the youngest Seeker to ever be invited into the organization.

Abeo was used to standing out, just not for positive reasons. Around his neighbourhood, people gossiped about him, claiming he had given some dark power from a demon. His family often referred to him as "Lucifer"—the light bringer. This name carried two connotations: his pale complexion and the fact that he could see what others could not. More than anything, it meant he was different. It was not a name that he carried with pride. As he aged, Abeo continued to be tormented for his faded features. The other children ridiculed him relentlessly. Even now, the voices of his harping peers echoed in his mind. Bullies fed off the audiences who ignorantly stood by, oblivious to their role in the entire ordeal. He often wondered why he looked the way that he did. His mother had been as dark as any other local of Crepusculum and, although—as a result of his precipitous passing—Abeo barely knew his father, he had been assured by those who knew the man that he was "as normal as any other person."

Abeo's distaste for others only escalated as he matured. He began to detest the stupidity and ignorance of his peers. He witnessed friends fall for devious ploys and outlandish gimmicks; he watched herds of people passionately flock towards spiritual communes in the hopes of answering the questions they were too inept to answer on their own. He saw how volatile a relationship, and how fickle a friendship, could be. He awed at how easily greed could corrupt, and how blind those in power were to the struggle of the many. For him, how such a minuscule degree of empathy could exist was a mystery. To have so little of a heart as to watch another person tortured on the way to inevitable death, was incomprehensible; it made his innards churn.

For these reasons, he always found solace away from society. Competition for jobs, food, and social relationships tended to bring the worst out in people. He felt the onset of nausea every time he was forced to integrate into the social machinery. It was Cura who gave him the strength to endure the daily norms. She was his rock. Thinking back on it, he could still recall the first moment they met.

Foedus had hosted a post-expedition party. It had been Abeo's second journey, but the first time he had reached Paradise Valley. He could still recall the shockwave that was sent through his body as he soaked in the panorama. At one point, he could have sworn that he saw a blue spiral shape on the horizon, but too often their view was cut off by the canyon walls.

Unfortunately for Abeo, he had joined the Seekers in the days when their value had already waned. He had missed the prime of Imperial excitement for Seeker expeditions. The Seekers as an organization had not found anything of importance since the discovery of the Carbo Caves. It was there, some twenty generations prior, that they had found a much more flammable type of ignasaxum which they named carbo. Those strange black rocks, with their explosive power and confined energy, fueled the Imperium's ever increasing military might and thirst for territorial expansion. As his tenure waxed on, problems in the Imperium began to take precedent. The few Seekers who did remain clung on to the job they loved.

As such, the Seekers were responsible for singing their own praises. Foedus often invited the others to celebrate any successful—which just meant deathless—expedition. He always insisted on Abeo's presence.

"You know I'm no good at those parties, Foedus," Abeo recalled pleading. "I always just end up making someone hate me when I give them a cool hard shot of reality."

"Well," Foedus replied, "you know you don't have to throw your contentious opinions around so liberally. There is such thing as self-control, not that I know much about that in other regards," Foedus snickered.

"I'm allowed to leave when I want, understood?"

"Understood," Foedus responded, elated that Abeo had agreed to attend.

The party began much as Abeo had expected. He made small talk with others, biting his tongue at someone's misguided opinion or weak attempt at humor. His eyes continually veered from his conversational counterparts, searching for an exit. Then, he saw her. As soon as she walked in, Abeo's eyes caught hers, and their stares lingered for more than a moment. He broke first, darting for the floor. Embarrassed and nervous, he navigated his way through Foedus' opulent home and made his way to the bar.

"Whiskey straight," he mumbled to the bartender. Abeo took a sip of the caramel coloured liquid and felt the burning on his tongue.

"I didn't know going past the Murky Mountains made your skin pale," a soothing voice serenaded from behind him.

He swung around and saw her standing in front of him. Her chestnut hair fell gracefully on her shoulders, and her crimson dress lay perfectly on the curves of her body. She gazed up at him with gentle emerald eyes and smirked seductively with her cherry lips.

"It doesn't. I just don't go outside very much," he managed to choke the words out with a nervous smile.

She innocently laughed and extended her small hand. "I'm Cura. It's quite an honour to meet a real Seeker of the Unknown. The host tells me you're quite the talent."

Now it all makes sense; Foedus is setting this up, he remembered thinking. As much as Abeo tried not to like the captain, there was something magnetic about him. His charm and his wit perfectly disguised any flaws he may have.

"He just wants his party to seem high profile. I assure you I'm nothing special," he calmly replied.

"I wouldn't say that. I've never seen someone look as you do. That's special, isn't it?"

"Depends on who you ask, I suppose."

"Then ask the right people," she responded with a smile and touched his shoulder gently. "I didn't catch your name," she prompted.

"Abeo," he said awkwardly.

"Abeo. Abeo! Abeo!" Cordatus shook him as he awoke from his slumber. "Abeo, the winds have picked up, we need to get moving again or else we'll risk getting caught in this storm. There is a cavern up ahead, do you remember it? We can rest there. Are you able to move?"

Abeo struggled to adjust to a seated position. "Can you re-wrap my ankle? I've lost circulation in it and can't feel it at all."

"Read my mind," Cordatus responded. He removed a bundle of tape from his bag and wrapped Abeo's foot.

"Prod," Foedus called out dictatorially, "you and Veritas will have to take turns carrying Abeo."

Prod nodded assuredly at the captain, but Abeo could tell the young man was not pleased by the assignment.

"Why don't I ride Airam instead?" Abeo suggested. He cringed as he adjusted his position. The circulation had returned to his foot; the feeling and the pain both rushed in like water over a breached dam. "The others can take some of the supplies she's carrying to make room for me. That would be much easier than lugging me along anyway."

Foedus agreed.

Prod sighed in relief and got up to unload the supplies from the mule's harness, giving no gratitude for Abeo's suggestion.

"Ungrateful brat," Abeo mumbled quietly to himself. Despite his apparent dwindling hearing, Abeo noticed a smirk emerge under Cordatus' grey beard.

The men loaded Abeo onto Airam's back and continued their trek down the vast expanse of protruding rock. The tall walls on either side were like giant waves suspended in time, ready to crash down upon them at any moment. A brisk wind began to bite into Abeo's skin, while a frosty tickle imposed itself on his nose. He noticed a single snowflake fall on his hand and watched it quickly transform into a droplet of water.

"We need to move," Abeo said anxiously.

Within minutes, snow came barreling down on them. Combined with the gusting wind, the chill felt like miniature icicles were raining from the sky, intermittently inserting into each exposed orifice.

Abeo threw his gray hood over his head and faced downwards to try and relieve himself from the vexatious chill. Foedus led the way, with Anin and Atnip obediently maintaining their proximity to the group. As the winds picked up, the men huddled behind a small alcove in the rock, providing them with temporary relief from the piercing wind. Everyone panted heavily; their faces were covered in wet snow. Abeo could feel the miniature icicles around his nostrils. Every time he blinked, his eyelashes would momentarily stick together. The temperature continued to drop.

Cordatus spoke first. "The storm is worsening quickly," he yelled weakly through the wind. "If my memory serves me correctly, there is a cavern, farther along. We're almost near it."

"How sure are you?" Foedus inquired.

"Quite positive. The snow has been somewhat disorienting, but once we see three large boulders, we will have to cross the river. The cavern should be there shortly after."

"It's too soon to cross the river; the ice can't be thick enough. We have to keep going. We can't cross until the ice gets thicker," Petram cautioned.

"We've done it before. The ice is thin, but we will just have to be careful," Turpis pointed out. Everyone glanced nervously at Foedus, awaiting his decision.

Foedus nodded at Turpis. "We have no choice; we have to try it. We can't stay out here much longer."

Suddenly, an exploding burst of air forced its way through the narrow valley and swirled around them violently. Foedus went over to Abeo, who quietly watched from atop Airam.

"You look paler than ever. How are you feeling?" the captain asked.

"Fine," Abeo responded sharply. "Let me take the lead."

"You're in no shape to be doing anything of the sort," Foedus replied.

"At least let me travel beside you so I can guide us."

Foedus shifted uncomfortably and wiped his brow of melted snow. "Let's pick up the pace then," he replied.

The team advanced along the bank of the river, keeping huddled together as close as possible. The winds howled while the sound of crashing snow and ice echoed above. The visibility declined to the point that anyone five steps away appeared to be swallowed by the ghostly ether. In the distance, Abeo began to see three irregular spheres of ash coloured rock; its jagged edges protruded through the hazy storm. As they continued, three massive boulders emerged into view. The stones sat on the opposite side of the river bank, detached from the rocky walls cradling them. Like massive vessels lingering in a frozen harbour, they lay statically afloat on the snowy ground. Abeo wondered how such large stones could have got there. What kind of journey had they taken? His reverence of the natural world never ceased to diminish.

"Let's cross here!" Cordatus yelled. His beard was covered in white powder, and his eyes were half open.

"Abeo, what do you think?" Petram inquired.

Abeo stared across the river from atop Airam and shook his head. "Hard to tell!" he yelled. His voice was barely able to overcome the swirling winds.

"Let's do it! The storm's only getting worse!" Prod yelled. His muscles had tensed so much that he was beginning to resemble a tree rooted in the ground, swaying in the wind to and fro.

Veritas, on the other hand, looked completely comfortable. The young man calmly walked up to the edge of the river and tested different pressures on the icy shore. His weight appeared to have no effect, so he gave a sign of okay. This was little reassurance to the six others who were heavier than him.

The men looked towards Foedus, eagerly awaiting his decision. The captain was not convinced it was safe to cross, but with the winds howling harder and harder, he had little choice but to approve. "Let's go two or three at a time," he commanded, "each trip taking a mule. Make sure we're spreading out as much as possible!"

Turpis grabbed a bundle of rope from a supply sack. "Tether together, just in case," he said. He threw the rope at Prod who caught it awkwardly.

Petram and Prod went first. They accompanied Abeo, who tentatively agreed to guide his furry freight across the crackling ice. As they crossed, they nervously listened as each heavy clop was met with crunching and cracking sounds that reverberated through the entire valley. Abeo watched carefully for any fragments starting to form in the ice, but the frozen sheet maintained its rigor. The three men made it across safely and immediately took shelter behind the largest of the three boulders. Prod untethered himself from Petram and pulled out a second rope from his sack. He wrapped the rope around a large rock and pulled to test the knot's hold on the marbled stone. Then, he shook the rope to signal to the others that it was safe. They were to use the line as a guide.

Shortly after, a second group emerged from the haze. Veritas' silhouette broke through the dense fog with Turpis tethered to him. The young man guided Atnip; the mule clumsily clopped on the volatile surface. Breaking through the chilly steam, the two men rushed to find shelter with the rest of the group. As they approached, Abeo noticed his Discipulus' face consumed with concern.

"The ice is beginning to crack; I don't think it's safe for them to cross!" Veritas yelled, his voice fighting a contentious battle with the battering wind.

"They don't have a choice at this point; the storm's getting too intense!" Abeo yelled back.

"I'm going back to warn them!"

"No, you're not! It's too risky!" Abeo cautioned.

But before Abeo could grab him, the young man had already darted swiftly back towards the shore. Veritas disappeared into the milky nebula.

21

Foedus could see the outline of the three enormous boulders poking through the thick fog but not much else. With each step, the frozen floor beneath his feet moaned and creaked in agony. He looked down and saw an emerging crack in the river and moved away from it. As he did so, the distance between him and Cordatus increased. They were tethered together, but the rope had enough slack he could easily lose sight of the old man in the dense mist. Then, emerging from the thick fog, was Veritas.

"What're you doing!?" Foedus yelled, trying not to make any violent motions.

Veritas slowly slid towards him, stopping when he was close enough to yell a reply. "The ice in front of you is far too thin and starting to crack. You'll have to veer your path. Follow me."

Foedus looked back to see how far away Cordatus was. He could barely make out the old man's trudging silhouette in the distance.

"Cordatus!" he hollered, motioning for him to come his way. Cordatus turned and waved and made his way towards them.

A sudden burst of wind forced its way across their path causing the captain to stumble. As he fell, he inadvertently pulled the harness of Anin. The mule exhaled an exasperated neigh and desperately shook her head, trying to loosen the rope's grip around her snout. Foedus clumsily picked himself up; his arms irritably tingled from the hard fall. To make matters worse, Cordatus was nowhere to be seen through the dense fog. As he attempted to peer towards the old man, the windblown snow ravaged his eyes forcing them closed. Nonetheless, the captain kept moving, trying to monitor the tension in his tether. He could see that it was heading in the same direction he was, so he continued towards the barely visible shore. Ahead of him, Veritas tried to guide his path, keeping as much distance between them as he could. Prod's guide rope was nowhere in sight—the captain feared how far he had diverged from the others.

Another violent gust of wind lashed against him. Foedus attempted to maintain his balance, but instead slid and fell flat on his stomach. As he did, a loud crack echoed throughout the valley. He unwittingly jerked the harness and lost his grip on the rope. In a panic, Anin, free from her bondage, sprinted away. Veritas ran after her as the mule clopped heavily on the fragile ice. The stomping of her heavy hooves echoed intermittently between breaks in the fierce gusting wind. Disoriented by the opaque fog, the captain had no clue which direction was the right way; all he had to guide him was his loose tether to Cordatus, which continued to slither along the icy surface.

Foedus pushed his hands against the turquoise ice and forced himself up from the ground. As he looked down at the frozen glass, he noticed small fractures spreading their arms. Cautiously, he rose to his feet and moved towards what he hoped was the shore. After a few steps, he felt his foot fall straight through the ice, sucking his right leg down into the piercing liquid below. Scrambling around, he grabbed ahold of a rut to prevent himself from falling in farther. All around him the glacial water vigorously ruptured. He carefully crawled on to a sturdier patch of the frozen river and got back to his feet. The captain was on an island of solid ice, the eye of the storm, while chaos cracked around him.

Carefully, Foedus shuffled forward. As he peered ahead, he began to make out hazy silhouettes waving at him. Pushing on the ice, he gauged its durability. Step by step he inched closer to the shore, following a volatile path. He attempted to locate Cordatus. The old man was close, but the blowing snow made it impossible to see him. A few strides from the shore, Foedus began quickening his pace.

"Foedus! Here! We're here!" he heard they others yelling.

As he took one more step, he suddenly felt a tug around his waist and was violently wrenched sideways. Landing painfully on the hard ice, he slid uncontrollably as the rope pulled him away from the shore. The captain grabbed the rope and pulled back on it, staying on his knees so not to be jerked forward. Suddenly, emerging through the mist, he saw Cordatus' half submerged body struggling to stay afloat. Foedus wrapped both of his hands around the rope and pulled with every ounce of strength he had. Each successful pull was met with a subsequent slip forward. With all of his might, he heaved Cordatus out of the water, grabbed his ice-cold hands, and dragged him across to the shore. Pulling the old man into his arms, he tried to extinguish Cordatus' violent shivering, but it had little effect.

"We're here!" he screamed in desperation. The old man shook uncontrollably, his hair was crusted with ice, and his eye were glued shut. "Here!" he yelled again. The captain wrapped his coat around the old man, attempting to inhibit the overwhelming chill.

Finally, out of the haze, the others appeared.

"What the hell happened?" Petram exclaimed. He rushed to his Praeceptoris and also wrapped his coat around him.

"He fell through the ice. If we don't find a fire and some shelter he'll freeze," the captain responded.

"Even if we do," Prod mumbled, stoically staring at the trembling old man.

Petram gave him a scornful look.

"Petram, do you know where this cavern is?" Foedus asked, his voice, too, began to tremble from his relentless shivering.

"Yeah, it's just up ahead. We can't be far," Petram replied.

"You and the kids get to the cave and take Cordatus with you. Turpis and I will bring Abeo and the animals. Has anyone seen Anin? She escaped my grip in all the commotion," Foedus commanded.

"She's here; she's safe," Veritas replied as he emerged from the fog. He had managed to wrangle the rogue mule.

Petram nodded at the captain. "The cavern can't be more than half a league. Stay close to the wall, you should see the light of the fire," Petram instructed. He and the two young man carried Cordatus and disappeared into the murky fog.

"You okay?" Abeo inquired.

"Fine, why?" Foedus replied.

"You're freezing. Your heart is barely beating."

"Don't worry about me," he shot back. Foedus hated being pandered to. "You're the one who should be worried, not me."

"I've never felt so warm in my life," Abeo mumbled back with a wry smile.

"Grab a mule and get a room," Turpis grumbled at the two men, wrapping his thick hand around Atnip's harness.

The three of them advanced forward, pushing hard against the gusting wind and pelting snow. Every step seemed to completely drain the blood from their body, only to be renewed by the next thrust forward. Finally, after a fierce battle between tenacity and nature, they saw a warm orange glow refracting through the snow. The wind was so strong that walking against it seemed futile. Reaching the entrance of the cavern, they walked into the luminous tunnel and eventually found a large alcove off the main path. There, sitting around a fire, Petram, Prod, and Veritas silently stared at Cordatus. Wrapped in blankets, his hair still soaked, and his complexion ghostly white, the old Seeker barely moved.

Petram looked at Foedus earnestly and shook his head in disbelief.

22

Silence filled the cavern. The only thing audible was the intermittent outburst of the ravaging storm and the subtle splash of falling dew drops echoing as they exploded on the rocky surface.

Petram looked at Cordatus. The old man was wrapped in a wool cocoon beside him. For now, the warmth of the fire and the shelter of the cavern were soothing, but they provided temporary relief. The cold winds continued to creep in forcing them to delve farther and farther into the cavern's murky depths. Petram's whole body clenched as he recalled his incident with the cave lion — he had narrowly escaped with his life and did not wish to roll the dice again.

Foedus, pretending he was not unnerved by the icy incident, tried to remain positive. Despite his optimism, the captain spent most of his spare time pacing the cavern, sporadically reminding the others that the break was impermanent.

In Petram's mind, it was clear that both Cordatus and Abeo needed time to heal. He had no desire to abandon his companions, but he knew the mission was the priority. Hopefully, that difficult decision would not need to be made.

Abeo, on the other hand, had remained relatively buoyant. He had taken it upon himself to explore the cavern with the Discipuli, hoping to strengthen his ankle in the process. He told the others that honing his skills in the dark would give him the energy to heal, and they felt it best not to question his methods.

Time dilated as each Seeker attempted to settle into the new environment, pondering both what had happened and what was to come. Turpis began rifling through the food supplies like a rodent looking for scraps. Foedus delegated the job of inventorying to the big man—a job Turpis always enjoyed doing because he could secretly snag some excess food for himself. How Foedus didn't clue in on this, Petram never understood. Perhaps he knew and just wanted Turpis to be happy. Who was to say?

Cordatus shifted on to his side and groaned in discomfort. "P...Petram," the words barely squeaked from his dehydrated tongue. "Petram," he swallowed with difficulty, "in my bag, the bottle...the blue bottle."

Petram rummaged through Cordatus' beige sack. In one of the front pouches, he found a small blue flask that contained a dark liquid.

"Do you need to drink this? Is it medicine?" Petram inquired.

Cordatus nodded. "Just a swig."

Petram guided the bottle to Cordatus' lips and let a splash of the drink enter his mouth.

Cordatus swallowed and exhaled in relief.

"What is it?" Petram inquired.

"Port," he replied with a smile.

To Petram, it was astonishing how a man of such great age, who had seen so much tragedy in his life, and who was suffering from the chilling cold, could maintain his enlightening aura. Despite the icy bath he had involuntarily indulged in, the old man's spirit refused to dampen. Cordatus closed his eyes, supplanted his sanguine smile with a subtle simper, and settled slowly into a sedated sleep.

"Petram!" Foedus shouted in a whisper. "How long have they been gone? I feel it's been a while."

"I was thinking the same, to be honest. They couldn't have gotten lost, Abeo and Veritas can see too well. I haven't heard anything to suggest a cave lion. Maybe they're just killing time. Doesn't matter, does it? Cordatus won't be fit to go anytime soon."

Foedus sighed. "We wait until the storm subsides. If he's not better by then, we'll throw him on one of the mules. Abeo should be good to walk again soon, even if it is at a hobble."

"And if he's not?"

"We'll just have to take turns helping him along. We can't wait here forever; our supplies are as limited as is. After what just happened to us, we're going to have to find a route around the Emerald Lake. I don't trust getting across that sheet of ice."

"I ain't carrying that son of a bitch, that ain't my job." Turpis' rough voice resonated inside the cavern walls. It was obvious he had been slipping himself swigs of whiskey from the supplies.

"Your job is to take orders, and if I order you to do so, you will." Foedus shot back.

Turpis grimaced angrily but returned to his "important" task.

The captain returned his attention to Petram. "Get some sleep. You've barely slept since we got here. Cordatus will be okay; we all just need to catch up on our rest. The storm will subside soon enough."

Petram wiped his crimson forehead and nodded in agreement. Despite the lingering fatigue, he had been experiencing acute insomnia—the dark had mangled his internal clock. Time seemed to erode away in a punctuated equilibrium. Even with his eyes open, images in his mind danced into and out existence. He could see the dazzling stars and emerald lights; they soothed his worries and guided his internal journey. Then, finally, his mind faded into complete darkness.

***

Petram awoke to the sound of voices in the distance. Lying on his side, his back faced the fire—whoever was talking couldn't know if he was awake. Barely lucid, he was too groggy to turn around, but he listened to what seemed like a contentious conversation.

"What… I mean, well… how?" one voice whispered.

"I don't know. I don't even really know where to start. I mean, do you see what this means?" the other retorted.

"It means we have something to report to home base."

"Well, let's wait and see what more we can find out first. We don't want to send something without all the details, right?"

"For now, yes, I agree."

In his comatose state, Petram thought maybe it had been a dream, but his conscious wonder overrode his apathy and forced him to get up to see what all the commotion was about. He turned over and looked across the fire.

"What's all the whispering about?" he yelled.

"Shut it!" Foedus shot back at him. Lying on the ground next to him, Turpis snored like a tranquilized animal beside his half-complete inventory pile. Cordatus, meanwhile, remained in his same cocooned position. Abeo, standing next to Foedus, was whiter than he had ever seen him. He looked frail, but he had an enthusiastic countenance.

"Abeo and the kid, uh…" Foedus started.

"Veritas," Abeo interjected

"Yes, Veritas, right. They, well, they found something."

"What?" Petram pleaded for them to end the suspense.

"Come with me," Foedus nodded towards the interior of the cavern.

Petram followed his captain down a narrow corridor. The path was so dark that he could barely make out the surrounding walls. As they ventured down the tunnel, he saw see the heat radiating off Veritas and Prod. Buried in a nook in the wall, they stood overtop another emanating object.

"What am I looking at?" Petram asked.

"This," Foedus responded, lighting one of their few remaining lamps. Orange light illuminated the entire tunnel. Petram looked away to protect his eyes from the sudden brightness, and then slowly peered through the cracks in his eyelids. In front of him stood both Discipuli. They held their swords in an antagonistic fashion at a shaking creature huddled in the corner. The creature's skin was ghostly white, covered in a thin coat of coarse beige hair. Its hip was wrapped in ivory bandages stained with its own blood. Draped around its shoulders was a heavy animal hide covered in coarse chestnut hair. The creature moaned uncomfortably in distress. Petram had never seen anything like it. Its head was buried in its shaking muscular arms, and the base of its spinal disks protruded through its pale skin. An assortment of mahogany paint covered the exposed portions of creature's body, formulating intricate designs of spirals and crosses.

"What is it?" Petram prodded inquisitively.

Before anyone could answer, the creature raised its head from behind its folded arms and looked up at him. Staring back at Petram were the blood-red irises of what looked to be a man.

M.A.T. REESON

BOOK 3
THE PEOPLE

23

The moment kept replaying itself in Abeo's mind. He, Veritas, and Prod had been sent to explore the cavern to look for a sheltered spot, one that didn't leave them exposed to the creeping cold. After some preliminary surveying, the three of them decided to venture deeper into the cavern. Eventually, the tunnel forked into two diverging paths; one reeked of dank, warm air—potentially the lair of a cave lion—the other exuded the seductive sound of trickling water. With their supplies beginning to dwindle, Abeo and the Discipuli agreed that the latter path was the best to pursue.

Descending down the rocky tunnel, Abeo heard the soothing sound of the steady stream sliding down the slick rock. Although very little heat radiated off the walls, Abeo was able to discern the cave's subtle structure if he relaxed his mind and focused intently.

Prod, too proud to ask for them to wait, fell behind. He had developed the habit of using his hands to feel his way down the tunnel, always trudging along at a conscientious pace.

After making their way through a few narrow shoots, the tunnel opened up, and eventually revealed a cliff. Directly below, a pool of water rested in a rocky bowl. On the opposite side, an opening exposed the grotto to the cool outside air. The light of the stars reflected off the water, illuminating the hollow. White and blue lights danced jubilantly on the cavern walls, reflecting off the interfering waves of water. An enchanting stream slithered down the rocks and gently trickled into the pool.

Abeo and Veritas looked on silently, admiring the subtle beauty, but their admiration was short-lived. Through the opening, a peculiar sight grabbed their attention. An ivory-skinned man, short and muscular, approached the glimmering pool. A chestnut animal hide rested upon his broad shoulders, and he held a tall sharpened stick in his thick hand. Abeo was astounded by what he saw. The man appeared to be human, but he had ghostly white skin, wispy blonde hair on his body, and piercing red eyes—the same eyes Abeo had seen so vividly in his dreams.

Veritas stared on in disbelief, and Abeo knew that the same cogs were churning in his Discipulus' mind. He had grown to appreciate the company of the young man; there was a deep similarity between them.

The two Seekers observed from above as the man waded into the pool, stopping when the water reached his knees. He stood tranquilly and gazed intently at the glassy liquid. From their perspective, he was examining nothing but the skin of a stagnant pond. Then, with prodigious speed, the man stabbed his stick into the water. When he lifted the weapon out of the pool, a squirming fish wriggled on its tip. Green liquid oozed from its flesh and its struggle slowly ceased to a halt. The man dropped his catch into a basket and returned to his predatory posture. By the time Prod finally caught up to them, the man had caught six more.

"This is cool!" Prod yelled. He looked upon the grotto with a triumphant pose, as if he had just conquered some remote island in the sea. No doubt, he was just happy to be out of the dark.

"Quiet!" Abeo hushed, dragging Prod down behind the sheltering rock. He nodded towards the white man, who had taken note of the sudden sound echoing through the cave. For a moment, they thought their cover was blown, but they remained still and listened intently. The calming sound of the trickling creek was all that could be heard. After enough time passed, they heard the swishing sound of the spear return. They remained unknown.

"What is it?" Prod whispered. He poked his head past the rocky facade to take a look, but every time he crept upwards, Abeo pulled him violently back down.

"We don't know. We'd like to find out, but if you don't stop being a damn moron, it's doubtful we'll even get a chance." Abeo sternly looked into the chestnut eyes of the boy in front of him. That's all he was: a boy. He had been dragged into an exciting adventure with the prospect of glory. But did he really know what he was getting into? Of course not. How could he? What did he know? He was aware of almost nothing. He didn't comprehend danger; he barely understood his own mortality. Naivety was his strength, recklessness his weapon. Nonetheless, lessons needed to be learned. Abeo gave him a hardy look, one that spoke without words. Prod received the message, though it was evident he was not pleased with what had been transmitted.

The whipping sound of the spear ceased, so Abeo instructed Veritas to take a look. He realized the boy's thin body would make him the best candidate for deception.

Veritas crept towards the far end of the cliff where a narrow opening allowed him to observe without the risk of exposing himself. He peered into the crack and watched. Creeping back towards Abeo, he motioned towards the location of the man. "He's counting his catch. We should go now, better not to miss him," he whispered.

Abeo nodded in agreement and turned to Prod. "You stay here and cover us. We're going to sneak down and try to ambush him. If we get exposed, I need you to threaten him with the rifle. Don't shoot unless he tries to run. If he does, legs only. Do not kill him. Can you handle that?"

"Why can't I come down, there's no way he could outrun me even if we did get exposed," Prod demanded.

"That's not what I asked you," Abeo sternly responded.

Prod stared back at his senior with contempt.

"We're running out of time. Please, Prod?" Veritas plead.

"Fine," he agreed, still glowering at Abeo.

Abeo and his Discipulus began their climb. They descended through a small groove in the rock wall. They clambered down, trying to find the perfect balance of quiet and speed. As they reached the bottom, they snuck behind a large boulder and peered over the top. The white man, gutting the fish he had caught, threw the entrails back into the pool.

"Draw your weapon quietly," Abeo whispered.

Veritas unsheathed his sword slowly, making as little sound as possible. Abeo quickly grabbed two thin knives from the scabbard around his ankles. He motioned towards Veritas, and they began their careful pursuit. Advantageously, the man's back faced them, but every step closer brought with it the increased audibility of the sediment cracking below their feet. Abeo inched closer and closer to his adversary. Grabbing one of the knives, he placed the sharper point between his thumb and index finger, ready to throw it if necessary. Veritas' thin sword stood awkwardly in the young man's hands. He was not a fighter, this was evident, but he refused to allow cowardice overtake his pride.

Abeo increased his pace and Veritas followed. They closed in and, at the exact moment it became too late for his escape, the white man turned. Screaming in fear, he attempted to swarm them off with his spear, nearly slashing Abeo across his eye. Abeo fell backward, jerked by the involuntary reaction of his body. Veritas waved his sword randomly, hoping to make contact with the spear knowing the thick metal would ravage the thin wood. Despite his best efforts, he could not make contact. The white man stabbed at the Veritas, who just barely avoided the attack.

Suddenly, a loud bang echoed in the hollow, followed by a streaking sound zipping from behind them. Prod's shot struck the white man in the hip. He screamed in a dialect, but Abeo could not understand what he was saying.

Abeo grabbed the spear, threw it into the pond, and stood over top of the man as he writhed in pain. Cherry-coloured blood dribbled out of his fresh wound and pooled underneath him. The man opened his brooding bloody eyes and gazed up at Abeo in fear. His open palms were placed beside his head submissively, and he whimpered like a wounded animal, begging for mercy from a battle he never asked to be a part of.

Staring at the trembling man, Veritas' bright blue eyes were fixated on the ground. Oozing from the white man's hip, gushing blood amalgamated with the gutted fish viscera strewn about the stony floor.

24

Foedus' eyes were fixated on the white-skinned man. Lying on the ground below him, the captain watched as Cordatus carefully removed the bullet from the man's hip and bandaged the wound. The stressful procedure induced a weariness in all of them, the white man most of all.

Standing beside the captain, Abeo observed and shook his head in frustration. "The kid is reckless," he complained. "He didn't need to shoot him; we had it under control."

Prod defended that the shot was necessary, but Abeo's skepticism refused to diminish.

Foedus attempted to ameliorate his friend's reservations, reminding him of Prod's inexperience. "Hey, at least he didn't kill the thing, right?" Foedus prodded.

"Mm," Abeo mumbled back.

"Now, the question is, do we go looking for the others on our own or do we get him to take us to them?"

"Considering we shot him, I don't think he's going to be overly anxious to take us to his people," Abeo croaked.

"True. Not to mention we don't understand anything he's saying, and he has no clue what or who we are. I'm feeling confident," the captain said with a charming smile. For a moment, he thought he saw a grin on Abeo's face—a sight almost as uncommon as the one sleeping in front of them. "If we let him go, then he'll have to go back to where he lives, right?" Foedus continued, "back to wherever he calls home. We could just pretend to lower our guard, let him escape, and then follow him."

"It couldn't be all of us, that would be too difficult to conceal," Abeo replied.

"Agreed. Cordatus isn't ready to travel yet anyway. Some of us would need to stay here."

"Let me go on my own," Abeo proposed.

"I can't let you do that. It's too risky. If you get lost, we'll have no idea where to even start looking for you. Take one of the kids. And Turpis."

"Not Turpis. He's far too conspicuous, and he's unpredictable. I'll take Veritas, Prod's skills are not nearly developed enough."

"Then I'm coming with you. That kid can barely hold his sword. I don't trust the two you if things get dicey."

"So big bad Foedus is going to protect me," Abeo jabbed sarcastically.

"Someone has to," he responded sharply.

They discussed the plan with the rest of the group. Foedus, Abeo, and Veritas, were to make their way down to the grotto and wait. Meanwhile, the others would pretend to fall asleep. The hope was that the white man would have the will to risk his escape. From there, it was up to the covert crew to follow him back to whatever place he called home. Everyone agreed to the plan, although Turpis, of course, had reservations not being chosen for the expeditionary squad. His disappointment was alleviated by the promise of a bottle of whiskey from the captain's private stash. Petram was happy to monitor Cordatus' health, while Prod was delegated the task of trying to catch fish like the white man had done. The final variable would be the odd-looking human himself.

***

"Let's go," Foedus commanded.

Abeo and Veritas eagerly awaited an opportunity to truly test their skills. They knew that the farther into the unknown they went, the more ethereal the darkness would become. To them, the fear of the void was eclipsed by the prospect of discovery. Wherever they were to go, it would be to a place that no Seeker had ever laid eyes upon. The enticement of that opportunity was motivation enough.

Abeo followed Foedus down the dark tunnel. He calmed his mind and allowed the darkness to envelope him. Looking forward, he saw the glowing outlines of his two companions. As he slowed his breathing, their full flaming figures materialized before his eyes. He continued trekking in darkness until he felt the sound of a trickling creek tickle inside of his ears. As they approached the entrance to the grotto, Abeo stopped to embrace its quiet beauty. The flickering of the stars seemed ever more prominent as their reflections scattered over the glossy surface of the water. The entire cavern radiated from the reflecting light.

"Incredible, isn't it?" he said.

Foedus just nodded.

"Where should we hide?" Abeo asked. "There are some large boulders on the far side of the pond that could provide cover. Only problem is we'll need to cross a big portion of empty space, and that'll leave us exposed. He can't know we're following him."

"But if we wait too long there's a chance we could lose him," Veritas added.

"Hmm," Foedus pondered, stroking his thickening beard. "Let's see if we can find something outside the cave."

They descended the same path Abeo and Veritas had when they first encountered the white man. The dribbling water followed the contours of the rock and coalesced at an eroded basin down below. Foedus noticed small potholes filled with different colours, resembling a collection of ink pots.

The three Seekers exited through the opening and looked upon the resplendent sky. White and blue lights quickly shot across the dark tapestry, propagating into and out of existence. Pearl and indigo ribbons of light intertwined with the neon green waves they were accustomed to seeing. All three men were completely awestruck by the brilliance that lingered above. *What were all those lights? What was causing such dazzling phosphorescence?* The vexing questions were universal—it was what made them the same.

Breaking away from his stupor, Foedus noted a crevice large enough for them to hide behind. The entrance to it was well hidden, and an eroded hole in the wall provided a perfect view of the grotto. From outside, the illuminated cavern looked even more brilliant.

The three Seekers took turns watching for any sign of the white man. Despite Foedus' orders not to leave their spot of cover, Abeo continually wandered outside the crevice to study the sky. Time passed like molasses crawling down a gentle slope, and still there was no sign of the creature.

Foedus gave Veritas a break and took a turn on watch. The captain began to have doubts about his plan. It assumed a lot of variables, and it made him nervous. He worried that the white man might take an entirely different path; he obviously knew the lands better than they did. The captain continuously scrutinized his plan and bullied his mind—confidently destroying his confidence. Then, just as he was about to transition his watch to Abeo, he saw him.

The white man frantically scrambled down the wet rock with incredible grace and balance. Continuously checking over his shoulder, he never stopped moving forward.

"We're on," Foedus alerted the others.

"You see him?" Veritas affirmed.

"He's just reaching the exit, get ready to go," the captain replied.

The white man scrambled out of the opening and looked around in a berserk manner. Foedus waited for him to head towards them. Instead, with unparalleled speed, he turned and scrambled up the rock wall and disappeared on the balcony above.

All three Seekers scrambled out of their hiding position and ran over to the spot where the man had suddenly vanished. They analyzed the cliff for a way up, but the vertical wall looked nearly impossible to climb. Abeo was at a loss for how the man could have scampered up the face so quickly.

"Do we try it?" he asked.

"I don't think we have a choice," Foedus responded. He walked over to the spot where the man had disappeared. The glitter of starlight on the moist rock revealed a small groove that, if proceeded with care, could be scaled. "Worth a shot, no?"

Abeo nodded.

Veritas offered to go first; his light weight made him the most agile climber. Observing the wall, it was difficult to see the contours in the rock. Each step had to be tested cautiously, and each grip had to be thoroughly approved.

Abeo ascended behind his Discipulus, trying his best to follow his follower's lead. As Veritas climbed, he inadvertently jarred loose a few rocks that tumbled down and narrowly missed Abeo's head. Eventually, after negotiating their way up the cliff, they reached an overhang. Veritas analyzed the contour of the cliff and searched for any easier way.

From Abeo's view, the only option was to risk leaping up to the overhang and hope that there was something to grab ahold of on top. He watched as Veritas solidified his footing into two well-defined grooves and reached as far as he could towards the protruding rock.

"Think you can do it?" Abeo called up from below him.

Foedus' heavy breathing echoed below, and his thick frame slowly came into focus. "Oh, even better," he jabbed as he looked at the task ahead of them.

Veritas continued to feel around. Suddenly, his eyes widened, and a smile grew on his face.

"Any luck?" Foedus called up.

"There's a handle of sorts. I think it's secure enough," Veritas called down anxiously.

"Be sure," Abeo cautioned.

"Okay," Veritas sighed, "I'm going to give it a shot." If he were to slip, or the rock handle were to break, the young man would undoubtedly fall to his demise.

Abeo watched as Veritas pushed off the rock wall with surprising force and swung—one arm clinging to the rock, the other free—across the face of the overhang. For a moment, he hung in mid-air, suspended by the feeble attachment of one arm, but he managed to throw his free arm over the cliff and latched on to whatever he could find. Using his strength to capacity, he pulled himself upwards until his legs were high enough to push up on the rock. The young man fell forward and disappeared over the top.

"Are you alright?" Abeo called up at him. No response came.

"Veritas!" Foedus called from below.

Still, no response. Abeo gave Foedus a dumbfounded look. Then, from behind the protruding cliff, Veritas' head poked out. His ocean blue eyes glared brilliantly like the stars in the sky above him.

"What's up there?" Foedus demanded.

"You're not going to believe this!" he responded excitedly.

Abeo scrambled out of his safe checkpoint and began the final stage of the climb. After a few contentious moments, he reached the overhang. He was a confident climber but knew this was no time to be reckless.

"There is a handle here you can grab on to, but you're going to need to push off the rock and swing your other arm upwards. I'll grab it and help you up," Veritas instructed.

"How is there a handle there?" Abeo questioned.

"It looks like it's been carved out of the stone. Something—or someone—punched a hole in an existing bulge."

Abeo felt around and found the handle. His hand was slightly too large to comfortably fit, so he was forced to grip with only three fingers and his thumb. He exhaled deeply and then pushed off the wall, swinging upwards and blindly flailing his left hand in the air. For a brief moment, he felt that he was going to lose his grip and go flying down the cliff, but an instant later, Veritas' emaciated fingers wrapped snugly around his wrist and wretched him upwards. He painfully pushed his knees into the jagged rock and clumsily scrambled forward. Laying on sodden rock, he caught his breath and pushed himself up so he could observe his surroundings. All around, the slab of stone sloped smoothly upwards, pinnacling twenty paces away. Above him, the familiar stars and lights danced, but something was different. Then he noticed, poking over the horizon, a magnificent ball of light.

"What is it?" he asked Veritas.

"I wouldn't even know where to begin," the Discipulus croaked back.

"How in the hell am I supposed to do this?!" Foedus interrupted from below.

Veritas educated the captain about the handle. He and Abeo grabbed his swinging arm and helped thrust the heavy man onto the plateau. The captain grunted and pushed himself up. "We need to find a better route," he joked.

Neither man responded. Abeo quickly turned and ran towards the top of incline. Veritas and Foedus followed him anxiously. They approached the top of the ridge and looked on in sheer astonishment. Below them lay an immense valley cradled by the surrounding mountainous peaks. Across their vantage point, a mighty mountain dominated its rocky entourage. Its black spine meandered perpetually upwards, while its dark base blended seamlessly with the horizon. The men admired the panorama. Their bodies, paralyzed by the vista, became as rigid as the rock upon which they stood.

Inspiring particular awe was what hovered above the ominous peaks. Illuminating the sky, a humongous spiral-shaped cloud, glittered with colours encompassing the entire visible spectrum, bewitched their attention. Composing the center was a radiating sphere of white and gold. Emanating from the central hub, blue and violet arms stretched radially outwards. The men stared in wonder for what seemed like an eternity. No one spoke, no one broke their gaze—they were entranced by this siren of the sky.

"Look!" Veritas shouted suddenly.

"What do you think I've been doing," Foedus responded wryly.

"No, not that. Down there! There are fires, tents, and people!"

Abeo seemed even more blown away by the sight of the exact thing they were looking for. They were so bewitched by the cosmic object that they had completely missed the colony buried in the basin. Situated at the base of the valley, multiple rows of white tents were illuminated by the orange glow of the fires within them. In the middle of the settlement sat a large domed domicile that was ten times bigger than all the others. Beside it, a smaller and majestically decorated structure radiated as if it was encrusted with resplendent jewels.

Abeo noted the movement of people congregating in different pockets of the settlement. He could feel that the air was much warmer than he had been accustomed to. The basin appeared to shelter them from the piercing chill of the wind.

"What do you see, Abeo?" Foedus asked.

"Very little. Seems like there's a high concentration of them in the central structure, but I can't make out how many."

"They're probably just finding out about us, whatever their comprehension may be. I mean, if we don't even really know what they are, what's going on in *their* heads," he scoffed.

"My guess would be somewhere between seventy-five and a hundred," Veritas calmly stated.

"What?" Foedus questioned.

"That's how many I counted," he responded.

"How can you tell?" Foedus demanded.

"I can tell."

Foedus gave Abeo a skeptical look but decided to take the young man at his word. "Well, we know where they are now. We should go back and discuss with the others. It'll be best to go as a group with a plan of attack."

"What do you have in mind?" Abeo inquired.

"Plan A will be to bear some gifts, try to offer our peace to them, and show them that we're here for diplomatic conversation—not that they'll have any concept of that—but I suspect if we bring something to trade we should have no problems."

"And if we do have problems?" Veritas asked.

Foedus looked sternly at the young man and put his hand on his shoulder. "Kid, have you ever fired a rifle?"

25

The group was resting upon their return. Petram blinked softly to moisten his dry eyes and delegated his attention to his three companions, eager to reveal their discovery.

"It's incomprehensible! The beauty, the magnificence, and the awe!" Veritas blurted out.

"Keep it in your pants, kiddo," Turpis slurred. With Foedus away, Turpis had indulged in an ample sample of whiskey. The captain was usually adamant that alcohol not be consumed, at least in excess, during the expeditions because it dulled the mind and numbed the senses. Nonetheless, packed alongside the food and supplies were twenty large bottles of fine rum and whiskey.

"Are you actually drunk right now?" Foedus asked impatiently.

"I'm just buzzed. My tolerance is down, okay?" Turpis responded harshly, wiping the sweat off his leathery skin.

"What did you find?" Petram inquired groggily.

"A small community buried in the basin of the mountains," Abeo responded. "Veritas believes there to be close to a hundred of them living there."

Petram looked back in disbelief. *How could there be so many? How did they not know about this before?* The questions battered inside of his head but refused to escape the tip of his tongue.

"It's our job to try and find out as much as we can about these beings," Foedus lectured. "From what I can tell, they seem to have enough intelligence to construct a community and organize themselves. We will bring what goods we can spare and offer them to these things peacefully. Hopefully, they respond in kind."

"And if they don't?" Turpis asked.

"Then we need to be prepared to protect ourselves," the captain replied, deepening his voice.

Turpis licked his lips at the opportunity for violence.

It is an insecure man who feels the need to purge his internal anger with physical brutality, Petram thought.

Foedus continued and explained to them his strategy for initial contact. He went on to demonstrate to the Discipuli the process of firing and reloading a rifle. Petram, himself, had always found a gun to be a tedious weapon, requiring insurmountable accuracy in order to maximize efficiency. Each shot followed by a reloading process that even the most skilled rifleman needed adequate time to accomplish. Foedus passed a weapon to each of them. Veritas' feeble fingers wrapped around the barrel uncomfortably; he placed the butt on his shoulder and peered down the sight. The gun looked awkward in his grasp, as if he were holding a severed limb. Prod, on the other hand, gripped the rifle with a voracious confidence. He continuously practiced swinging it from behind his back into ready shooting position, no doubt peering down the sight at an imaginary adversary, mentally preparing for the real thing.

Had he not been recruited by the Seekers, Petram had no doubt that Prod would have been drafted by the Legion. The military body of the Imperium looked for young men who had little regard for their well-being. They, being immature and ignorant, truly did not comprehend how tenuous their grasp on life was. Budding and innocent seemed to translate into merciless barbarity when it came to the battlefield. "Conquering for the Imperium!" This was the mantra of the Legion. The slogan did nothing but legitimize the justification for the violent conquests.

Foedus delegated jobs to each Seeker, and they began packing their belongings. The men were excited to end the stagnant period of the expedition. The mules were especially relieved to be moving again; they had begun to get restless from their extended stay in the cavern. Prod occasionally took them down to the grotto for a drink of water while he attempted to catch fish like the white man had done. Despite his confidence, his efforts were to no avail. It seemed the esoteric skill required was more than the supercilious young man could muster.

"What have I missed?" a sanguine voice gently probed. Petram turned in astonishment to see Cordatus standing beside him. The old man looked extremely frail; he had lost at least ten pounds off his already fragile body. His skin was faded ebony, yet his eyes remained full of vigour.

"You're awake!" Petram shouted. All the other Seekers looked over curiously to see their veteran companion weakly standing, wrapped with a warm blanket.

"How are you feeling, old man? Are you capable of traveling?" Foedus asked.

"I am sore beyond belief, and my energy levels are less than ideal, but, perhaps with the aid of a mule, I could find myself ready to continue on our voyage. I must say, though, I am less than enthused about the impending traverse across another sheet of ice."

Petram laughed and placed his hand on the old man's shoulder. "We have a surprise in store for you."

They filled Cordatus in on the events that he had missed in his comatose state. From the discovery of the white man to the community buried within the mountains. Upon hearing the news, his eyes lit up like fireworks, radiating with jubilance. A jovial aura seemed to invigorate his body and mind, replenishing the energy chasm that he had fallen into. The old man questioned them continuously, naively believing they had much more information than they did.

"Patience, my friend," Abeo responded warmly. None of them had seen Abeo so positive before; he was far from his usual bereaved self. It was as if their discovery had rejuvenated the dwindling flame burning within his core.

The group packed up their entire inventory and began trekking towards a new and intriguing destination. Seven men departed to make the first contact with a colony of unknown creatures.

26

The Seekers of the Unknown trudged up a steep slope barely wide enough for their animal companions to comfortably move. Heavy exhales polluted the cool night air as each man forced himself up the incline. Slowly, they reached the precipice of the slope.

Foedus felt the burn in his legs as he pushed his arched sole against the ground. Light from above penetrated through the clouds and tickled the subtleties of the stone facade around him. The bright reflecting glow of the Spiral Cloud was beginning to come into their field of vision, bringing with it palpably warm air.

"What is that?" Prod blurted out.

"Nothing but your eyes can answer that question," Foedus quietly replied. He reached the top of the incline and awaited his lagging companions. As the rest of the group reached the crest, they stopped and basked in the magnificent panorama. Glistening stars twinkled on and off, surrounding the captivating cosmic cloud. Their pendulant jaws hung idly, but nothing was said.

The captain cut their stupefaction short, ordering them to find a path down to the camp. Ahead of them, a clear trail jutted out of the rock. It hugged the stone wall, switching back and forth, inching down to the mouth of the basin. For them to go unnoticed seemed impossible, but they had no other choice, it was the only way down.

The Seekers began their descent, making every effort to assure discretion. On occasion, the sound of a dragging toe would be followed by a slight stumble; each man struggled to discern the subtle contours of the path. The mules, too, had difficulty with the steep trail. Airam carried Cordatus on her back, while Prod and Turpis accompanied the other two mules.

The captain could feel a growing unrest stirring within the latter two men. Prod exhumed an increasingly disdained disposition towards him, while Turpis developed the nagging habit of groveling about any arduous task. Foedus felt as if nothing could stand still. If he gave priority to one person it just made another unhappy. He felt as if his job were to calm the waves of a rippling pond—the more he tried to flatten the disturbance, the more chaotic the water became.

The group continued down the rocky switchbacks until they reached an opening at the bottom of the hill. Before them, an open plain stretched out towards two massive boulders sitting adjacent to each other. Together, the colossal stones acted like watchtowers guarding the entrance to the village.

As they approached the quasi-fortress, the men huddled together and discussed their ready positions for the first contact. The plan was for Cordatus and Petram to linger behind with the animals and guard the goods. Three loaded rifles were strapped to the Anin's harness, ready to be used if necessary. They agreed that Foedus and Abeo would engage in discussions first. Turpis, Prod, and Veritas were to stand close behind and guard against any rear attacks.

As they approached the boulder-guarded entrance, Foedus felt his body starting to jitter. The mammoth rocks gradually grew; every lunge forward generated an added heartbeat in the captain's chest. There was no sign of anything; no movement, no sound. On the other end of the entrance, Foedus saw a glittering pond. Beyond that, the hazy glow of the village called. The captain turned around to make sure that his entire crew was with him when, suddenly, a whizzing sound stimulated his ear and caught his attention.

A sharpened soaring arrow crashed against the ground and ricocheted away. Anxiously searching the source, Foedus threw his head up and scanned through the darkness. Another whizzing arrow was followed by two more. The group frantically scattered and ran towards the boulders, hugging them for cover. Suddenly, a screeching scream reverberated through the entire valley; the silhouettes of two creatures appeared perched atop the boulders, firing down upon the

Seekers.

"Get low and find cover!" Foedus yelled. He scrambled towards Petram and grabbed one of the loaded rifles. Blindly, he fired a shot towards the silhouettes. The bang of the rifle echoed deafeningly, and a cloud of red smoke wisped effortlessly away from the barrel of the gun. Without hesitation, the captain grabbed the second rifle and fired it again. Everything became a standstill. Foedus hurriedly grabbed the third rifle and prepared to fire one more time, but the onslaught seemed to have ceased.

Scanning their surroundings nervously, the Seekers waited in an inauspicious haze. Then, emerging from darkness, came five powerful human-resembling creatures. They were shorter and stouter than the Seekers, and their appendages seemed smaller in proportion to their bodies. Nonetheless, they were intimidating all the same. The white men walked cautiously towards the group, arrows drawn and pointed.

In the middle of the oncoming posse stood an imposing man. He had a silver pelt wrapped around his shoulders and was taller than the rest of his entourage. His eyes were a magnificent shade of vermilion and were situated under thick blonde eyebrows. His soft white skin seemed to illuminate the air around him. In his hand, a tall wooden spear, emblazoned with ribbons of gold and violent, firmly stood by his side. All five of the white men wore necklaces composed of dagger-like teeth. Foedus noticed immediately that the leading man's chain had more teeth than the others.

The leading man yelled something incomprehensible and pointed his spear aggressively at the Seekers. Foedus looked around at his companions with a dumbfounded look. He put down the rifle gently and passively raised his hands. To his left, Turpis and Prod aimed their guns at the white men, refusing to break their gaze. The captain could tell it was bothering their counterparts; they looked on at the weapons with fear and intrigue. Foedus motioned his companions to lower their rifles. Prod and Turpis did so begrudgingly. The white men lowered their arrows in response, but the leader continued to stand before Foedus with his hand securely wrapped around his spear.

"Abeo," Foedus motioned to his friend.

Abeo carefully approached. He stared at the white men intently, trying his best to assert confidence without inducing violence. Taking off the bag strapped around his shoulder, he opened it up slowly and removed the items inside. A bundle cured meat, a loaf of bread, dried fruits, and a few silver coins were all presented before the foreign posse. Abeo offered the items to the lead man who instructed one of his contemporaries to take the items. With much vacillation, a second man walked over, took the goods, and brought them to the group for inspection. They looked at each other confusedly but decided to rummage through the offerings.

Abeo motioned for them to ingest the food. They looked at each other incredulously, hesitant to try the foreign cuisine. Despite their reservations, their leader motioned his approval and encouraged them to ingest the gifts. The stoic man who took the basket obliged. He took the meat and tore a tiny piece off, placing it on his vibrant pink tongue. He chewed hesitantly once and then stopped, smiled, and shoved the rest of the slab of meat in his mouth.

The leader looked back at Abeo with distinct curiosity. Staring his darker adversary up and down, he nodded and beckoned them to follow his companions towards the village.

Foedus exhaled deeply and nodded in agreement. *This is the job; this is the bond*, he thought to himself.

The other Seekers emerged from the cover of the boulder wall and revealed themselves to the white men. Carefully, the aliens observed each other.

Then, Veritas emerged from the darkness. Foedus heard one of the white men cry, "Sanuye! Sanuye!" He called to the leader, trying to get his attention. They all pointed feverishly at Veritas.

Sanuye turned in amazement and locked his red gaze with Veritas' blue eyes. The white men chattered amongst themselves, constantly whispering the word "Wakan."

Veritas looked back incredulously at his new-found admirers.

27

Dozens of red eyes stared in horror and awe as the seven Seekers were escorted into the village. A welcoming crowd awaited their arrival, eager to witness what none of them had ever seen—dark-skinned men. Whispers escalated to enthusiastic chattering as Veritas walked by. Men and women blatantly pointed towards the young man, muttering in excitement. Why they had such bafflement in blue eyes and not brown or green seemed odd—all were completely foreign to them.

For Abeo, the entire experience felt mystical. His eyes refused to cooperate; they darted eagerly at the abundance of visual magnificence. Outlining the camp, rows of conical tents were illuminated by the fires entombed within them. Painted on their beige coverings, images of people, animals, mountains, and the Spiral Cloud were etched in black and red. At the center of the camp, sparingly filling the vast meadow, an assortment of exotic animals grazed and wandered. The massive muscular creatures periodically drank from a small pond. Replenishing the water withdrawal, multitudes of meandering streams funneled down from the surrounding cliffs. Some animals had large tusks protruding from their head, lining their rounded noses and flat faces. Others resembled mules in appearance, only not as big and with thicker fur.

Perhaps most peculiar was what the animals ate. Rooted in the ground, thousands of rounded shrubs grew in a variety of sizes, with larger shrubs growing closer to the pond. Abeo curiously observed as he slowly walked past a thick patch. Emanating from each shrub, bifurcating roots interlocked with those of the others. The roots coalesced into a complex web, forming an interwoven network that united the different plants into one.

Yet, it was not the flora that captivated Abeo. The people themselves were an elaborate system of social beings. Some gathered food and fed the animals; others carried large bundles of chopped roots, piling the bundles in front of specialized workers who used sharpened stones to mould the roots into spears and arrows. As far as Abeo could tell, they were not animalistic at all; they were intelligent and civilized.

Passing through the meadow, the group approached the epicenter of the camp. Situated in the center of the settlement, an illustrious tent, ten times the size of the ones they had seen, proudly stood. It did not have the conical structure of the others; instead, it stood as a large cube. Its four corners were firmly pinned to large rocks that formed the tent's scaffolding.

Beside the Central Tent was a small and elegant structure. The outside was covered in paintings of spirals and stars, and it was embroidered with gold and crimson ribbon. Embedded into the skin of the tent, an assortment of glittering jewels softly reflected the incident light of the night sky. Abeo felt momentarily bewitched by its presence.

Demanding their attention, the man named Sanuye led the group down a winding path towards the front entrance of the Central Tent. Here, two physically dominating creatures stood guard, spears in hand. In the background, the chatter of the other white-skinned people was relentless. Their appetites for curiosity seemed insatiable.

Sanuye motioned for them to enter. Abeo looked at Foedus for support; the captain confidently motioned for him to continue, and Abeo hesitantly walked inside. As he entered, one of the guards grabbed his arm and shook his head at the mule. The animals were not to be brought inside, so Foedus delegated the responsibility of watching them to Prod. Unsurprisingly, the young man was less than pleased.

Abeo entered the structure anxiously. Inside, two curved benches created an ovular encasing of a large pit; an active fire tranquilly raged in the space between. On one bench, five pale-skinned men stoically sat, each wearing distinct necklaces decorated with magnificent jewels.

The men looked much older than those they had just met. Four of them had wispy grey beards to match their flowing silver hair, but the man sitting in the center was unique in his appearance. Covering his face, a broad moustache curled around his lips and descended towards his chin. A charming smile hid underneath, and his soft pink eyes looked upon his guests compassionately. With great civility, he motioned for the Seekers to sit on the bench across from them. The other white men stood attentively on guard, deliberately standing close to—what Abeo assumed were—their leaders.

The bearded men stared at Veritas and whispered to each other. The moustached man motioned for them to cease their secrecy and show some respect to their guests. Even so, he paid a noticeable amount of attention to the blue-eyed boy. Breaking his gaze from Veritas, the white man cleared his throat and spoke a word that none of them had ever heard. After receiving no reaction, the man repeated the word, this time gesturing his hand towards himself as if to welcome them.

Foedus nodded and smiled, not knowing what to say. One of the warriors brought over the gifts that Abeo had offered and placed them in front of the bearded men. The meat was nearly gone.

The white men mumbled and motioned to each other before indulging in the food. It did not take long for them to seem satisfied. One man even attempted to throw a piece of meat in the air and catch the soaring pellet in his mouth.

The moustached creature smiled and motioned towards the entrance of the tent. Limping towards them came the same man that Prod had shot in the grotto. He hobbled towards them with a scowl on his face, begrudgingly carrying a basket. Placing it in front of the Seekers, Abeo looked down astonishingly at the assortment of shimmering jewels inhabiting the basket.

The moustached man made another peculiar sound and motioned towards the Seekers, insinuating that the jewels were theirs to take.

"Thank you," Foedus blurted out awkwardly. The white men looked at each other incredulously but smiled back. Body language and facial expression seemed to be the only form of translational arbitration.

After eons of awkward silence and uncomfortable murmuring, Foedus motioned for the group of Seekers to see themselves out. The first contact had been a relative success, and he didn't want to spoil a good thing. The white men seemed upset the Seekers were leaving, but did not make a concerted effort to prolong their visit.

As he exited the Central Tent, Abeo noticed Prod staring aimlessly at the sky, paying little attention to the animals he was supposed to be chaperoning.

"Prod!" Turpis yelled aggressively.

"What?" the young man turned in surprise.

"Calm down," Foedus instructed both of them. "No need to make a scene in front of our new acquaintances," he warned.

Turpis snarled at the captain's command.

The white men escorted the Seekers out of the camp, following the same path they had come in from. The village was quiet; most of the other people had retreated to their tents. Even so, the odd admirer poked their head out and stared as the dark men walked on by. The Seekers exited towards the boulder gate, uncertain about where they were to go.

As they started back up the trail, Abeo noticed the white men trying to get their attention. As he turned around, he saw them motioning towards the ground, followed by what appeared to be the outline of a triangle.

"I think they want us to camp here," said Abeo.

"Here?" Foedus inquired, pointing to the ground and yelling—as if saying it louder would help them understand. Yet, somehow it did. The white men nodded and even offered to assist with their tents.

Not long after, a fire raged, stew cooked, and men snored. The Seekers owed their respite to the hospitable white-skinned beings. Their generosity seemingly knew no bounds. How oddly trusting they were of people that they did not know. Truly, it was a great moment of friendly cooperation.

After they settled, Abeo found time to lay down next to the fire and stare at the blanket of stars. His ankle was sore from so much walking, but he didn't care. His mind continuously veered away from the pain and focused on the wonder of what he had indeed just witnessed. Since the debacle through the snowstorm, he had not truly had enough time to lay down and appreciate the sky. It was the reason he enjoyed the expeditions; it was the motivation for his mind. As he gazed up at the flickering lights, he wondered what these cosmic quandaries were. Maybe they were other planets, just like Unum, or even something similar to Stella. Whatever they were, they were beautiful, no matter where he was.

28

A vibrant aura resonated throughout the group. The men engaged in vivid conversation as they enjoyed their first respite in what seemed like ages. Petram watched as Foedus and Abeo discussed at length about how to proceed with the white men—or Rubeus, as they had agreed to call them on account of their red eyes.

Abeo proposed they spend as much time as possible learning about "the people," as he referred to them. The others were not so quick to adopt what they deemed an overly complimentary term. In fact, Turpis made it his duty to remind them that the Rubeus were savages and sub-human. Nonetheless, Abeo fervidly believed they had much more to learn and were in no position to transmit information to Christoph.

The captain, however, disagreed. As far as he saw it, it was their duty to report any important findings to their superiors. Foedus knew it was essential to inform Christoph of the abundant riches the Rubeus ignorantly sat upon. Trading goods for jewels would bring in enough of a profit to keep the Seekers afloat for generations. No doubt, the white men had a poor understanding of the financial significance of such sought after stones.

Each Seeker posited his opinion on the matter, but it seemed the only suggestions given any credence were those of Abeo and Foedus. Turpis and Prod supported Foedus' claim, while Veritas backed his Praeceptoris. Petram looked to Cordatus for council, but the old man was barely paying attention. Instead, he was busy shuffling through an old book, hastily scanning each page.

"What are you looking for?" Petram inquired.

The old man raised his index finger to ask for quiet and continued scanning the pages of the antiquated anthology.

The background quarreling died down, and Abeo grew tired of the debate. Getting up, he left the fire to walk around and explore the surroundings. He had made a habit of indulging in solitary strolls; the walks helped him sharpen his senses and strengthen his healing ankle. More than anything, they gave him time to be alone with the night sky.

After Abeo's departure, Foedus poured himself a glass of whiskey and exhaled a sigh of relief as he sat tiredly upon a boulder. The captain had let the group open one of the bottles whiskey for "celebratory reasons." No doubt, his reasoning was simply an excuse to indulge in his favourite temptation.

Petram sipped on his own glass and immediately began feeling its effects; remaining abstinent since the beginning of the expedition had significantly lowered his tolerance. He looked over and saw Prod downing his third glass. The young man eagerly prompted Foedus for a refill.

"Why don't you tell us a story, Prod," Foedus blurted out as he poured the brown liquid into Prod's cup. The captain, too, slurred his words and relinquished control of his verbal volume.

The young man scratched his chiseled jaw and grinned as the gears rattled around inside of his durable skull. "Have any of you ever gone hunting before? Like, big-game hunting?" All except Foedus shook their head to indicate they hadn't.

"What have you hunted?" the young man asked his captain.

"In Cirfa," Foedus replied, "I saw one of the largest, most savage animals I've ever laid eyes on. It had eight large pincer-like teeth, claws that could pierce your skull, and a growl that would leave you dumbfounded. I saw it, tracked it, and put a bullet right through its head." There was melancholy way in which Foedus told the story. The narrative felt heroic, yet the tone was anything but—perhaps he regretted what he had done.

Prod, enthused by the story, was eager to match with his best merciless tail tale. He went on to enlighten them about his inglorious hunt of a cave lion. Prod claimed that he and his father had tracked one inland from Crepusculum and followed it for several sleeps. They eventually pursued it down a dark cave where light ceased to exist. It was there that he had truly discovered his ability to see subtleties in the darkness—or "dark light," as he had called it. He and his father eventually cornered the creature and pierced it with twelve arrows before it slowly fell to its death. They beheaded the animal while it still breathed and asserted their interspecies dominance.

When the story was over, no one said a word. The atmosphere spoke for itself. Prod's opinions on hunting were not entirely shared, but they were not completely lost either. In fact, big-game hunting had become a major fad in the Imperium. Men and women would travel great distances to track and kill an animal, only to take its carcass as a trophy, manifesting their unconscious desire for superiority.

"In my opinion, an animal is good for one thing: meat," Turpis grumbled.

"At least I cook my meat when I eat it," Prod jabbed. "You guys missed it when you had your fun little meeting, but I saw one of those things take the heart out of a dead animal and bite into it raw. If you're asking me, they're more animal than man."

Once again, no response was given. The men were deep in thought, considering the real voracity of the question. Indeed, the answer on what to do about the Rubeus was not evident. Petram pondered both sides of the argument. On the one hand, the Rubeus seemed to value both their own existence and that of other creatures. They decorated their homes with paintings of their environment and culture, and they appeared to have a fully functional social structure. On the other, they congregated and carnally consumed cold carcasses to comfort their carnivorous cravings. *Savage and sane, just like the rest of us*, he thought. The similarities between the two groups increasingly dawned on him.

After getting some much-needed rest, the Seekers were twice visited by their courteous hosts. On their first stopover, a group of warriors, led by Sanuye, brought hides of exotic animals for their foreign guests. Each skin was covered in chestnut brown fur and was large enough to cover two men comfortably. Petram packaged the Rubeus a bag of food, but they could see the group had little to spare and graciously declined.

"Thank you," Petram said to the stern looking man.

Sanuye stoically nodded and retreated to his camp.

It was Sanuye who also led the second welcoming party. On this occasion, however, he was accompanied by two of the bearded men from the council, as well as three women bearing gifts. Two of the women were older; they had long, pale blonde hair and thin wrinkles embedded into their pasty-white skin. The third woman, however, was younger and possibly the most beautiful thing any of them had ever seen. Her golden hair fell gently onto her thin shoulders, caressing her delicate skin. Cherry-red lips curved into a gentle smile, and her striking strawberry eyes were splotched with gold and orange specks. Her gaze was paradisiacal. She caught notice of the men staring at her, and her cheeks radiated a soft hue of pink.

The other women timidly placed the baskets of the food on the ground and retreated to the safety of their escorts. Foedus, ever the charmer, approached the group with a warm smile and nodded. "Aren't you just magnificent." The captain leered at the young woman. She blinked softly and averted her eyes, clearly having never been in such a precarious position before.

"Veritas, bring me that small bag attached to Airam," Foedus demanded, shooting another charismatic smile at the young woman.

Veritas emerged from the darkness with Foedus' bag and handed it to him. Not once did he look at his captain. His eyes were firmly locked on the young woman and hers on his.

Foedus, who took no notice of the young man's asphyxiation, removed two large bottles of whiskey from his bag and handed it to Sanuye. "Be careful with this stuff," he said jokingly.

The Rubeus warrior curiously inspected the bottle, seemingly intrigued by the glass container more than the fluid inside. He handed the bottles over to the two older women and nodded at Foedus. "Thah unk you," the words stumbled out of his lips.

"You're welcome," Foedus replied with a smile.

The baskets the Rubeus had brought contained an assortment of meats and strange vegetables that came in all sorts of colours and patterns. Petram admired the medley of edibles, wondering how such alien things could grow on his home planet.

It didn't take Turpis long to sample all of the food given to them. "It's savage food, but it's not the worst thing I've ever had." Debris sprayed out of his mouth as he spoke.

During the periods when they weren't being visited, the Seekers spent their time wandering the surroundings. Foedus made it mandatory to go in pairs, but Abeo insisted that he was old enough to be left alone.

For most of them, the landscape seemed surreal. Jagged rocks jutted chaotically throughout the valley, many of them covered in a thick carpet of blue vegetation. The plants drew nutrients from within the stone walls and drank the melting snow that trickled down from the mountain's crest. To some, the ominous enclosure could well be seen as a claustrophobic nightmare, but the dazzling sky and the majestic Spiral Cloud seemed to inhibit any fearful feelings.

Despite their positive encounters, Foedus began to get anxious. As the captain, he felt forced to make a decision regarding the Rubeus. He asked the others to congregate in order to make a final stance. Every man took part in the conversation; every man except for Cordatus who continued to scan through his books. The old man insisted he was listening, though never clarifying to what degree.

"I think it's important that we inform Christoph of our findings," said the captain. "We've learned enough about these creatures to at least give a preliminary report. We know that trade is possible and, with enough effort, communication may come in time. I'm sure linguists of the Imperium would have a better chance of learning their language than any of us would."

Most of the Seekers seemed to be in agreement, but Abeo vehemently objected. "If Christoph finds out about these people, and the riches buried in these mountains, the entire Legion will be upon them before they know it. There will be no will to learn their ways. The Rubeus will be taken advantage of. If it were up to me, I wouldn't be telling Christoph anything at all. Leave these people in peace, Foedus."

Foedus looked at his friend incredulously, no doubt wondering how he could be so dishonorable to the Imperium. "You're saying we should just pack up and head home, tell Christoph we found nothing? And what happens when the light reaches this place and the entire Imperium has moved this far? We're just supposed to say 'oh, we must have missed that entire colony of living beings and the horde of riches they're sitting on?'"

"They've stayed a secret this long. Perhaps they'll just move deeper into the dark as the light approaches. What business is it of ours to intervene with their lives?" Abeo retorted.

"Where is your loyalty?" Foedus cried.

Petram attempted to mediate. "The captain is right. We can't just come back empty handed after everything we've seen. But I also agree with Abeo; we can't make hasty decisions here. We need to be a bit more aggressive in our communication effort. I'd be happy to join an ambassadorial party to the camp. I know we don't have much of a jumping off point, but we can start by drawing pictures and writing down translations for common words."

"Like whatever *that* is," Prod interrupted, pointing up at the luminous Spiral Cloud hovering in the sky. "I'd like to figure out what I've been staring at incessantly."

After much debate, Foedus begrudgingly agreed to partake in a diplomatic effort to learn more about the Rubeus. "We can give it a shot," he said, "but I wouldn't get anyone's hopes up. As Petram noted, we don't even have a jumping off point."

"Or do we?" Cordatus interjected.

"What have you got for us, old man?" Petram asked excitedly.

"This." Cordatus turned his book towards the group and showed them an open page. On the left, scribbled in their native language, was a ballad written by the ancient historian and philosopher Worobus. On the adjacent page was what appeared to be the identical ballad, only drafted in a language none of them had ever seen before.

"What about it?" Turpis growled.

"This is an ancient ballad that has been long forgotten. It tells the tale of a group of people that once lived before the time of the Imperium. They were the first settlers of Crepusculum, and they had a keen ability for seeing in the dark. Thousands of years ago, these people were ousted by those of the Interior. They were pushed west across the Murky Mountains to the land of darkness and ice, never to be seen again. My father used to read this poem to me and told me many times that he believed we were descendants of these people. He told me that, like him, and his father before him, I had possessed some ability that had been passed down from generation to generation. Of course, no evidence ever existed for such a thing, so I always figured that it was a myth to explain why I was different than the rest. Being different isn't easy for anyone, as I'm sure most of us know."

Each man listened intently, keen on every word coming from the old man's mouth.

"I think it's pretty clear," he continued, "that these people are the remnants of an ancient civilization and that we have a piece of them in us."

"The old man's officially lost it!" Turpis spat. "Look at these things; they're mutants! They're shorter than us, they have pale skin, and blood red eyes; they're not humans, they're animals."

"No more than you or I," Abeo stated calmly.

Turpis disregarded anything Abeo professed, preferring to roast in his rage.

"It's an interesting theory, I'll give you that," Foedus conceded, "but unfortunately hard to believe. Also, I don't see how we're supposed to use that as a jumping off point."

Cordatus smiled gently and pointed to the left-hand page of the book. "This here is a translation of the poem into an ancient language thought to be used by those antiquated people. Their vernacular may have changed, but there is a chance that the Rubeus language is rooted in the discourse of these pages. We can reverse translate into the common tongue and start building our knowledge from there. This poem can be our key to unlocking the mystery of these people. I have to think it's worth a shot."

Abeo smiled jubilantly. "You're always full of surprises, old man."

Foedus stroked his face and nodded in agreement. "Then it's settled. After some rest, we will bring the book to their leaders and attempt to break the dialect deadlock. Failing that, I will have no choice but to send a letter to Christoph and inform him of our findings."

Everyone but Turpis seemed satisfied with the plan. The groveling man had grown tired of taking a backseat on important tasks. Whether it had been the incident with Abeo and the rope or just the fact that Foedus loved to play favourites, he continuously found himself on the outside looking in.

The men retired to their tents for some much-needed rest, while Foedus and Abeo stayed up discussing the plan, continuously debating the logistics. Despite their disagreements, the two old friends had remained fairly amicable.

After the others had retired to their tents, Petram wandered off to find a spot to empty his bladder before he slept. He tucked himself behind a large rock and stared up at the glittering sky. Suddenly, he heard the sound of flapping wings overhead. He had not seen a single bird, other than their own, since they had crossed the Murky Mountains. He could only speculate where it came from or where it was going.

29

The Rubeus emerged from their tents to gossip and observe every time the Seekers made an appearance at their village. Each man tried his best to act nonchalant, but their celebrity status made it difficult not to crumble and smile.

Veritas, as always, was the focal point of attention. The young man had done his best to avoid the spotlight, but most of his attempts were futile. Only Sanuye, and the man with the moustache, were able to resist the urge to gush and awe at his blue eyes.

The Seekers made their way to the Central Tent to impose an unannounced visit on their hosts. As they approached, they were welcomed by the moustached man who smiled with excitement. He motioned for them to join him in their sacred conference room. Interestingly, as he turned to lead the way, he stumbled. It seemed the Rubeus had taken kindly to the bottles of whiskey Foedus had given them.

The Seekers entered the tent and sat down on the curved bench. Facing their faded hosts, it appeared they had arrived just in time for the party. The five men of the council were all laughs and smiles; they yelled audibly at each other, never giving one another chance to say more than two uninterrupted words. It was only Sanuye who remained sober. The stoic warrior stood quietly behind his drunken superiors, staring upon the Seekers with discontent.

Foedus, who did not notice Sanuye's galled glare, put on his charming smile and laughed alongside the group. "I told them to be careful with it."

The moustached man quieted his peers and motioned towards

Foedus, probing him for the reason behind their impromptu visit. The captain motioned to Cordatus, and the old man handed him the antiquated book. All the men of the council looked intently at the black script. Foedus opened up to the correct page and turned the book to the council. Pointing towards the page, he passed it over for the Rubeus to inspect. The bearded men congregated excitedly and observed the text.

"Do you understand? Is that your language?" Foedus asked, pointing at them and then back down to the book. One of the bearded men pointed at the pages and muttered something to the others. The man with the moustache looked up at Foedus with wide eyes and smiled.

Cordatus excitedly snatched the book back and began scanning through the poem. He located the word "water" and looked across the page to find the corresponding word. Placing his finger on the word, he turned the book and showed it to the man with the moustache.

"Ohneka," the man read aloud.

Abeo grabbed his canteen and poured water into his cupped hand. "Ohneka?" he inquired.

The Rubeus smiled and nodded in agreement.

An invigorating rush proliferated through Abeo's spine. The language barrier had been fractured, and the floodgates were open.

One-by-one, every word in the poem was decoded into a useable vernacular. Not every word translated perfectly, but they were able to determine most of the text. Cordatus eagerly spelled out each translation as best as he could, logging both the meaning and enunciation. The key was far from perfect, but it provided them with enough information to initiate the bridge building process. By the end of the meeting, over two hundred terms had been directly translated.

Once they were able to communicate, the Seekers quickly learned a lot about the Rubeus. For one, they called the land they lived on Abya Yala. The chaotic landscape was sacred to the white men, or, as they called themselves, the Atanak.

As expected, the man with the moustache was the tribal leader, and he went by the name Powhatan. Powhatan and his contemporaries, the four bearded men, were collectively known as the Onontsi. Just as

Cordatus had suspected, the Onontsi formed a kind of chiefdom that made important decisions for the tribe. The other four members had unique names like Sak, Boox, Jua, and Kedalak. Remembering all their names was sure to be a challenge, but Abeo was eager to master the language as fast as he possibly could.

Interestingly, the man who had been shot by Prod in the cave turned out to be one of the most invaluable translators. His name was Arawak, and he had a knack for the common tongue.

A prominent linguist in the midst of savages, Abeo thought. For him, any doubt that these people were anything other than human seemed insular.

After enjoying the fervour of the first translational pow-wow, the Seekers began making it a routine to visit with the Rubeus to further understand their culture. The process was grueling at first, but growth was exponential. Each man compared notes after a session and argued about what they thought they had heard. Cordatus had the unenviable task of compiling a master codex based on a host of subjective translations.

For the most part, the Seekers struggled with the Rubeus language. Their words were awkward to pronounce, and the syntax was oddly structured. Abeo, however, had a natural affinity for the vernacular; he soaked up the dialect like a sponge. Foedus—usually a cunning linguist—was able to jerk out sentences with enough reference to his notes but had trouble effectively verbalizing. Luckily for his pride, the captain's struggles were overshadowed by Turpis, who often gave up in a fit and demanded that the savage beasts learn *his* language, as he so graciously put it.

The Rubeus, on the other hand, learned the names of the Seekers with great ease. Their enunciation was poor, but their verbal memory was unmatched. Most preferred to call the Seekers by the nicknames they had given to them. Abeo was bequeathed the name Skan—the Rubeus word for "sky"—which was no doubt attributed to the countless moments he spent staring at the celestial ceiling. Foedus, on the other hand, was given the name Wohitika, or "brave." The captain didn't rush to dispute the distinction.

Over time, the other Seekers were assigned names that had a variety of meanings. Turpis was designated a name to mean "beast." He initially took it as an insult, but Foedus managed to spin it in a way that effectively pacified his under-stimulated ego.

Most intriguingly, however, was the name given to Veritas. The Rubeus referred to him as Wakan—a word they had not yet translated. In fact, no word even close to this was found in the book or any of the added words they had deciphered. Abeo and Cordatus worked diligently to try and figure out the meaning of this name; they became overridden with a desire to win the challenge they placed upon themselves, but the word's meaning kept eluding their pursuits.

Despite all their progress, Foedus became increasingly anxious, incessantly reminding them the importance of sending Christoph updates. He claimed that enough time had passed and not nearly enough headway had been made.

Abeo knew if he couldn't continue to make breakthroughs on the translation front, he would lose reasonable cause to oppose the captain's request. After one particularly unproductive session, Foedus gave Abeo his ultimatum, telling him that he had no choice but to send something to the admiral.

"What are you going to say?" Abeo asked.

"Hmm, let me think on that. Probably something regarding the colony of living beings we found, maybe mention that life is viable out here, or that there are resources and riches to be traded for and, most significant for us, reason to increase our funding and keep the Seekers afloat. I know you have become infatuated with these people, but you need to keep your priorities in order. We're here for us first and foremost. Don't forget that," the captain warned.

"You can't tell them about the jewels," Veritas interjected, "if you do, it won't be us coming out here anymore; it will be the Legion. The fight for control will lead to violence, and these people will be left in the dust."

"I can do whatever I damn well please, just in case you forgot," Foedus shot back. He stared ominously at the young man.

Veritas' blue eyes never broke their returning gaze.

"Nothing bad will happen to these people. They will be absorbed into the Imperium and reap all the benefits that the rest of us do," the captain assured.

"That's a very naive outlook," Veritas shot back, showing vigour that he had never revealed before.

Foedus laughed. "What do you know about anything? You're a kid."

"Maybe. But you grew up in Lux, surrounded by riches, culture, sunshine, and prosperity. I grew up in Opus Dorum. I doubt you've ever dared to set foot in that city. There, no matter where you go, people are miserable. They're born into an environment where they have no choice but to work long hours in the ignasaxum and carbo mines. No one can farm out there, almost nothing grows. Men and women endlessly slave away; pushed to their mental capacity, their psyche waivers on the precipice of suicide and survival. I have to say, it's pretty incredible what the human mind is willing to endure for a glimpse of what maybe one day could be. What do they suffer for? So those living in the Interior can reap the rewards and riches, right? The Imperium doesn't care about them; why would they? And that's what they do to their own kind, captain. What do you think they will do these people?"

Abeo and Foedus stared back in silence. They were utterly astounded by the uncharacteristic rant from the normally reserved young man.

Foedus cleared his throat and gave Veritas an endearing smile. "Alright, son, I guess it wouldn't be the worst thing for me to withhold some information from Christoph. I suppose if I don't inform him about the jewels right away I could bank it for my next correspondence and spread out the positive news. That will buy you guys some time, but not a lot. I'm going to have to tell him eventually. I'm sorry, it's the best I can do."

Veritas scowled unappreciatively and stormed away, but Abeo assured Foedus they were thankful for his diplomacy. He knew that his friend's hands were bound in the situation, but he also believed that he had to fight for what they thought was right. Often, he wondered if what was right in his mind was truly moral. Maybe he was just another immoral being, bathing in his own delusions. In his time, he had witnessed the hands of men do more wretched things than his mind had the capacity to bear. He had seen the dark path of desperation in the eyes of the dead, dying, and delirious. Who was he to be an ethical compass? The best he could do was measure himself against those things he sensed were wrong. But what if what he sensed wasn't right? How could he be sure? Deep down, he felt as if the fight was futile. Nonetheless, to his death, he knew he would need to resist to the last atom for the minuscule mound of serenity left to fight for. It was the only way forward.

30

Gazing out at the tangerine sky, Christoph watched the mesmerizing horizon with great reverence. He sipped gently on a glass of whiskey and clenched his cheeks as he swallowed the caramel liquid. In front of him, lying on his desk, were two handwritten notes. The one on his right had just arrived; it was a message from Foedus, the first he had heard from him in ages. It was common to go long stretches without receiving any word from those on the expedition, very often there was nothing to report. This time, however, was different. The admiral snatched the letter off his desk and brought it close to his face. It read:

Admiral Christoph,
My apologies for the extended duration between this and our last correspondence. Much has happened.
First off, we've had extensive injuries. Petram, Abeo, and Cordatus all had incidents: Petram was attacked by a cave lion and barely managed to escape; Abeo fell from a great height and fractured his ankle; Cordatus survived a dramatic fall through ice and is still feeling the effects. We took temporary shelter in a cavern which led us to a miraculous discovery—a white-skinned man.
We followed the man and found an entire colony buried in the mountains. We know very little about these people thus far. Our communication with them has been minimal. We haven't been able to find a suitable means of breaking the language barrier, but efforts are in place to alleviate this.
Miraculously, life has found a way to flourish in the void.
As of right now, there is nothing more of significance to report. I will

continue to update you as per your request and reply.
Sincerely,
Captain Foedus

The entire thing was stupefying to Christoph. Living creatures in the dark? How could they not have seen them before? How could the Imperium not have known about their existence?

Foedus' letter should have induced excitement in the admiral. With a single stroke, the group had found justification to continue expeditions and fund future Seekers. Their existence was paramount to the interests of the Imperium. Interestingly, Foedus' letter induced little fervour in the admiral. In fact, he was not at all surprised. He had read, in greater detail, the same thing already. A more loyal Seeker put it upon himself to go behind Foedus' back to inform Christoph of the full story.

With his long fingers, he grabbed the second letter from his desk. Christoph had read it over ten times, but he felt compelled to etch the words in his mind one more time:

Dear Admiral Christoph,
I know that writing this letter to you is an impeachment of Seeker law because Captain Foedus has ordered that none of us correspond with you until he has done so. That being said, I feel I have no choice but to send this to you.
To get to the point, we have found a colony of living beings deep in the mountains. They are odd, white-skinned creatures, but we have already made significant progress communicating with them. They have a strange language, but Cordatus has done well to translate what he can.
Most importantly, these creatures have found a way to mine rare jewels and minerals from the mountains. Without a doubt, there would be vast riches in these items; riches that could be used to fund all of us so that we would never have to worry about finances again.
I write to you now because I worry that Abeo and his loyal Discipulus, Veritas, are untrustworthy. They continue to side with the creatures over their own kind. It's treasonous in my mind. If nothing is done, Foedus could be

swayed to side with Abeo, forcing us to lose our exclusive knowledge of these great riches. I implore you to act quickly.

The letter was not signed, but Christoph knew very well who his loyal servant was. The words resonated in his mind over and over. The admiral fantasized about the possibility of endless riches at his fingertips. He ogled at the thought of being the one to inform the Imperator that the men under *his* command had found not only hope for life in the Murky Mountains, but vast treasures as well. He would be the most famous man in all of the Imperium—a hero to be paraded down the golden boulevards of Lux. But how to solve the problem?

Christoph ran his fingers through his jet-black hair and furled his lips as he tried to concentrate. He had never really liked Abeo. Sure, he respected the man's abilities, but the two had never seen eye-to-eye. Abeo had vocalized his suspicions surrounding Tenax's death many seasons ago, and it aggravated Christoph to have such a stubborn thorn constantly prodding his psyche. As he had told others, he truly believed that a piece of Abeo died when his son passed; the rest left this world with his wife. In Christoph's mind, Abeo was nothing but a slowly rotting corpse aimlessly wandering until time was finished with him.

More troublesome than Abeo's provocations, Foedus' betrayal stuck in Christoph's mind. It was rare for him to open up to a friendship. People were parasitic as far as he could tell; their intentions were inherently selfish whether they knew it or not. Instead of persisting in the delusion that he was a moral person, Christoph accepted that he would always act in his best interest. Yet, Foedus had been the one man he had seen as a friend. Now, he knew; he had learned his lesson—there was no one he could trust but himself.

He grabbed a long quill, dipped it in carmine ink, and began etching a reply:

Captain Foedus,

It's come to my attention that there is more to your story than you are letting on. In fact, it would seem that you omitted a fair number of important points. Why you felt you needed to lie to me, I do not understand. Perhaps it is the influence of that problematic friend of yours: Abeo.

It has also come to my attention that your first officer has forgotten who he is and where he belongs. As a result, you have left me no choice but to take drastic actions.

Your orders are as follows:

1. You are to send me a full report on the extent of your knowledge about these beings and the riches that they sit upon; I want to know as much as you know and then some.

2. You are to send me coordinates and directions to your location. Be as precise as possible, use references in the sky, and include a guide to any markers you have lain.

3. Any valuables obtained are to be inventoried and recorded. No personal gifts shall be kept.

4. No Seeker is to fraternize with these creatures unless for educational purposes. Cordial activity is prohibited.

The admiral admired the flaming sky one more time. Over to the east, he noticed a soft yellow glow creeping on the horizon. To the best of his memory, he had never seen this hue in Crepusculum.

Once again he fantasized about the riches and fame that potentially awaited him. He smiled and laughed to himself, amused by his own excitement. Nothing could ruin this. *No one* could ruin this.

Christoph returned to his letter and proofread his orders. Dipping his quill into the bloody ink one more time, he scribbled down a fifth and final commandment for Foedus:

5. Should anyone oppose these commandments, it is my direct order to have them imprisoned. If anyone resists, they are to be terminated.

Sincerely,
Christophorus
Lord Admiral for the Seekers of the Unknown

Book 4
The Rising Sun

31

A warm fire peacefully crackled within the confines of Petram's tent while the outer skin flapped gently on its wooden frame. The winds had become unbearably cold; even the Rubeus retired indoors to escape squall's biting chill.

"Fascinating, isn't it?" Cordatus whispered to Petram. The old man lay comfortably on a bed of animal furs and blankets. Despite his general enthusiasm, it was clear that Cordatus' health was deteriorating. He had made a preliminary recovery since the icy incident—perhaps it was the stimulating discovery that had temporarily heightened his spirits—nonetheless, his physical condition declined with each passing sleep.

"What's fascinating?" Petram asked.

"Everything. Before this expedition, all we knew was our home and the void beyond the Murky Mountains, nothing more. Now, everything has changed. What I wouldn't give to be the first person to study these people and understand how life developed out here. It's so miraculous, and I'm sad that I only got to see a small part of it." A tear leaked out of the corner of his eye, and he wiped it away with his wrinkled hand.

"But you did get to see it," Petram smiled, attempting not to get emotional himself. "That's something, isn't it?"

"It is your time now, my young friend. I hope I have taught you enough that you can discover the world and write books from which others can learn. Just remember, you can never stop trying to understand what is around you. If you think you've reached the end of the journey, then you've fooled your mind into believing such nonsense. The world has presented us with a puzzle of infinite complexity, yet we somehow found a way to model its structure. We function because the commonalities of the objects around us are constantly moulded into a dynamic database that categorizes our perceptions of reality. Somewhere, deep in the past, our minds found order in the chaos. But the mind itself is made from the fundamental pieces that comprise the system upon which it abstracts. It is like a reflection without a mirror. You see, the pieces of the universe are very narcissistic; they have taken a keen interest in themselves. In a sense, to not pursue the truth of reality is to deny your own programming." Cordatus winced in pain as he adjusted on his bed. "I remember the moment my perception of the world changed. It was, of course, found within the pages of an old book. But it was not what the words said that intrigued me; what truly fascinated me was how the symbols on the page somehow corresponded with a tangible object. How we turned the sounds our throats make into specific and intricate models of the world. We study the natural world as if it is some alien entity distinct from us. How blind we are to ourselves."

Petram grinned but gave no response. His Praeceptoris cast a formidable shadow, one that would be difficult to escape. At the same time, Cordatus' legacy was a giant upon which he could stand. Petram's fear was not rooted in ineptitude, it was in the future of learning and reason. As he matured, he watched as society increasingly devalued the importance of intellectual inquiry. Religious institutions continued to push their agenda, staying tightly wound around the governing body of the Imperium. Cordatus maintained this would continue to be the case until individuals modified their perception of the spiritual. The people needed to grasp the irreparable harm inflicted on society when cults dictate enlightenment. Sure, the old man was aptly religious; he constantly revered the universal omnipotence that he believed imbued the world. It was the institution that bothered him. "Man is so easily swayed to believe illogical arguments," he would often say. For the two of them, accepting the justification for such beliefs was too arduous of a challenge to reasonably accept.

The group had often debated the issue. Some were piously religious, believing that any disinterest in God stemmed solely from a lack of faith and understanding. Foedus, who was a staunch critic, often laughed at the idea of praising an invisible being. His worship was directed to himself and his work.

Abeo fell in a similar realm as the captain, but he was far less outspoken. Once when asked what he did believe, he simply pointed towards the glistening sky. No living person was more in tune with the natural world than Abeo; it was mainly why Petram respected him and refused to accept Turpis' slander.

Probably most pious of them all was the one man not present on the expedition. Christoph often lectured the group on the importance of spreading God's message and converting all non-believers into loyal subjects. For him, faith in religion was another example of loyalty to the Imperium. No doubt, justifications for the Imperium's colonial activities were rooted in some infallible book.

Petram wondered if the Rubeus invented similar stories to explain their world. Their experience, so different than his, made their fundamental model drastically different. *What wonderful tales could they have conjured about the heavens?* Petram pondered. The question continued to pester him. After epochs of learning and observation, Cordatus' contagious preoccupation for absolute comprehension had successfully consumed Petram's conscience.

***

Once the cold finally subsided, the Seekers were again visited by their faded counterparts. The Rubeus brought baskets of jewels in the hopes of exchanging goods, but they knew the Seekers had little to spare. Interestingly, they seemed to have a particular lust for the intoxicating brown liquid the captain had gifted to them. Had he contained the necessary supply to quench their thirsts, Foedus would have no doubt continued to exploit their humble valuation.

Abeo, eager to advance his understanding of the Rubeus, engaged in an avid conversation with Sanuye and Arawak. Over time, the three men took a particular liking to each other, especially Abeo and Sanuye. The two were eager to discover as much as possible about the other's culture.

With relentless work, the Seekers came to learn much about the Rubeus. Most significantly, they determined where and how they mined the precious gems. For generations, the white men manipulated a network of caves into a complex system of valuable resources. Deep in the labyrinths, vast mines were built to excavate the horde of jewels embedded in the mountains. The Rubeus' ability to see in the dark made it easy for them to navigate in the depths. Those with particularly strong vision were told to delve deep into the caves and collect the lustrous stones. But the Rubeus did not use the jewels for themselves. For the most part, the stones were used to decorate the unique structure that stood beside the Central Tent. The mysterious pavilion was infused with jewels resembling the Spiral Cloud. The remaining jewels were divided amongst the Onontsi and other important members of the tribe. The colored stones acted as a symbol for merit and respect.

Petram noticed that Sanuye often wore an elegant cloth strapped over his shoulder. Embedded into the fabric, three ocean-blue stones mimicked three exceptionally bright stars in the sky. The stellar alignment was said to be great warriors who had ascended to the heavens for their bravery and heroism. Sanuye wore the cloth in honor of his revered ancestors.

After some negotiation by Foedus, the Rubeus granted the Seekers a tour of the mines so they could witness the splendour for themselves. Petram marveled at the complexity and breadth of the rocky tunnels. As they investigated the hollows, they came to realize that the cavernous network was not solely used for jewel extraction; many of the tunnels led to hidden grottos that acted as reservoirs for the white men. The air, warm and humid near these pools, acquired its heat from small volcanic outpourings at the base of the water. The strange structures spewed warm clouds out of tiny holes at the bottom of the basins. Directly around these objects, marine vegetation grew—food for the ivory fish that inhabited the ponds. The rounded shrubs they had seen in the camp extended vast networks of roots and vines all the way back to the bowls of warm water. Somehow, the outpourings provided the energy source necessary for life.

Walking alongside Sanuye, Petram inquired about the necklace of sharp teeth the warriors all wore. Sanuye had a difficult time explaining it to his dark counterpart, but from what he could determine, the teeth came from some giant beast—killing one was a sign of strength and readiness for duty as a warrior. Although they had not seen any other tribes of Rubeus, they had been informed that rival bands battled for control of the caves and resources. Warriors were expected to be prepared to protect their people from potential raids, but it wasn't all hostile; Sanuye also mentioned friendly tribes that lived nearby. Many of their distant relatives made up different civil bands; marriage and familial relationships often determined tribal compositions.

The complexity and sprawl of such a small community was nothing short of miraculous. Their social unity was astounding; every person had a role in benefiting the group. Younger men and women toiled in the caves looking for food, hunting all sorts of creatures that lived deep in the valleys. The older women prepared feasts for the masses, while the children made clothes and decorated the tents with paintings of the Spiral Cloud.

The more time they spent with the Rubeus, the more they learned about their astounding culture. The Onontsi, who had shown initial trepidation towards the Seekers, became their strongest companions. They came to learn much about the council of elders: Two of the bearded men, Sak and Jua, were analogous to teachers. They enlightened the younger generation about the patterns the stars made in the sky and on the origins of the Spiral Cloud. Both wrote books filled with diagrams of stars manifested into interconnected shapes and accompanied by mythical stories.

The other two, Boox and Kedalak, were experts on strategies of war, diplomacy, politics, infrastructure, fauna, and flora. Most importantly, they were in charge of deciding when and where they would move their camp when the cold season came.

Perhaps the most intriguing character in the Rubeus tribe was

Powhatan's wife: Shima. She was considered a healer and was highly respected among the tribe. Her thin white hair nearly reached her broad hips, and she had the most magnificent magenta eyes. Shima knew better than anyone which combination of herbs and chants would help alleviate illness and pain, always carrying around with her a sack full of powders and plants. Cordatus, keen on learning about the medicinal compounds, spent a significant amount of time trying to absorb what he could from her. He even volunteered to try a strange umbrella-shaped herb. After he consumed it, he spent the majority of his time walking around utterly enthralled by everything. Afterwards, all he said to the rest of the group was that reality was much more complex than their perception seemed to be able to capture.

Finally, there was Wicasa, the oldest man in the tribe. Covering his skin were deep crevices and cracks—biological imprints from his long life on Unum. His role within the community was difficult for the Rubeus to explain. It remained a mystery but seemed to be related to the name given to Veritas and the intriguing tent that they had yet to set foot in.

Veritas, himself, became increasingly preoccupied with the beautiful blonde girl they had met from before. Her name was Taree, and she was the daughter of a prominent warrior named Tian. Despite his best efforts, the blue-eyed boy's subtlety in his affection for Taree was minimal. Foedus cautioned the young man to not to get too close to her. The captain agreed that the Rubeus were docile beings, but to intermingle with them romantically was still considered taboo.

"I'm just getting information and learning, no different than the rest of you," Veritas plead, but Foedus was not fooled by the ruse. He saw in the young man's eyes the same absent logic that overcame Abeo when he had first met Cura.

Abeo, meanwhile, was ecstatic with how much progress they had made in such a short time. He wasn't concerned with Veritas' gallanting; his priority remained focused on preventing the arrival of Christoph. Time was of the essence, and he knew that making breakthroughs with the Rubeus would give him, and them, more time to prepare for the coming storm. He was thankful for Cordatus' wisdom; without the translational aid of the book, it would have taken eons to learn so much about each other. For him, this unity in language was more than enough proof that the Rubeus were broken from the same mould as he was. It made too much sense.

Upon the return of the warm winds, the atmosphere among both groups became jubilant. The Seekers could not remember a time when the entire crew had been so relaxed during an expedition. After one particularly productive session, Sanuye extended an invitation to the Seekers. They were asked to come to "the Great Feast of Wakan," the most important celebration for the Rubeus. Even Turpis, who had resisted the urge to fraternize with the white people, began to enjoy himself.

As they mingled together long into the evening, the Seekers and the Rubeus coexisted harmoniously. Like the different coloured stars embedded in the celestial ceiling, the world was more beautiful as a whole.

32

Abeo stared into the cold bedroom, trying his best to comprehend the emptiness that permeated the atmosphere. Glowing gently within the ashen chamber, a thin line of orange light glimmered through the single weakness of the window's blinds. Floating effortlessly, motes of dust hovered unconsciously, continuously suspended in a sunbeam. Toys and clothes were strewn about the floor; the only exception, the stuffed owl his son had been so fond of. There it lay, abandoned and alone in an empty crib. Abeo continued to glare into the icy heart of the room; his gaze refused to break away from the small impressions still moulded into the mattress.

The soft sound of sobbing penetrated through the wall of the adjoining room. Cura had become inconsolable. Abeo tried to make his presence felt in an attempt to blunt her sorrow, but the harder he tried the worse he seemed to make it. This frustrated him, and caused his cold persona to rear its ugly head. The positive feedback of negativity had become ethereal—it imbued the air he breathed.

"Abeo," Cura called.

"Coming," he replied, breaking from his stupor. "What can I do to help?" he asked as he entered their bedroom.

"There's nothing you can do; there's nothing to anyone can do," she mumbled through her tears.

He sat beside her and wrapped his arms around her shoulders. She gingerly nestled her head against his chest and buried her face within the warmth of his embrace. He could feel the vibrations of her jittery breathing as she struggled to fight the waves of emotion that continued to slam her body.

"Abeo, there's something I have to tell you."

"What's that?" he replied, trying to hide the anxiety that washed over him with such an ambiguous statement.

"I'm going to join the Leagum Rotundum. I'm tired of sitting around and allowing this regime to decide what's best for everyone else. We need to develop new ideas that revolve around individual choices."

"Cura, I don't see how that's going to solve anything. You're going to put yourself in danger."

"Abeo, you worry more than needs to be worried. Most of what they do is meet in secret to discuss and build a plan. No one is going to fight the Imperium without a plan. They've learned from the failures of the past. They understand the need to have a system ready to replace the old. Nothing is imminent; right now, everything is just talk. But they need reasonable minds to shape that goal correctly. My sister has already become ingrained with the Leagum. More than anything, I want to be there to keep an eye on her. You know how Lepidia can be; sometimes she dives into the pool head first without checking if there's water."

"You would be a good voice for them to have, I have no doubt about that, but even talk can get you into serious trouble. You know that as well as I do."

"So what?" she asked aggressively.

"So, I don't want to lose you. We've both lost too much already; I can't possibly bear the thought of seeing you arrested for treason or executed at the expense of someone's else's pursuit of power."

"That's not a way to live, Abeo. What is it you always tell me? The quest for the unknown is the only path forward in life. I can't just sit back and be complacent with a life where one group's beliefs get to determine the fate of my child!" Cura's sobbing restarted. Her breathing became choppy, and she struggled to normalize it.

Abeo wrapped his arms around her and gently kissed her neck. Nestling up next to her ear, he whispered, "breathe with me, follow my breath."

At first, her body resisted, but as she focused on his deep breaths, her inhales matched his inhales. She reached her hand upwards and grazed his cheek.

Abeo sighed and softly placed his hand under her chin, raising her head so that she looked up longingly at him. He looked into her mesmerizing green eyes, delicately brushed her mocha hair behind her ear, and slowly let go of a shy smile.

"What?" she asked playfully.

Abeo sat there for as long as he possibly could. He knew this moment was fleeting, but it was exactly that which made it so perfect. Her aura reached out and grabbed him, and together their energies coalesced into one. What was it about her that was so perfect? Her eyes called like a siren. The physical intoxication that just her stare could induce was proof enough for him that she was all he needed to fulfill his purpose in life.

She nervously looked away, but brought her gaze back to his, instilling in him a piece of innocence that drew indescribable meaning—she was a flower to be protected. His heart raced and his veins pulsed, but his breathing remained in line with hers. Together, they were two floating gasps bobbing up and down over a gentle current. He wanted to tell her that she was everything to him and that losing her was more than his conscious could bear. He wanted to reveal to her the agony that warped his viscera at all moments when he was not around to keep her safe. No one understood him as she did; no one loved the person he was like she did. If he were to lose her, he would lose a part of himself—he would lose the scaffold around his fundamental structure. Truly, he loved everything that she was.

Cura smiled back at her husband. She wiped an emerging tear from his eye and softly placed her palm on his coarse cheek. "What's on your mind, my dear?"

"Nothing," he whispered. "I love you, that's all."

Never again did the opportunity arise where Abeo's heart was able to reveal its true feelings.

33

Foedus swiftly struck a match and lit the herbal concoction embedded in his pipe. Inhaling deeply, he watched as blue smoke levitated towards the dazzling sky. Then, he noticed a swift blue streak fly urgently across the dark ceiling and rubbed his eyes in astonishment, startled by the fleeting flying flame. The sky, perpetually in motion, was a living entity.

    The captain sat alone near his tent, firmly planted on a rock. Next to him, pushed by the soft breeze, an unraveled scroll seesawed gently. He had read the letter from Christoph ten times over and still was in disbelief. Not only was he baffled as to how his superior knew so much, he couldn't get over the final order. The idea of actually having to "imprison"—or worse "terminate"—a member of his squad was nothing short of insane.

    Foedus fixated on the betrayal. He ran through his options, trying to determine his treacherous crewmate. Logically, it was Turpis who had sold him out. The grumbling beast of a man fought every order he gave, especially those that put the Rubeus ahead of himself. Foedus was privy to Turpis' contempt, but a good captain knows where his crew members are best served. He firmly believed the needs of the Imperium and the Seekers outweighed those of the Rubeus, but their docile demeanour made it difficult to justify violence. Most of the Seekers had taken well to the Rubeus; they embraced their community and maintained a keen effort to learn about their customs. To Foedus, the whole situation felt as if it had escalated out of nowhere. With Christoph now in the fold, diplomacy seemed impossible. Foedus contemplated how to handle the external forces opposing his every move. Duty to his job and allegiance to his friend squeezed his conscience. After extensive internal debate, the captain decided it would be best to inform Abeo and warn him of the impending danger.

He owed his friend this, at the very least.

Foedus walked across the camp and entered Abeo's tent. Abeo was busy reviewing his notes from a previous conversation with the Onontsi.

"Captain," he welcomed Foedus flippantly.

"Where's the kid?" Foedus asked.

"I think he went to go get some water from one of the grottos."

Foedus could tell Abeo was lying.

"Something wrong?" Abeo asked.

Foedus sighed. "I received a response from Christoph. It's not good."

"How could it be bad? You barely told him anything, I thought?" Abeo accused.

"I didn't, but someone did. Someone told him everything; now that I've flat out lied to him, he has me under his thumb. Needless to say, if I don't abide by these orders, it will be the end for us." Foedus handed his friend the scroll and let him peruse through it.

Abeo's eyes widened as he scanned through the edict. "He can't be serious about this?" he said.

"Well, he is. I'm showing this to you now in the hopes that you'll listen to me when I say my hands are bound on this one. Don't put me in a situation I don't want to be in, Abeo. For both of our sakes."

Abeo's green eyes stared back at his captain. "You know what will happen if you give him the coordinates? He'll bring the Legion with him. They'll see the riches and resources here and push the Rubeus out of their homes. When the light touches this land, the white-skinned people will be but a fading memory."

"And what's your alternative? We lie to our people and our bosses; we abandon everything we've ever known, who we are, and where we came from? For what? Some random group of people we know nothing about? I know you hate the Imperium, Abeo, but abandoning your home is not the answer."

"This is my home. I have always felt there was something out here for me, and now that prophecy has seen itself come true. I'm sorry, but I can't just step aside and watch these people fall victim to the lust of the Imperium."

"Abeo, please listen to me. If you resist, I will have no choice but to have you arrested and dealt with once Christoph arrives. You know the Imperium does not treat treasonous individuals well. Think about yourself here."

Abeo placed his hand on Foedus' thick shoulder and looked at him with reverence. "You are a great friend. You have always put up with my bullshit and been there when I've needed you the most. But this is still my life, and I have to make my own decisions. Just know that this is not in contempt towards you."

"But it involves me!" the captain shot back, showing a rare glimpse at his labile side.

"Not unless you let it. Pave your own path, my friend." Abeo grabbed his bag and exited the tent.

Foedus sighed. "Where are you going?"

"I have plans to meet with Sanuye. It's for informational purposes, you can tell your admiral that if he asks."

"He's your admiral, too," Foedus mumbled back. Sitting alone in the tent, Foedus wiped his brow and sighed.

***

Gathering the Seekers together, Foedus informed them of Christoph's commands. The news was understandably met with disappointment when they learned they were no longer to partake in recreational activities with the Rubeus.

Petram and Prod were particularly upset that they would no longer be allowed to play the new sport they had just learned. It involved sticks, a flat disk, two nets, and a lot of slashing and hacking. The Rubeus played it on the icy pools with sharpened stones tied to their feet. It was a physical, yet elegant, sport that they particularly enjoyed.

"Can I still partake in learning about the Rubeus if I find it recreational?" Cordatus inquired with a smug grin.

Foedus' perturbed glance answered his question thoroughly.

Most apparent to the group was the absence of Abeo and his blue-eyed Discipulus. Turpis was particularly upset the two were missing, knowing full well they were breaking the exact rules the rest of them were being lectured on.

"The rules apply the same to everyone. I will discuss this with both Abeo and Veritas," Foedus assured.

Turpis spat on the ground. He was not convinced by Foedus' promises.

"Despite the hospitality we have been treated to here, we must remember who we are and who we respond to," the captain continued. "We still have a job to do and orders to follow. It is up to us to police ourselves and hold each other accountable. I am counting on all of you to act professionally and remember your loyalty to the Imperium."

"So this means we don't get to go to the feast tomorrow?" Prod asked.

Foedus paused to consider Prod's question sincerely. "Because we are running short on our food supply, I will allow it. It'll be the best time to negotiate food and water rations with Powhatan. Hopefully, this will suffice until Christoph arrives."

The men murmured amongst themselves. The news had not sat well, but they were temporarily appeased at the notion of a celebratory send-off to their otherwise amicable relationship with the Rubeus.

As they retired to their tents, Foedus grabbed Turpis and pulled him aside. "Couldn't just come to me first could you?" the captain demanded.

"What?" Turpis asked, incredulously.

"I know it was you. I know you sold me out, and I won't forget it. Watch your back."

"What the hell are you talking about?" Turpis spat back, pushing Foedus away from him.

"You know damn well what I'm talking about. Remember chain-of-command? Get yourself in line."

"Right. Chain-of-command. Like how Abeo's little pet has somehow climbed the ranks over the rest of us. Funny how that happens. Maybe you should be more concerned about the two traitors breaking the rules right now instead of ringing me out for obeying orders."

"Don't worry about those two. I will take care of them," Foedus reassured.

"I hope you do. Because if you don't, I will."

34

Sanuye placed a brown bowl filled with bite-sized fruits in front of Abeo. The spherical pods came in an assortment of colours ranging from emerald green to ruby red. Abeo tossed one into his mouth and felt the skin of the fruit tear, allowing sour and sweet juices to erupt onto his palate. His counterpart grinned as he could tell Abeo enjoyed the taste. More than that, they both smiled as another thread was woven into their friendship.

From the outside, the two men couldn't be more dissimilar. Abeo, taller and thinner, was covered in a caramel skin that suctioned around his sunken cheeks, while Sanuye's chalky complexion wrapped firmly around his wide jaw. Abeo's dark bushy hair stayed rigid in the cold, while Sanuye's wispy blonde mane blew carelessly in the breeze. Using only physical features, they were two distinct organisms. But when pale green eyes observed cherry red, the two inherently understood a simple message—the chemical reaction of fruit juice on tongue was good. Nothing needed to be said, no language needed to be translated. A smirk and a look would suffice.

Abeo continued to pester his new friend, hoping to decipher the meaning of the word Wakan and how it related to Veritas. The young man was held in great esteem among the Rubeus community, for what reason remained a mystery.

"Wakan?" Abeo inquired.

Sanuye shrugged. The Rubeus warrior grew weary of the conversation. His common tongue was strong, but it was still tiring for both sides to maintain lengthy discussions.

Abeo pondered a way to stimulate the conversation. Then, it struck him. *What had they not discussed? What part of his community was missing from theirs?*

He grabbed Sanuye by the arm, dragged him away from the fire, and headed into the open meadow. Hurriedly, Abeo pointed across the opening at the peculiar tent they had yet to set foot in.

"What is this? What's it for?" Abeo inquired.

Sanuye struggled to find a word. Instead, he flattened his hands and pointed his upturned fingers at his forehead. Moving his hands upwards, he turned his palms toward the sky and spread his arms wide, basking in the light from the heavens. Then, he pointed at the Spiral Cloud. "Wakan," he whispered.

"Where did you come from, Sanuye? What created this world?" Abeo knew that asking such existential questions would doubtfully lead to a satisfying answer, but he felt that was on the right track.

"Wakan make all," Sanuye pointed at the cloud. "Wakan watch and care for Atanak. Does Skan know?"

"I think I do. Wakan is your God."

"What God?"

"Good question," Abeo smiled as Sanuye gave him a bewildered look. "Wakan is not Atanak, is he?"

"No. Wakan not Atanak. Wakan not he. Wakan watch and be. That all."

Abeo looked up at the Spiral Cloud hanging high above the horizon. It was dazzling. Long blue arms speckled with yellow stars whipped around the glowing core. The cloud looked back at Abeo, and he stared into the heart of the unknown. The thrill of curiosity nearly toppled him off his feet.

"What about Veritas?" Abeo asked. "Why is he called Wakan?"

"He be Wakan, here to watch, here to protect Atanak."

Abeo scratched his chin and tried to wrap his head around the entire thing. The Rubeus seemed to believe that Veritas was a manifestation of their God, but why?

"How do you know?" he asked.

Sanuye pointed at his eye. "Great story says Wakan come here and be Atanak."

"What story?"

The Rubeus warrior turned and motioned for Abeo to follow him. Leading him across the trickling creeks, Sanuye approached the mysterious tent and walked inside. Abeo anxiously followed. As they entered, Abeo saw, rising on both sides, three subsequently taller altars. Each alter contained a different assortment of jewels, all shaped exactly like the Spiral Cloud. The smaller spirals were composed of emeralds and amethysts, while the larger ones were filled with rubies and topaz.

Opposite to the entrance, stood a miraculous shrine that reached towards the roof of the tent. Abeo was unsure of Rubeus customs, but Sanuye nodded it was okay for him to approach, and he did so slowly. Walking along the alters, he admired the brilliant décor. Then, he reached the shrine. Standing in the middle, a perfect replica of the Spiral Cloud was built out of lustrous stones. Diamonds and lazuli comprised flailing spiral arms while brilliant white stones encased the pearl epicenter. A black backwash curved around the cosmic facsimile; speckled with white and yellow jewels, it modelled the night sky. Abeo looked on in amazement at the craftsmanship. The entire tent appeared to twinkle with glimmering light.

Situated below the shrine, sitting on top of the chestnut alter, was a book. It was covered with a black skin and bound with white string—almost identical to the book Cordatus had used to translate their languages.

"What is this?" Abeo asked.

"Word of Wakan."

"Where did it come from?"

"Much time Atanak have. Where from, Sanuye not know."

"What does it say?"

"Many things."

Abeo laughed at the simplicity of his friend's answers. "What does it say about Veritas?"

Sanuye untied the string, opened the book to a particular page, and pointed at the foreign writing. Abeo's grasp of their vernacular was strong under the circumstances, but his ability to read the Rubeus language was still relatively poor.

"Can I take it? Cordatus can probably translate it fairly quickly."

"No. Must stay here, never leave," Sanuye responded.

"Damn." Abeo knew he would have to grab the old man. "I will come back," he explained to Sanuye, and he retreated from the tent and headed back to where the Seekers were camped. On his way, he saw Veritas emerge with a bashful smile on his face. The young man saw his mentor and diffidently walked over to him.

"Learn anything new?" Veritas asked.

"Turns out they might think you're some kind of God," Abeo stated rather matter-of-factly.

Veritas shot him a stupefied smile. "Interesting," he smirked and continued walking.

Abeo grabbed him by the arm. "Listen, Veritas, I know you're having a great time with this girl."

"Taree," Veritas interrupted. "That's her name."

"Taree, sure. Trust me, I get it. But things might get contentious pretty soon. We are all going to have to make a choice in the next little while. I need you to realize that I can't make your decisions for you, and I can't protect you."

"No one is asking you to protect me," the young man shot back.

"All I'm asking is for you to be careful, okay? Don't be reckless; you don't know the kind of trouble you could find yourself in."

"Thanks for the advice, but you don't need to worry about me. I can take care of myself." Veritas broke away from his Praeceptoris' hold and walked away.

"Do you love her?" Abeo called after him.

The question took Veritas by surprise. "Of course I do. What kind of question is that?

"I'm not asking if you like her; I'm asking if you love her." Abeo paused and looked up towards the sky, closed his eyes, and exhaled. "Does her presence make you feel more at ease? When you hear her voice, does it calm your anxiety? Does it soothe your soul? Are you powerless against her laugh? Are you often distracted by just the very thought of her in your mind? When you look into her eyes, do you see something merely aesthetically beautiful, or do you, for that moment, forget all of your hardships? When you are with her, does it feel like all that exists is the singular set that you two embody?"

Veritas paused to consider the question. "Absolutely," he responded. His chilling eyes glared back at Abeo, cutting through the darkness.

Abeo smiled and placed his hand on the young man's shoulder. No, he was not his son, but he could have been. For all the tragedies he had faced, for all the love that had been ripped away from him, he witnessed the same love continue to exist in the far corners of Unum, refusing to perish. He stared into Veritas' dazzling blue eyes and saw the same euphoria that had once grasped him.

As they continued back towards the camp, Abeo gave one final piece of advice to his young companion. "If you do love her, then you must be prepared to do anything to protect her. A flood is coming, and the world doesn't care if you sink or swim."

35

Gasping for air, Christoph reached the pinnacle of a daunting staircase and admired the massive palace towering before him. Across a white courtyard, an enormous arch stood subordinate to a golden dome. Behind it, an exorbitant tower nearly grazed the pink speckled clouds that populated the orange sky.

Christoph turned around to admire the panorama of Crepusculum. To the east, the city stretched beyond the horizon, baking in the light of Stella. To the west, a charcoal expanse of rock and ice loomed below the glistening sky—two conflicting forces melting together in the firmament's collage. Soaking in the view, he caught his breath and continued towards the entrance of Domus Imperium. Lining the expansive courtyard, large trees intermittently poked out of protrusions in the white cobblestone. Their chestnut arms bifurcated until they could divide no more, while verdant leaves blossomed at the terminal end of each branch.

Christoph approached the tower entrance where two guards stood. Both with sinister looks on their faces, they nodded in approval knowing Christoph from his frequent visits with the Princep. As if it were possible, the Imperator's son was far worse than his father. Not only did he inherit the Imperator's severe lack of empathy, he consciously carried himself as a virtuous gift from the heavens, seemingly brought to this planet so that others could bask in his presence.

Wiping the gathering sweat off his forehead, Christoph took a deep breath, attached a volatile smile to his face, and walked through the imposing ivory doors. As the doors opened, a loud creak echoed throughout the expansive hall situated on the other side. Christoph revered at the magnificent architecture inside the palace walls. All throughout the corridor, great pillars supported the immense arches standing on their shoulders. Intricate carvings of flowers and vines were engraved into the wooden curves, while gold and crimson strands wrapped themselves around the stain-glassed windows that symmetrically lined the outer walls.

On the opposite side, sitting atop an elegant throne, was the Princep. He was a short and stout man with a dark complexion. Thick chestnut hair fell chaotically on his broad shoulders, and a pretentious smile lingered under his wide nose. Sitting atop his skull, an extravagant silver crown curved around his thick head. Six guards prudently watched as Christoph approached his superior.

"Welcome, Lord Admiral Christophorus," the Princep said with a shrill voice.

"Your Grace," Christoph bowed his head and gingerly approached the throne.

"I hear you have great news. A nice change from the usual drabble I get from the Seekers of the Unknown." The guards snickered on command like trained dogs.

"I do, Your Grace. Great news in fact."

"Do tell, my loyal subject."

"I received word a few sleeps ago from Captain Foedus that evidence for sustainable life has been found within the Murky Mountains."

"Sustainable life? As in wild beasts? I thought you had news, Christophorus."

"No, Your Grace. I do not mean wild beasts. I mean vegetation, domesticated animals, freshwater fish, and some…" he hesitated, "well some form of intelligent being."

The Princep broke from his disinterested slouch and sat up on his throne. "Intelligent being?"

"I don't know enough details, Your Grace, as I have yet to see them myself. But from what I could ascertain, they are creatures very similar to us. They are organized and have learned how to manipulate their environment. They have a language that is slowly being translated. At this very moment, my men are working towards understanding what they can about these beings."

The Princep stroked his chin. "How unbelievably odd," he mumbled. "Well, this is excellent news for our people. With the light of Stella moving, we can migrate to these lands and begin the colonization!" he said with a casual malevolence. "I will give you fifteen men and all the supplies you need to go canvas the land and learn the ways of these beings, or whatever they are."

"There's more, Your Grace" Christoph interrupted. "Within the mountains are rich mines of jewels that these creatures know how to access." The admiral was well aware that the Imperium would have no choice but to continue to fund the Seekers if they wanted access to the riches buried in the darkness of the mountains.

"Is there now?" The Princep asked curiously. "Perhaps a hundred men would be a more reasonable number," he smiled.

Christoph nodded. "Thank you, Your Grace. That is most generous."

"Don't thank me just yet, Lord Admiral. There is much left for you to do. You will be accompanied by one hundred of my hand-picked people. Together, you are to find these creatures, learn their ways of domestication, food production, and jewel extraction. I want daily updates on progress."

"Yes, Your Grace."

"I also want one of your men to draw up a contract that will ensure Imperium ownership over any findings done by our men."

"Your Grace, I doubt these beings will accept such terms."

"Then make them agree," he barked. A sinister smile emerged under his prominent nose. "Have that captain of yours, Foedus, draw it up. He has strong diplomatic skills, much like his father. I liked his father, did you know him?"

"I did, Your Grace."

"Loyal man, very loyal. I like loyalty, don't you?"

"I do, Your Grace."

"Very good. Loyalty is significant to me. I hope you realize that anyone caught acting against my orders is violating laws of the Imperium and shall therefore be sentenced as a traitor."

"Of course, Your Grace. I wouldn't have it any other way." Christoph stroked his moustache and bowed to the Princep. "Is there anything else that you request of me?"

"No. For now, go and get some rest. Return in a few sleeps, and I will have my squad chosen and ready for you."

Christoph bowed again and turned to leave the hall. He returned to the elegant courtyard, descended the mountain of stairs, raced across the street, and entered the decrepit black building that was home to the Seekers. Ascending the spiral stairs to his office, he grabbed a glass and poured himself some whiskey. Downing the first glass, he poured another, walked over to his desk, and began to write:

Foedus,

I have just finished my meeting with Princep Aragon. He has given me an ample quantity of men and supplies to make it to where you are. I am to be accompanied by one-hundred members of the Legion, hand-chosen by the Princep, to come and assess the situation. I will attempt to use Cordatus' star-maps for direction, although I don't know what he means by "Spiral Cloud," and will follow any markers that you have left. Perhaps everything will become clearer as I venture onwards. I trust all is in order there and that the men are on board with all plans.

I have one final order for you coming straight the Princep himself. You are to draw up a contract that will give the Imperium rightful access to all jewels, food, and resources found. Any being who wishes to participate in extracting these resources is welcome to do so. If the beings refuse to agree to such terms, be sure to explain to them what military conquest is. Hopefully, this suffices in guiding their signing hands.

I leave soon. Keep well. Keep things in order.

Christoph

Using his thin fingers, he rolled up the letter, attached it to the talon of an owl, and watched as the beautiful bird flapped its violet wings and disappeared into the darkening sky.

Soon, he would embark on the long journey west. It would be cold and wet, and it would be difficult, but it would be the first step towards endless riches, greatness, fame, and conquest.

"For the Imperator and the Imperium!" Christoph yelled out the window as he raised his glass to the enchanting sky. He took a prolonged sip of the caramel liquid and felt it burn as it descended his throat. Squinting his eyes, Christoph stared indignantly at the world. "Fuck that," he muttered to himself. He took one more savory sip and whispered, "for me."

36

Abeo sat atop a large boulder and basked in the night sky. He admired the Spiral Cloud and the swirling mosaic of colours that comprised it. Behind the cosmic marvel, the stars twinkled in a probabilistic pattern, and the ribbons of neon green danced indiscreetly above. An electromagnetic orchestra played silently, and Abeo listened intently with his eyes.

Soon, he and the others were to join the Rubeus for "the Great Feast of Wakan." It was a time of pride and delight for the white people; their energy and excitement had become increasingly noticeable. The Seekers, on the other hand, were not to share the fervour. At least that was the command given by Christoph. Foedus supported his superior's orders, pleading his men to terminate their relationship with the Rubeus on an affable note.

To Abeo, the whole thing seemed so utterly ridiculous. As far as he could tell, the Rubeus were not unlike the people of the Imperium. Sure, their appearance and their customs differed, but their understanding of emotion, their ability to love and to communicate, to form bonds and feel pain, and to question and contemplate existence, were all so relatable. The Rubeus shared much with the Seekers, yet were continuously portrayed as a plague.

"I must remind all of you that this evening's events are for professional, not recreational, purposes," Foedus had announced to all of them. "Eat and drink tonight to stave your hunger and quench your thirst, but do not binge. Admiral Christoph will be here soon enough. Until that time, it is our duty to prepare for his coming by continuing to learn about the Rubeus, and, most importantly, the resources to which they have access. I expect every man here to follow these orders." The lecture had seemed cold juxtaposed to the emotional speeches Foedus usually gave to his crew. The words he spoke were not truly his, but he still felt comfortable delivering the message.

Abeo meditated on his rocky throne and awaited his companions. As they emerged from the darkness, he mentally prepared himself for the uncomfortable situation his captain had imposed upon them.

***

The seven Seekers walked as a group towards the entry of the camp. Foedus led the way, carrying a load of whiskey in his sack. Much to the chagrin of Turpis, the alcohol was the only commodity they had left to trade.

Abeo lingered at the back of the pack. Struggling to keep pace with the rest, Cordatus strolled alongside.

"Are you alright?" Abeo asked.

"Just fine," he calmly replied. "The cold weather is beginning to take a toll on this poor soul, but I believe I can make it okay."

"Are you ready to tell me what you found in that book yet?" Abeo asked. He had sent Cordatus to try and decipher, as best as he could, the holy book that held the clue to Veritas' fame. The old scholar returned with news that he had translated it into an intelligible story, but he felt it best to wait until they had a private moment to speak of it.

Cordatus looked around to make sure that no one could hear them. "The story in those pages was somewhat difficult to translate, but I think I got the main idea. As far as I can tell, the Rubeus believe Veritas is some manifestation of their God. The story says that their God—or Wakan—which seems to be linked to that magnificent Spiral Cloud, once came down to this planet and lived as they did. Wakan watched over the people, taught them lessons and told them stories about how the world had been created and how they came to be. The story claims that Wakan was discernible through one distinct feature—his blue eyes that resembled the Spiral Cloud. The book says that one day Wakan would return to them, and they believe Veritas is this God-like reincarnation come back to guide them again."

"So they think he is their God?"

"Well, some Rubeus manifestation of their God. Either way, they consider him to be above the people of this world."

"How peculiar," Abeo said with a smile.

"You've really come to fall in love with these people, haven't you?"

"I've never felt more at home."

Cordatus smiled momentarily, but his jubilance was interrupted with a sudden hacking cough.

"Are you alright?" Abeo inquired.

"Fine, just the dry air in my lungs," Cordatus responded. For a moment, Abeo thought he saw blood on the old man's hands, but he couldn't be sure his eyes weren't playing tricks on him in the dark.

As they approached the camp entrance, Sanuye and others welcomed them at the gate. They waved and gestured for the Seekers to come in, each with excited looks on their faces. Sanuye immediately approached Abeo and grabbed his hand to shake it. The Rubeus warrior was incredibly awkward with his formalities, but he was genuine in his warm welcome.

"Welcome, Skan," the white man stumbled through the words. "Exciting this. Good time we have." He pointed at his chest and then at Abeo's, signaling the growing unity between the two men.

Foedus cleared his throat audibly.

Abeo noticed his captain disapproved of the gesture, but he did not care. He placed his hand on the Rubeus' shoulder, "I'm hungry, my friend. Let's eat!"

Some of the other Rubeus attempted to shake the hands of the Seekers, following Sanuye's lead. Foedus begrudgingly allowed the greeting, but Turpis and Prod refused to touch the hands of "dusty-skinned animals."

Following their escorts into the center of the camp, Abeo observed an enormous fire raging. Men and women danced around and chanted, pointing upwards at the sky and singing. Their faces were decorated with red and black paint, while spiral shapes covered their bodies. In the background, drums beat viscerally. The atmosphere was electric, and Abeo couldn't suppress his excitement.

Sanuye had explained to him that the festival was held to celebrate the ascension of the Spiral Cloud. The massive cosmic object cyclically changed its position in the sky, reaching its highest point before descending towards the horizon. Whenever the Spiral Cloud dropped, the warm winds subsided, replaced by the unyielding chill of the dark season. During this time, the Rubeus retreated to caves to sleep for long periods. With its ascension, the Spiral Cloud brought energy that activated the Rubeus. In the dark times, they became increasingly dependent on their secondary vision. Without this skill, death was surely imminent. For now, light and life were aplenty. This was the time of Wakan, and it was extremely sacred to the Rubeus.

For Sanuye, Veritas' arrival had coincided too perfectly to be just a fluke. As the young man entered the camp, the music went silent. Hundreds of piercing red eyes drew their gaze towards him. The Rubeus all bowed their head and mumbled incoherently. Veritas could do nothing more than stand still and allow his worshippers to praise their God.

Abeo admired and observed the gathering crowd. He looked past the fire and saw Powhatan standing upon a large stone. The Rubeus leader wore a magnificent hat decorated with an assortment of jewels. His people quieted down, bowed, and watched in silence as he lifted his arms towards the sky and repeated a chant that reverberated throughout the valley. All the people rose from their bowing position, pointed towards the heavens, and copied the words of Powhatan. They repeated this process seven times, one for each arm of the Spiral Cloud, and then returned to their laughing, dancing, and singing.

Veritas looked at Abeo with a broad grin on his face. The wonder of such a uniquely distinct culture was not lost on him.

"Don't get too cozy kid," Turpis scowled at Veritas. "Your so-called followers are the enemy. Any man whose followers are the enemy is nothing but a traitor."

Veritas paid little attention to the jab. Instead, he made a bee-line for Taree whose curly blonde hair radiantly bounced as she jogged towards him.

"Veritas!" Foedus yelled loudly, drawing the attention of many of the nearby Rubeus. "Restrain yourself. You are here to follow orders, not to fraternize."

Veritas stopped in his tracks a few paces from his muse. He looked her square in the eyes and motioned for her to stop. She looked back at him confused, so he winked, and she reciprocated with a gentle smile. Veritas turned back and returned to the Seekers, much to the dismay of the Rubeus. To them, Wakan had showed subordination to one of the dark-skinned men. How could they make sense of their God bowing down to the orders of a mortal? The men and women chattered amongst themselves, but the stir was eventually eased, and the celebration continued.

Soon enough, a massive feast was sprawled out amongst a row of tables. In an orderly manner, the Rubeus lined up by social rank. The Onontsi went first, followed by the elderly men and women, the jewel miners, the animal farmers, the gatherers, and finally the children. The warriors were last to eat but were given the greatest share of the food.

The Seekers, being guests, were invited to eat first. Graciously, they approached the buffet to receive their long-awaited meals. Drawing in the hungry eyes of both parties, cooked fish, assortments of ripe fruits, and odd-coloured vegetation filled the tables.

Once they had their food, everyone congregated near the blazing fire. Powhatan stood upon a large rock and once again yelled for everyone's attention. He turned his back to the Rubeus and the flame and opened his arms wide as if to prepare for an embrace. He then stared up at the Spiral Cloud, yelled a chant seven more times, and waited for a communal echo to ensue. The Rubeus bowed at the cloud, repeated the words as their leader had, and then began to indulge in the delicious feast.

Once everyone's appetites had been satiated, the Seekers and Rubeus sat side-by-side around the raging fire, admiring the night sky, and drinking whiskey—Foedus' party favour. Abeo looked across the fire and saw his captain deep in discussions with Boox, Kedalak, and Powhatan. Petram and Cordatus sat beside him and listened intently on the conversation. Then, the six men retreated to the Central Tent; for what reason, Abeo did not know. Curiously, both Foedus and Petram took multiple rifles with them.

Abeo returned his gaze to the burgeoning fire and watched as its flickering flames blossomed like the petals on an ephemerally blooming flower. To his left, also observing the fire, was Veritas. He leaned against Taree while her blonde crown nestled softly on his shoulder. To his right, Prod and Turpis laughed belligerently, quarreling over equal partitions of their remaining bottle of whiskey. Unbeknownst to them, a full bottle lay a few inches from Turpis' feet, but they were too inebriated to notice it.

So much for not recreational, Abeo thought to himself.

Prod got up and stumbled off into the meadow to relieve himself.

"Beautiful light, Skan," Sanuye proclaimed. The white man stood before the Seeker, decorated elegantly with gold and crimson paint. Spirals and swirls enveloped his pearl skin, and his strong hands wrapped firmly around a towering spear. The weapon itself, decorated with delicate ribbon, had elegant jewels embedded in the shaft.

"Beautiful light," Abeo responded, offering his flask to Sanuye who vehemently refused. He had not said it, but Abeo had inferred that Sanuye was not pleased with the effects whiskey had on his people. It was not his place in the community to say so; he spoke about it through his actions. Despite his friend's rejection and concern, Abeo took another sip for himself, but his enjoyment was abruptly interrupted by a shrill scream.

Out of the darkness, Prod emerged. He violently grabbed Taree by her hair and pulled her backward onto the ground. Before Veritas could react, Prod landed a vicious punch square on the young man's forehead. The force suctioned him backward, and he yelled in pain.

"You knew the rules, and you blatantly defy them in front of all of us!" Prod spat. He kicked Veritas in the ribs as he attempted to get up, causing him to painfully cough.

The Rubeus warriors nearby yelled in alarm. Most were unarmed, but those who had their ceremonial spears and bows stood up and approached the scene.

With Prod briefly distracted by the closing mob, Veritas had time to unsheathe his falchion.

Prod turned to his smaller adversary in surprise. A gaping grin grew on his muscular face. "Oh, you want to play, little boy? You want to die for these chalky bastards?" Prod unsheathed a vast sword. The dazzling sky reflected off its silver exterior.

"They're just people! They're just like us! How can you not see that?" Veritas screamed at Prod, his face already swollen from the Prod's punch.

"People?" Prod spat on the ground. "They're god-damn animals. They're not us! You're the one who's supposed to be some prodigy. Use your eyes! They don't look anything like us, how can they be us? They're savages, just like this little bitch." He pointed his sword at Taree, forcing Veritas to edge closer. Despite being outmatched, Veritas stood bravely and firmly against his so-called companion.

"Prod! Stop!" Abeo admonished. He got up and headed towards the skirmish but was immediately tackled by Turpis. The beastly man lowered his thick forearm onto Abeo's neck, effectively pinning him to the stubborn ground.

"Sit still and watch the show," he snarled.

Abeo writhed to break out of this hold, but Turpis' weight and strength were too much to overcome. From his perspective, Prod's tall frame dominated Veritas' even more so. The former swung his sword with great force, nearly missing the latter's arm. Prod attacked twice more while Veritas dove left and right, barely managing to dodge the swipes. With his fourth swing, Prod sliced Veritas' upper thigh, forcing him to stumble. The slash cut deep, allowing crimson blood to ooze from the wound.

"WAKAN!" the Rubeus shouted frantically.

Prod looked anxiously at the mob.

Drawn in by the sound of chaos, Foedus and Petram emerged across the meadow. Petram fired his rifle into the air causing the mob to disperse in shock. Foedus swung his rifle around his shoulder and ran vigorously towards the shambolic scene. He and Petram both pointed their guns at the angry crowd, forcing the Rubeus to back away.

"Prod!" Foedus yelled. "Don't move another muscle."

Prod smugly smirked at Veritas. "Lucky for you," he whispered. Begrudgingly, he lowered his weapon.

Veritas struggled to his feet and raced over to Taree who continued to cry. Blood dripped down her forehead; Prod had torn part of her scalp off with the force he had pulled her hair. As she stood, a flood of blood rushed from the wound on her forehead, straight down her face, effectively covering her delicate white skin in a pool of red liquid. An elderly women cried in disgust and outrage, spitting at Prod. This was too much for the mob to see; screaming in distress, the Rubeus began to anxiously stir. Outraged men and women aggressively closed in, restrained by their more passive counterparts. Like a dormant volcano, the Rubeus, offended by the disruption of their most sacred celebration, were ready to erupt.

Then, emerging from the crowd, was Arawak. With incredible speed, he tossed a spear and watched as it whizzed straight into Prod's left shoulder. Prod stumbled backward and aggressively yelled in pain. At this, Foedus fired towards Arawak but missed. Instead, the bullet flew into the crowd, hitting a young man in the head and killing him — another innocent name thrown into the anthology of collateral damage.

Arawak grabbed another spear and ran furiously at Foedus. The captain calmly grabbed a reloaded rifle and shot again, this time hitting the Rubeus man in the chest. Arawak's limp body fell heavily on the rocky ground.

In sheer panic, the mob dispersed and frantically ran away from the violent epicenter. Smoke from both the guns and the fire amalgamated into a thick fog that enhanced the chaos. Abeo watched helplessly as Petram grabbed Veritas and slung him over his shoulder. Foedus did the same with Prod, and the four of them retreated away into the haze.

Using the commotion to his advantage, Abeo managed to momentarily break free from Turpis, but the mammoth man recovered quickly and grabbed Abeo by his ankles, bringing him down again. Turpis wrapped his strong hands around Abeo's scruffy neck, and malevolently smiled as he began squeezing his wind-pipe with sufficient force.

Abeo struggled to inhale; he felt as if he had swallowed a plug. He flailed his fists towards Turpis' looming skull, but the giant man would not be deterred. The more he fought, the harder the compression around his throat felt. Darkness began to ease into the perimeter of Abeo's eyes. His vision veered away from his adversary and moved towards the sparkling sky. If this was the last thing he was going to see, he was okay with it.

Suddenly, the plug in his throat was gone. Abeo painfully inhaled as much as he could and coughed violently as his body rejected the influx of dry air. He rolled over and felt warm liquid dripping onto his arm, followed by the cool breeze of compressed air blowing under Turpis' tumbling body. The imposing man fell onto his stomach and landed heavily on the ground.

Abeo looked up to see Sanuye's spear lodged firmly in Turpis' rib cage. The Rubeus tried to loosen the weapon out of Turpis' thick frame, but the big man thrashed away angrily, causing the stem of the spear to snap. With haste, the warrior offered Abeo his hand. Sanuye grabbed his friend by the wrist and pulled him out of the cloudy and chaotic carnage.

Turpis, still writhing in pain, didn't even notice their escape. Grunting vociferously, he removed the spear from his ribs and stumbled away from the scene. As he left, he bellowed a frustrated groan that reverberated through the entire valley.

Lost and forgotten in all this commotion, was poor old Cordatus.

37

Incessantly panting, Petram exhaustedly dropped Veritas who grunted in pain as he hit the hard ground. The gash on his leg, widened from the turbulent ride on Petram's shoulders, continued to periodically pump crimson fluid out of the chasm. Webbing across his thigh, the blood diverged into a multitude of narrow streams.

"Thank you," the young man said, barely squeaking the words out of his dehydrated lips.

"Don't mention it," Petram responded. He looked sternly into Veritas' cosmic blue eyes and then repeated himself, "seriously, don't mention it. I don't know what's going to happen, but you're in some deep trouble now. From this point on, my hands are clean from your dirt."

"Me? How can I be in trouble?! That idiot attacked me for no reason."

"You might see it that way, but I assure you your superiors definitely won't. You were disobeying orders in plain sight. I hate to say it, kid, but your defense is pretty minimal on this one."

"Insanity," Veritas whispered to himself. He cringed in pain as he readjusted his position.

Out of the darkness, Foedus emerged with Prod slung around his shoulder. The young man was bleeding badly; the spear, pulled from his chest, left a gaping gash that gushed relentlessly. Both men grunted as they struggled across the jagged floor, stumbling in unison when the captain's toe caught the protruding edge of an imposing stone.

"Petram, make us a fire and grab some water," Foedus ordered. His voice had no semblance of its normally blithe tone. "Where does Cordatus keep his medicine?"

"I'll grab it," Petram responded assertively, stopping suddenly at the haunting realization that now hijacked his mind—he had completely forgotten about the old man in all the commotion. As he ran into the tent to grab both the ignasaxum, and the burgundy bag that housed all of the medical supplies, his anxiety began to run wild worrying about his Praeceptoris. He lit the fire as quickly as he could and brought out three full canteens of water.

Foedus, meanwhile, worked on mending Prod's wound. The young man writhed in agony as the captain poured whiskey on his open sore. Foedus took a swig for himself before offering some to Prod and then began wrenching fragments of wood out of his gash.

"You're lucky these spears aren't hooked, or we'd be in a real mess," the captain mentioned, attempting to lift his spirits. Prod merely groaned and took another sip of the caramel liquor.

Veritas, still losing blood, squirmed uncomfortably on the callous ground. Petram grabbed a bandage and began wrapping the young man's leg, periodically glancing out to the darkness for a sign of Cordatus, but no one emerged. He finished wrapping the wound and immediately got up to look for his mentor.

"Where are you going?" Foedus demanded.

"To find Cordatus," he responded quickly.

"Stay where you are. No one leaves."

"But what if he's out there and hurt?"

"We wait. Cordatus knows his way back. Besides, we don't even know where Turpis and Abeo are. There's a good chance they're together."

"Doubtful," Veritas mumbled.

"What was that?" Foedus shot back, an enraged look overtook his tired face.

Veritas weakly struggled to his feet, leaned all of his weight on his uninjured leg, and stared his captain straight in the eyes. "I said doubtful. In case you haven't noticed, Turpis hates almost everyone, especially Abeo. I wouldn't be surprised if he tried to kill him given the ample opportunity the chaos provided."

Foedus' face morphed from incensed to surprisingly amused. He approached the young man, stood before him, and placed his hand on the kid's shoulder. "I know you think you know a lot about how things work. I know you believe you're this gift to these people because they praise the ground you walk on. But here, in my world, you're a subordinate. Nothing more. So, next time you perceive it in your best interest to tell me what I do or don't know about my crew, it will be the last time you perceive anything." He removed his steady hand from Veritas' shoulder and punched the young man in the stomach, forcing him to keel over and painfully cough. Foedus turned around and walked away. "Where the hell is Turpis!" he yelled furiously. His face became malevolently distorted, and his thick brow furled inwards, arching menacingly around his chestnut eyes.

Petram had never seen Foedus so aggravated. All this time, hidden beneath his stern exterior, was a pinch of disquietude.

Then, as if summoned by a conjurer, Turpis emerged from the dark. He panted heavily and clutched his ribs.

"What the hell happened to you?" Foedus yelled in disbelief.

"Chalky-skinned bastard blindsided me for no reason, jabbed his spear right into my rib cage," Turpis mumbled back. His deep voice sunk an octave lower than usual, making his sentences nearly impossible to understand.

"Really? For no reason?" Veritas asked accusingly.

"Shut your mouth!" Turpis yelled. He suddenly lost his balance and fell to his knees.

"God damn it," Foedus muttered to himself. He managed to catch the big man before he face-planted on the hard rock and immediately began bandaging his wound.

Turpis, barely conscious, stuck his hand out for a canteen. Petram passed one to him; he took one swig and spat out the cold liquid. "Whiskey!" Turpis' strained voice rasped. He violently tossed the canteen; the clattering of the metal on the hard rock echoed throughout the entire canyon. Petram brought him a bottle of whiskey and Turpis bit off the cork and chugged the brown liquid.

"Where is Abeo?" Foedus asked him, grabbing the bottle from Turpis' thick hands.

"How should I know?" Turpis grumbled back, already slurring his words.

"Did you see Cordatus at all?" Petram asked nervously.

"Nah. Didn't see him. I tried to get out after I saw you guys run off. Got completely blindsided."

"I find that hard to believe," Veritas shot back.

"You hold your tongue, kid," Foedus ordered him.

"What're you going to do with them?" Turpis mumbled to his captain.

"Who?" Foedus asked.

"The two traitors."

Foedus paused to consider the question. He sighed, wiped his brow, and delivered his verdict: "Veritas will be quarantined to his tent until Christoph arrives. The admiral will have the final say as to his fate."

Turpis chuckled, but his laugh was immediately interrupted by a coughing fit, forcing him to clutch his ribs in pain. "Kid, if your fate is in Christoph's hands, *and* your offense is treason… shit, would say nice knowing you, but it hasn't been." He turned and looked Veritas in the eye, and a wide grin emerged on his sweaty face.

"What do you mean by quarantined?" Veritas asked.

"I mean you won't be leaving your tent unless I say so or one of us accompanies you," Foedus commanded.

"Probably not the best idea to leave the two kids on their own," Petram whispered to his captain.

Foedus nodded in agreement. For the time being, he and Petram would need to take turns guarding Veritas. Hopefully, for them, Christoph would arrive soon. Their food stocks were beginning to run extremely low. Before the commotion, Foedus had been drafting a contract with Powhatan that would have provided them with the necessary supplies until reinforcements arrived. Now, thanks to the violent incident, they would have to depend on rationing and scavenging to get by.

After he finished wrapping Veritas' wound, Petram escorted the young man to his tent. His sword, his pride, his love, and the only family he ever had, had all been taken away from him.

Foedus took first guard, while Petram tended to the others. After Prod retired to his quarters, Petram finally found the time to accompany his captain at Veritas' tent. He brought with him warm cups of stew and sat down exhaustively outside the improvised prison.

"Do we have the rations to last until Christoph gets here?" Petram asked anxiously.

"As long as he doesn't get lost," Foedus replied with a nervous chuckle.

"What do you think is going to happen to the kid," Petram whispered, hoping Veritas wasn't listening, but knowing full well that he was.

"Hard to say. Treason is never a good thing, especially in the new regime. That being said, maybe he can plead complicated circumstances."

"Seems ridiculous, doesn't it?" Petram asked hesitantly, probing for Foedus' reaction. The captain showed no change in his expression. "I mean, all he was doing was courting some girl, what's the harm in that?"

Foedus sighed and turned to his companion. His eyes were coated with a thin layer of tears, but they did not reach the threshold to descend his weathered face. There was compassion in his eyes, even empathy, but it was buried deep beneath something else. He cleared his throat gently and stood up from his comfortable perch. "The law is the law," he asserted. The captain turned and retreated to his tent, leaving Petram alone outside.

Petram curled his arms and hands into his armpits to protect his extremities from the chilling wind. Accompanying the breeze, specks of snow bleached his black hair. As he sat guard, his eyes deviated from the light and the warmth of the blazing fire before him, to the dark, cold abyss that surrounded the light. The only constant was his concern for Cordatus.

38

"Skan! Skan!" A voice reverberated inside Abeo's head. He heard someone calling his name, but the sound seemed to come from a distant place, as if blowing in the passing breeze. Suddenly, he felt the strong mechanical force of a hand shaking his shoulder. His eyes slowly cracked open like baby reptile breaking out of its egg. Then, three white circles emerged into his line of sight. As his eyes focused, red eyes, thin noses, and blonde hair manifested the circular faces in front of him. He immediately felt a tender burn around his neck; Turpis' hands had ravaged the skin around his throat, leaving red and blue lines that were sensitive to touch.

Sanuye lowered a canteen to his lips and forced Abeo to drink the cold liquid inside. His throat burned as he swallowed, but the dehydration alleviation was worth the pain.

Abeo sat up on his bed and looked around. On the other side of the tent, Shima tended to Arawak. The Rubeus man had been hit by Foedus' bullet directly above his lung; he cried out in pain as Shima attempted to close the wound with herbs and bandages.

Beside Arawak, Cordatus lay motionless on a bed. His skin was severely faded, making the purple bruises on his body ever more apparent.

"What happened to him?" Abeo asked anxiously while pointing at Cordatus.

Sanuye looked at his friend sympathetically. "Old man fall. Stepped on many times," he said as delicately as possible.

"Is he dead?" Abeo asked.

"Dead? No. But maybe soon."

Abeo stood up from his bed but felt instantly light-headed and had to sit back down. He grabbed the canteen, chugged as much water as possible, and then made his way over to the bedside of his dear companion. Cordatus breathed slowly and intermittently, and his hand rested on his sunken ribcage. There were no obvious wounds on his body, but he looked battered like the exterior of a rotting apple. Abeo put his hand on the old man's and stared wistfully at the broken body of the brightest person he had ever known.

"Hello, Abeo," Cordatus whispered almost inaudibly, his eyes fractionally open.

"Don't speak, save your energy, my friend," Abeo replied.

"Nonsense," he whispered gently. "Energy is there to be used, not to be saved."

Abeo gave a kind smile. "Are you in pain?"

"Only when I breathe," he replied with a grin. "What happened? Where are the others?"

"I'm afraid I don't know much myself. From what I remember, Prod attacked Veritas for being affectionate with that young girl, Taree. The Rubeus were upset that someone was attacking their God, so Arawak attacked Prod, and Foedus shot at the crowd in response. The result was pretty much chaos."

"And how did you gain such lovely red lines around your neck?"

"It would seem my suspicion of Turpis was not ill-founded."

"He tried to strangle you?"

"Came pretty damn close too."

"So much malice in that man. For what reasons, I do not know." Cordatus coughed violently, clutched his ribs, and groaned in pain.

Abeo grabbed a canteen and gave the Cordatus some water in the delusional hope that it might help, but both men were aware of his worsening condition.

"Rest now," Abeo told Cordatus. "We can discuss this when you are feeling better."

"I'm sorry to ruin your optimism, but I don't believe there will be a later for me. I can feel life dissipating out of me like steam rising from a boiling pot. It will not be long now."

"Don't speak like that," Abeo reassured, trying to mask the tremor in his voice.

Cordatus lifted his eyelids and revealed his dark chestnut eyes; the bags enclosing them were saturated with endless wisdom. Cordatus looked at Abeo and placed his wrinkled hand weakly on his wrist. "None of that, now; no sorrow, please. I have been blessed with a lengthy, eventful life. I have seen the arrow of time work its magic on this world, sculpting and molding life into its chaotic continuum. I've seen some of the most fascinating people, met the most interesting characters, read the most intriguing books, and loved the most captivating companions. More than anything, I got to be here, at this moment, where civilizations met. This, the bridging of the gap between different people, will forever change our perspective. We are here for the paradigm shift; never forget that. It is how we handle this transformation that will define the world going forward. Stay the course, Abeo. Know that you are right in your outlook on these people. The rest of the world simply needs to catch up."

Through his gray beard, the old man shot Abeo one last sanguine smile. He reached weakly into his pocket and pulled out a letter that he wanted Petram to have.

Abeo did not dare to tell him that, under the current circumstances, there was a good chance he may not have contact with Petram ever again. Instead, he lied to the dying man, and allowed him to fade away thinking that all was well with the Seekers and that all would be resolved.

Cordatus shut his eyes and fell into a peaceful sleep. Soon after, his cumbersome breathing came to a halt.

***

The Rubeus agreed to keep Cordatus' body untouched, but it could not be left for long. They, too, were aware of the ill omens a dead body carried with it. Abeo knew he had to contact Foedus so that Cordatus could be given a proper burial. How he would do so without endangering both his life and that of the Rubeus was not clear.

The white-skinned people had also suffered losses. One of Sanuye's most trusted lieutenants, a man by the name of Malosi, was killed with Foedus' first rifle shot. The bullet penetrated the base of his neck and exited near the top of his skull. Suctioned to the rocky floor, his brain lay scattered in a thousand gooey pieces.

Meanwhile, Arawak's condition continued to decline. Shima worked tirelessly to conjure the right concoctions and murmur the right chants, but none of it seemed to work. The white man's wound continued to get worse; the smell of death and decay clung to him like a leech.

Once he was well enough, Abeo was summoned by the Onontsi for an important meeting. Trudging towards the Central Tent, he observed red eyes staring and pink lips whispering. The Rubeus had come to enjoy the presence of Abeo, seeing him as some paternal guide for Veritas, but he was not considered a holy man. Any doubts they had about the dark-skinned men had been amplified thanks to the incident at the feast. Abeo could feel the public opinion moving against him.

As the Seeker entered the Central Tent, the murmuring of the Onontsi ceased and their attention became fixated on him. Their white-skinned faces warily looked upon the Seeker; many glared with disdain at the dark and distrustful demon he represented. It was only Sanuye's face that brought him any sense of hospitality.

Despite their reservations, the white men invited him to join them around the blazing fire. Eager for answers, the Onontsi hurled questions at him, too anxious to wait for another to speak. Abeo tried his best to focus on one question, but their fragmented sentences made it virtually impossible.

Finally, Powhatan yelled to quiet the room, and the noise dissipated into the chilly night air. The Rubeus leader looked calmly at Abeo. "Why dark man want to hurt Wakan?" he asked. His thick eyebrows furled under his pasty forehead as he stared back at Abeo, anxious for his response.

Abeo pondered what to say. The words refused to manifest themselves in his head. He continuously looked back at the eyes lingering on him, unable to focus on a response.

Sanuye poked him gently, probing whether he had understood the question. "No get?" he asked.

"No, it's just… it's hard to explain, you know?" Abeo replied.

Sanuye shook his head, motioning in confusion, as he often did during their conversations.

"My orders, well, *our* orders, I suppose, was not to fraternize… I mean, be friendly with you."

"Not friendly?" Sanuye repeated curiously.

Abeo knew he could not reveal the real intent behind Christoph's protocols. How do you tell a group of people that they aren't worthy of your respect or your love? How do you say that their appearance, something blatantly outside of their control, was the sole reason they were seen as inferior?

"We must go back soon; you see? Back home," Abeo continued. "Our orders were not to get too close with everyone because it would be harder to leave."

"Leave? Waken not leave!" Powhatan protested vehemently.

"I'm afraid he must," Abeo admonished.

"Where Wakan?" Boox demanded.

"Back at the camp, I would imagine."

"Then we go get Wakan. Bring back here!" Sanuye declared.

The others nodded their head in agreement.

"It's not that easy," Abeo warned. "Foedus and the Seekers want Veritas for themselves. They won't let you take him back. Not without a fight."

"Then we fight," Sanuye stated.

"No," Abeo stoically shot back. "Far too dangerous. They have better weapons and may have more men at any point. It would be too costly."

Everyone in the tent shifted uncomfortably, clearly frustrated that they could be losing their deity. Somber faces filled the room; Abeo couldn't help but feel their disappointment. He had started this; his insistence on bridging the gap between the Seekers and the Rubeus was too much too fast. If only he could have been patient, no one would be in this mess. Then he remembered what Cordatus had said.

"Give me a moment," he requested and quickly left the tent. When he returned, he had Cordatus' coat and a bundle of blue flowers picked from the meadow. Out of his pocket, he pulled out a folded piece of parchment and a pointed charcoal stick. Quickly, he scribbled something down, folded up the paper, and handed it over to Sanuye.

The Rubeus hesitantly took the note from Abeo. "What this?" he asked.

"Take five warriors with you and take this note to Foedus at his camp," Abeo commanded.

"Will dark man shoot?" Powhatan asked concernedly.

"Not if you take this with you." Abeo handed them Cordatus' faded coat and put the bundle of blue flowers in the outer breast pocket. Placing blue flowers on the breast of a departed individual was a custom of the Imperium. Abeo knew that Foedus would recognize the sign and realize that Abeo was still alive. "Approach them cautiously," he warned his friend. "Show them this coat and give Foedus this letter."

"What say?" Sanuye asked.

"Just give him the letter and show him the coat. We'll find a way to get Wakan back. I promise."

39

Slurping his hardy stew, Foedus sat stoically in front of a small fire. He had grown extremely tired of the slightly salty taste of the rations provided to them at the beginning of their journey. He enjoyed his work, and he enjoyed the responsibility and the excitement it brought with it, but the length of the expedition was beginning to take a toll on the captain. His once muscular body had become frail and thin; his skin hung idly on his thick frame. Thoughts of fine wines, extravagant meals, and female companions filled his fantasies.

Unfortunately, with Christoph's arrival daunting upon them, Foedus' workload was going to grow. His hopes of returning home dissipated away from him. The admiral's last letter, arriving just prior to the frenzied feast, informed him that Christoph and the Legion had reached the Paradise Valley. Through the silence, Foedus almost felt he could hear their approaching march.

With Petram keeping guard over Veritas, the captain hoped he could finally get some rest. Then, before he could even close his eyes, five white bodies emerged from the darkness.

Foedus grabbed his rifle and cocked it, aiming it at the incoming posse. Four Rubeus warriors, led by Sanuye, carefully approached with their hands passively raised. Slung over Sanuye's shoulder was Cordatus' jacket. The breast pocket was filled with blue flowers.

"Oh no," Foedus whispered to himself. He lowered his rifle but kept his hand securely lodged around the barrel.

"He dead?" the captain asked, knowing full well the response he was about to get.

Sanuye nodded and put the jacket down on a nearby boulder. The light of the fire flickered on his painted face. His long white hair fell freely on his shoulders, and the orange light tickled his red eyes, making him appear incredibly intimidating. There was anger buried inside Sanuye's heart, and Foedus didn't want to be the one to unleash it.

"Where's Abeo?" he asked.

Sanuye reached into his sash and handed Foedus a folded piece of parchment. He unfolded it and immediately began reading. It was a letter to Petram from Cordatus. Scribbled in charcoal writing at the bottom, it read:

Parley.
~A.

The captain hesitated to move from his position. The Rubeus did not stand aggressively, their demeanour seemed peaceful, but he felt that they were masking some malicious intent. Nonetheless, he slung his rifle over his back and agreed to follow them into the camp. He did not inform any of the others about his leaving; the two injured men were sleeping, and he wanted to prolong having to break the tragic news to Petram. *Sometimes being in charge isn't so great*, he thought to himself.

The Rubeus warriors escorted Foedus into the camp, across the luscious meadow, and into a small brown tent situated near the center of the camp. Sanuye opened the flap and motioned for Foedus to enter. Inside, a fire gently crackled. On the opposite side of the tent, Abeo's swords lay atop a pile of furs—the Rubeus had set up a temporary home for the Seeker.

"Welcome," Abeo's cracking voice startled Foedus as he emerged in the entrance of the tent. Abeo entered, sat down cross-legged on the milky furs, and motioned for his captain to do the same. "Glad you decided to come."

"I didn't have a choice. I have two severely wounded men and two others missing. And now I find out, through your messengers, that one of them is dead. Not to mention your Discipulus breaking every single order I give and still having the audacity to think that he doesn't deserve to be punished for it."

At this comment, Abeo's face distorted into anguish. "What did you do to him?" he asked aggressively.

The captain averted his friends' eyes.

"Foedus, look at me. Where is Veritas? Look at me!"

"Calm down!" Foedus yelled suddenly. He scrunched his dark face and locked his tired eyes upon Abeo's. "The kid is fine. I have him quarantined to his tent until Christoph arrives. At that point, it's out of my hands what happens to him."

"Well that's convenient for you, isn't it? Not having to make any of the hard choices, just letting everyone else do it for you."

"I'm just doing my job; I'm doing what I've been asked, no, ordered to do. Maybe you should do the same sometimes instead of always having to be a maverick. Believe it or not, there is a reason for structure. If every person just did what they wanted, nothing would get done."

Abeo scoffed. "Give him back to us, Foedus. Let us run away with these people. They have no idea what's coming for them. You will have access to all the jewels and resources you want. Let us run away," his voice shook as he pleaded his friend to grant him one last favour.

"You can't just run away, Abeo."

"Why not? There's nothing left for me in the Imperium. We both know that. I'm at peace here; I'm at peace with these people. Let me live out my days on my terms. Isn't that all anyone can sincerely hope for?"

"I'm not going to drag you back to camp and give you up. But I can't give you back the kid. My life could already be on the line for the pandemonium of the other night. Turpis knows I have him in my custody right now. If I let him go, that'll be it for me."

"Then come with us! What's left in that world for you? You remember when we were younger? We used to always fantasize about finding a place of solitude. A place away from politics, war, corruption, and greed. Look around you! We don't have to dream anymore, Foedus."

Foedus bit his lip and wiped the sweat from his brow. Inside, he was weeping, but his hardy exterior prevented him from leaking a single tear. "I warned you. No, I begged you not to put me in this position, not to make me have to make the hard choice. I told you what would happen. Now, here we are," the captain paused and looked away from Abeo. "What do you want from me? Do you want me to go back on my word, betray everything I stand for, and abandon my home? I'm sorry, my friend. I truly am. But there is nothing that I can do for you."

"You can let us go," Abeo retorted.

Foedus sighed. "Here is my best offer: Pack up with these people and get as far away as you can. Christoph is close. With women, children, animals, and supplies, you will need the head start. I will buy you some time. I will say that communications have broken between the Seekers and the Rubeus, but Veritas must remain with me. I will ask for him to be treated fairly as a prisoner. You know this is the best I can do, please understand that."

Abeo looked up empathically at his companion. Both of them felt that this would be the last time they ever spoke. It was an unjust conclusion to a great friendship, but it was a mandatory one all the same.

Foedus extended his hand, and Abeo accepted it. The captain then pulled him for an embrace, patted him on the back, and whispered in his ear, "good luck, old friend." He gave Abeo an enervated smile and got up to exit the tent.

"I will have Sanuye arrange for Cordatus' body to be returned to the camp," Abeo called after him.

"Let me tell the men first," Foedus responded thankfully.

Sanuye met the captain outside and offered to escort him back to the camp.

"I'll get back on my own just fine," Foedus coldly replied. He leisurely crossed the meadow, fighting the urge to take one last look back at his friend. If he had, he would have seen Abeo in the doorway of the tent, blowing warm air into his cold fists, leaning down to pick up a folded piece of paper on the ground.

40

Petram sat outside of Veritas' tent, occasionally indulging in a drink of hot water cut with caramel whiskey. The obstinate winds forced the tent's skin to rattle violently on its scaffold. The sound of the flapping cover and the crackle of the inviting fire seemed to resonate in unison.

As he again sipped on the warm liquid, Petram stared up at the stars. He noticed that the Spiral Cloud's height in the sky had markedly sunk. When they had first arrived, the cosmic swirl was readily apparent above the ridges of the valley. Now, the bottom quarter was cut off from view.

Petram probed the surroundings for any sign of Foedus, but there was still no sign of the captain. *Where could he have gone?* he wondered.

Suddenly, a rustling sound came from Veritas' tent, and it grabbed his attention. The anemic boy poked his head out of the flap to see Petram staring back at him.

"How's it going?" Petram asked casually.

"Well, I'm pretty sore. Not entirely happy about being quarantined to this tent counting down the minutes until I'm inevitably executed. But other than that, pretty good."

Petram attempted to give the young man a half-hearted smile, but he could see genuine fear buried beneath Veritas' sardonic mask.

"As much of a hard-ass as he can be, I know Foedus will do what he can for you. You may have broken his rules, but he always cares about his men, whether or not people realize it."

"I don't think there's all that much he can do for me. He said it himself, it's Christoph's call. I made my choice," Veritas replied.

Petram felt the sorrow emanating from Veritas. He understood that young man's melancholy was not related to his inexorable execution; it was the death of young love that injected despondency into his soul.

"Can't just let me out, can you?" Veritas nervously asked.

Petram let go of a quick laugh and turned to the young man. "I'm sorry, you know I can't."

Veritas accepted his fate with quiet maturity.

Petram felt dispirited seeing such innocence fall victim to unfortunate circumstance. "Are you hungry?" he asked.

"No, not particularly, but I should probably eat," Veritas mumbled.

"Alright, I will cook you some stew."

"Just to change it up," Veritas replied. He shot Petram a somber smile and retreated into his temporary prison.

Petram emptied a can of viscous stew into a boiling pot and stirred it as it simmered on the gentle flames.

Not long after, Foedus emerged from the darkness. The captain headed directly to Prod and Turpis' tent and woke them up, asking them to join him at Veritas' confines.

"This better be important, I was finally getting some sleep," Turpis grunted.

"I think you'll live," the captain shot back. Clearly in no mood for jokes, Foedus' demeanour was serious as ever.

Prod begrudgingly emerged from his tent. Petram noticed the young man looked unusually sickly. His normally dark complexion had transformed into a faded gray, and his eyes struggled to stay open. Prod trudged over to the group and laboriously sat down.

Foedus, naïve to Prod's malady, continued. "I have just returned from the Rubeus camp on a diplomatic discussion. Unfortunately," Foedus continued, looking at Petram, "I have some somber news. It appears that among the commotion of the feast, Cordatus was," he struggled with the words, "Cordatus was trampled, and his lungs collapsed. He passed away not long ago."

"How do you know?" Petram begged.

The captain pulled Cordatus' dark green coat out of his bag and handed it to Petram. The elegant blue flowers, stamped down, were firmly placed in the breast pocket.

Petram's eyes immediately watered. He took a deep, sputtering breath and grabbed the coat, placing it on his lap. "Why the hell didn't we wait for him!" he yelled in frustration.

"It was a panic; I thought he was with us. I should've checked, I know." Foedus conceded, hanging his head in disappointment.

Petram sobbed quietly, burying his face in the jacket. "Where did you get this?"

"The Rubeus approached me. Abeo sent them. He wanted to meet and discuss terms."

"Terms?" Turpis interjected. "You can't negotiate with that traitor!"

"Well, I'm the captain, so yes, I can. But more than that, I needed to make plans to retrieve Cordatus' body so we could give him a proper burial."

"What did Abeo have to say?" Prod asked weakly. The wound on his shoulder had become infected almost overnight. His white sweater had an egg-shaped stain above the left breast. Pus and blood resembled a yellow yolk residing within a brown shell.

"He said he would not return to us and that he would not accept his punishment like a man," Foedus responded. "He said he'd rather run and hide and be banished from his home forever."

"So, what now?" asked Prod.

"We go and get his ass is what we do," Turpis snarled.

"No." Foedus shut him down. "Leave him be; he's made his choice. Exile can be his punishment."

"Bullshit!" Turpis interjected. "You can't just let him get away with how he's acted. He helped those fucking creatures. He tried to have me killed. He-"

"Shut up. Shut the fuck up!" Foedus yelled in a way none of them had ever heard before. His eyes were severely bloodshot and the bags underneath had become increasingly noticeable. The full extent of his malnourishment was as apparent as ever. "I'm tired of your lies! He didn't try and kill you; you tried to kill him! If it were up to me, it'd be you quarantined to this tent!" The interminable stress was beginning to wear on the captain. Like an old vessel, his bow and stern pulled away from each other, subsiding to the relentless force of the sea.

"Whatever he said, it was to save his own skin," Turpis replied quickly; the words blended as they swiftly escaped from his mouth.

"Just stop! Stop the lying," Foedus plead. "I saw the burn around his neck; I saw what you did. And for what? Some woman? You loved Cura, didn't you? And you could never let it go. Jealous bastard."

Everything became hauntingly silent. The observers collectively held their breath.

"What the hell are you talking about?" Turpis asked, squinting at Foedus.

"You know very well what I'm talking about. You purposely dropped Abeo off the cliff. You tried to kill him when you thought the opportunity was prime. You told me you loved a woman once, but she was taken from you, and now she's dead. You loved Cura, and you could never forgive Abeo for taking her from you."

Turpis chuckled incredulously. "Is that really what you think?" He cleared his throat and wiped his forehead. "No, I didn't love Cura—at least not in that way. She was a great woman, though. It was her sister who I loved."

"Lepidia?" Petram asked.

"Yes."

"She died in the revolution, did she not?" Petram inquired again.

"She was a lieutenant in the Leagum Rotundum," Foedus mumbled. "She was one of the biggest advocates of the revolution. How the hell did you two get along?"

"She shouldn't have been!" Turpis spat. "I warned her not to get wrapped up in it. I warned her that it was just a matter of time until the Imperium gathered the strength it needed. I begged her not to get involved."

"I had no idea you two were even together," Petram interjected, his eyes still red as he clutched Cordatus' coat.

"She loved me once, and I loved her. But she fell more in love with the revolution and the idea of change. The very ideas that Abeo poisoned both of their minds with."

"Abeo?" Foedus questioned.

"He ranted all the time about how bad the Imperium was; how they cared for no one but themselves. All he would do is complain about what was wrong with the home he had been given, by the society that tried to embrace him. He just pushed it away. He infected both of their minds with his propaganda and got them both killed."

"So this all is about vengeance?" Foedus questioned.

"No. Not vengeance. It's about retribution. It's about being a man and paying for the lives that you are responsible for."

"And you're the one who's going to make him pay, are you?" Petram asked with a tinge of mockery.

"I am. I am the undertaker here to take what's mine. He owes me his soul. If I have to march into that camp and slaughter every damn one of those chalky bastards to get to him, I will." He spat into the fire and took a swig of whiskey from the bottle that hadn't left his hand since he had awoken.

"I'm with you," Prod wheezed.

"You need to get better first," Foedus interrupted condescendingly. "Here, drink some of this, you're starting to get too pale." The captain passed Prod a small flask of medicine, and he sipped it appreciatively.

"I'll go on my own if I have to," Turpis grumbled.

"No," Foedus commanded. "I'm sorry for your loss, Turpis, I really am, but enough of this nonsense. We've removed ourselves from the Rubeus and will remain that way until Christoph arrives. Until then, the only thing we need to concern ourselves with is staying fed and keeping our prisoner a prisoner."

Turpis fumed, but Foedus was sure the large man was in no shape to try anything brash—at least for the time being

"Now, I wrote up a schedule," Foedus continued, reaching into his jacket pocket. "Um, hmm..." He felt around, tapping his chest and sides trying to get a feeling for what he was looking for. Despite the self-induced pat down, he ended up empty-handed. "No matter," the captain murmured, "I had it memorized. Turpis, you're on next watch. Petram, take time to get some rest. When you're ready, I have other items of Cordatus' that he left to you. Prod, drink that medicine and get some sleep. I'll take watch after you, Turpis."

The captain was back.

Turpis begrudgingly nodded, seemingly not wanting to acknowledge his superior.

Foedus grabbed the bottle from his thick hands, took a swig, and sat down beside him. "One way or another, we will all get what we want. I promise," he whispered.

Petram, listening intently, found the remark peculiar. For a while, it seemed like Turpis and his captain were at odds. Foedus consistently chose other Seekers for important tasks, relegating the big man to menial jobs. Petram had overheard them recently quarrelling, but he couldn't determine what the disagreement was about. All he heard was Foedus frustrated with Turpis in regards to something with Christoph.

Disregarding the comment, Petram retired to his tent to get some much-needed rest. He caught his breath and found some solitude. Then the full weight of Cordatus' passing fell upon him. Unable to control the flood of emotion, he let go and wept, violently trembling as he did. The old man was the best friend he had ever had, the only one who ever really understood him. He had saved Petram from the abysmal life he had been trapped in. Petram could feel the yawning vacuum the old man's absence inflicted.

Eventually, the emotional waves subsided, and Petram was able to pull himself into a calm state and ease off into sleep. Falling into a deep rest, images of red eyes projected on the back of his eyelids, while swirls of neon green and sparkling lights illuminated inside of his mind. Suddenly, he was flying among the stars and the clouds, ripping through the sky on a celestial cruise. As he soared, he looked ahead and saw, staring back at him, the Spiral Cloud. The swirl rotated around a black center that suctioned in the surrounding cloud of colours. In a seamless transition, the cloud blinked and became the eye of a giant. He stared back into the great eye, and it peered back at him. Its sheer size should have produced ominous feelings inside of the dreaming man, but instead, he was at peace. A calming connection linked the two; they were one and the same, separated merely by lines drawn in the sand. He smiled at the great eye, and somehow he could tell that the elated expression had been reciprocated.

When he awoke, Petram continued to ponder the dream. Looking up at the real Spiral Cloud, he couldn't remember if it had always looked the way it did, or if his new perception of it had permanently changed his contemporary memory. Nonetheless, he was captivated evermore by its beauty.

Leaving his tent for the first time in what seemed like ages, he gathered his mind and went out to see Foedus planted by the fire staring into its warm core. His face was expressionless; his mind was elsewhere.

***

For the next while, the captain maintained a strict schedule for each job. Between the four of them, one man kept guard of Veritas, and the other two gathered ignasaxum, retrieved water, or attempted to catch fish in the grotto. Their food supplies, too, ran dangerously low. They were not excited about Christoph's arrival, but the supplies he was bound to bring were sure to be a welcome sight.

Petram, once again assigned to guard Veritas, sat quietly on a smooth boulder. He heard Prod aggressively cough and worried about the young man's condition—his health continued to decline despite the captain's best efforts to treat him.

Turpis, on the other hand, recovered nicely from his injury. For a man of his age, Turpis was still tougher than nails. Foedus decided the big man was fit enough to accompany him on a resource expedition, so they disappeared and left Petram alone once again.

Sitting silently under the night sky, Petram felt at peace. The entire camp remained quiet; all that could be heard was the occasional soft howl of the chilled wind, the ambient crackling of the fire, and the soft trickle of the nearby creek. The evening was serene; simply midnight, the stars, and Petram—a rendezvous with the cosmos.

Poking through the silence, he heard Veritas shuffle restlessly behind him. Petram opened the flap to check on the young man, but Veritas lay motionless in a deep sleep. Then, while watching Veritas rest, Petram heard the sound again. He removed his head from the tent, looked around anxiously, and wrapped his fingers around the shaft of his rifle.

All he saw in front of him was darkness, but the sound of dragging footsteps continued to tease him from every which way. Trying to calm his mind, he focused on the movement of any potential predators lingering in the dark, but his anxiety prevented him from concentrating fully.

As his heart rate began to rise, so did the pitch of his voice. "Foedus? Turpis? Is that you?" he called out insecurely.

Suddenly, emerging out of the darkness, Sanuye approached; his red eyes pierced through the darkness. Petram lifted his rifle and pointed it at the white man, but before he could even yell a threat, he felt the cold sensation of steel pressed against his throat. A sharp knife pushed just hard enough to tear away at the first layer of skin on his neck, letting loose a small trickle of blood.

"I wouldn't," whispered a familiar voice.

41

With his left hand firmly secured on Petram's shoulder, Abeo placed the knife around his friend's neck and pressed it aggressively against his skin. Up to this point, the plan had worked to perfection. When Foedus had left the Rubeus camp, he had dropped the guarding schedule for Veritas. Abeo couldn't be certain whether his captain left the plan intentionally or not. There had been emotion in his friend's eyes when they had parted ways; perhaps the full weight of empathy had finally broken through his firm determination to play by the rules. Nonetheless, it was an opportunity that Abeo couldn't pass up; Veritas had become incredibly important to him. More importantly, the Rubeus had become inconsolable with the loss of Wakan and likely wouldn't quit until he was returned to them. Getting him back before Christoph and the Legion showed up was imperative.

Luckily, the Rubeus knew the land's topography better than the Seekers did. Sanuye led Abeo to multiple vantage points where they surveilled the Seeker camp. It dawned on him that the white men, encouraging the Seekers to set up camp where they did, had been secretly spying on them all along. Ever the cunning creatures, the Rubeus continued to impress.

Despite not having the schedule with him anymore, Foedus managed to maintain a relatively rigid routine, almost exactly on point with the one in Abeo's hand. The only deviation was Prod's role. He had initially been put on watch every second cycle but had spent most of his time resting in his tent. This was advantageous for Abeo because it gave Petram more opportunities to be on watch. Petram, the most passive of the group, was the best option to ambush. More than that, his watch tended to coincide with the absence of Foedus and Turpis.

Now, with the others away or resting, Abeo and Sanuye, accompanied by two other Rubeus Warriors—Shujaa, a young and capable fighter, and Tian, Taree's father—decided to initiate their plan. Following a hidden trail, they snuck around the Seeker camp and approached from the rear. Sanuye and the others made noises to distract Petram and draw his attention. Then, while his rifle was pointed at the oncoming Rubeus, Abeo snuck up behind his companion and poised him to put down his weapon.

"We're taking the kid. Don't fight it; I don't want to hurt you any more than you don't want to be hurt," Abeo said.

"Traitor," Petram spat.

"Don't talk like them. You know this is the right thing."

"How could I possibly know that? No one knows what that means. You act like you hold the key to some moral handbook; you act like you're some infallible deity. What makes your morals so much better than mine, or Foedus', or even Turpis'?"

"Don't kid me about Turpis; you can't possibly defend his scruples."

"You know why he wants to kill you? Because he thinks you're responsible for innocent lives. He thinks that your carelessness and big mouth poisoned the minds of honest women. All he wants is justice. And, you know, I'm almost inclined to agree with him."

Abeo swallowed a stone and pressed the knife harder into Petram's throat. "So that's it? I'm responsible for killing my wife, right? You don't think I've thought about that before? You don't think that the thought overtakes my mind? You don't think it makes it impossible for me to think of anything else? Why do you think I am the way I am? I lost my wife; I lost my son; I lost everything. I've suffered nothing but pain my whole life. I've paid my debt. One way or another, we're all interconnected. You don't just do something without it somehow affecting another person. It could be completely menial, or it could be the most significant moment in their life. We have to live with chaos, my friend. We are it."

As the two Seekers talked, Sanuye ripped open a hole in Veritas' tent. The young man poked his thin body out of the opening and gave a horrified look when he saw Abeo's knife pressed against Petram's throat.

"Please, don't hurt him. He has been kind to me, you know he has a good heart, he…"

Before Veritas could finish, Abeo pushed Petram away, releasing him from the threatening grip. "We all have to make our own choices about what we think is correct, but you know, as I do, what is truly right here," Abeo said.

Petram nodded, and his face contorted with emotion. The group snuck off but, before they could leave, he grabbed Abeo by the arm. "Can you at least beat me up a bit? You know, to make it look like I didn't just let you go."

Abeo gave a wry smile, put his left hand on his companions' shoulder, and then punched him in the side of the head with his right fist, knocking Petram out. Sanuye caught him before he could hit the ground and gently placed the Seeker against the tent.

"Goodbye, old friend," Abeo whispered as he crept away into the darkness.

The group journeyed back towards the path from which they had come. Sanuye led the way; his knowledge of the terrain was unmatched within the tribe. Once, he had told Abeo that he spent his spare time as a child exploring hidden passages wherever the tribe set up camp. Over time, he had developed an innate ability to find obscure paths.

Behind Sanuye, Shujaa and Tian carried Veritas. The young man's energy levels may have been lower than normal, but, had he wanted to, the Seeker could have continued on his own. The Rubeus, however, were not prepared to let Wakan out of their sight anytime soon. Like a mother who had just been reunited with her lost child, the Rubeus' biggest fear was losing him again.

Quietly, the group ascended the jagged ebony rock. Abeo focused his mind in the dark, watching as the contours revealed themselves as different variations of purple and blue. The rock was slick from the trickling water that weaved in and out of the fragmented stone. Each step had to be taken with a confident foot. Eventually, they reached a narrow plateau that overlooked the entire valley. Softly nestled into the basin, the dim fire of the Rubeus camp glimmered like a distant star.

As they continued to climb, one side the rock wall protruded, suctioning in and out, making the path narrow and widen like a wave. On the opposite side the trail, a cliff overlooked nothing but darkness.

"Watch your footing," Abeo called out. Particular portions of the path were barely narrow enough for one person to shuffle through. Nonetheless, Sanuye kept the pace up, somehow being careful and reckless at the same time. Each man focused intently, cautiously trying avoid a misstep.

Sanuye delegated himself to guiding Veritas through the contentious parts of the path, so Shujaa took the lead. The trail curved around the wall, and a plateau revealed itself ahead.

Suddenly, a blinding flash emerged from behind the bend, followed by a roaring bang. In an instant, a whizzing bullet powered through Shujaa's stomach. The force of the bullet suctioned him backward violently. He stumbled off the cliff, one hand clutching his wounded gut, the other reaching upwards. The white man fell helplessly into the darkness. There was no sound of his body hitting the ground; the height of the cliff was simply too great.

Immediately, the others ran toward the plateau trying to find cover behind the jutting rock. Another flash and boom emerged again from the darkness, and another bullet seared through the cold air, narrowly missing Tian. The Rubeus warrior dove and rolled with incredible grace, concealing his body behind a nearby boulder.

Sanuye grabbed Veritas and ran for cover. From the shadows, Turpis and Foedus emerged, rifles at the ready. Turpis fired another shot at the boulder causing fragments to explode outward. A piece struck Sanuye in the forehead, and he fell awkwardly on the hard ground. The Rubeus warrior clutched his head while crimson blood oozed out between the cracks of his ghostly fingers.

Foedus aimed to fire again, but before he could get the shot off, Tian threw a small hatchet with great speed; it struck the Seeker captain in the arm. The rifle flew out of Foedus' hands wildly, and he screamed in pain. The hatchet lodged itself securely into his thick wrist.

In a panic, Turpis turned around to fire at Tian, giving Veritas enough time to scramble behind the covering rock. The young man called for Sanuye to come to him, but the warrior hesitated, costing him a chance to join the others. Turpis readied his rifle and pointed it at where Sanuye lay. Courageously, instead of making a desperate break for the others, the warrior emerged from behind his meager cover and stood proudly in front of Turpis. He puffed out his toned chest and beat his heart with his right fist. Turpis placed the rifle against his shoulder and aimed down the narrow sight.

"Easy, big fella," Abeo croaked as he pointed Foedus' errant rifle at the massive man. "You're here for me, not him. You want to settle this, then let's settle it, but let them go."

Turpis smirked, "always have to be the hero, don't you? How about I kill this white-skinned piece of shit and then I come over to you and finish the job."

"These people have done nothing to you. You're here for me. Don't let your feeble mind confuse you. You know why you're here and why you came on this journey. You wanted to find a way to kill me from the very start. You needed to find a way to get what you wanted without any repercussions. But, I mean, you're the real man here, right? You're the debt collector ready to do good. Don't lecture me about trying to be the hero. You want me; I'm here. But not until they go first."

It went completely quiet for what seemed like an eternity. Then, Turpis, the massive mountain of muscle, fat, bone, and viscera, nodded, put down his rifle, and freed the giant axe strapped to his back. "If we're going to do it, we're going to do it for real."

Abeo unsheathed two thin swords and prepared for battle.

They stared at each other for a moment, both hesitating to make the first move. Each inched closer and closer. Then, Turpis charged. He swung violently downwards, forcing Abeo to dive out of the way, nearly sliding to the edge of the cliff. He picked himself up and juked away from Turpis, narrowly avoid another violent swing of the giant axe. Orange sparks exploded like fireworks as the metal clanged violently against the stony ground. After dodging a third attack, Abeo swiftly swung his sword and sliced Turpis' thick leg, inducing a hardy gash. The big man momentarily stumbled but regained his balance and grunted aggressively.

Aggravated, Turpis spun the giant axe above his head and forcefully brought it down. The sharp steel caught Abeo' right shoulder, causing a large patch of skin to be sliced off like a peeled potato. Abeo clutched his arm in pain and fell backward, landing awkwardly on his side. Turpis approached quickly and swung down again. Abeo blocked the attack by crossing both swords together, but the force caused one sword to fly out his hand, clanking loudly against the rocky floor. He scrambled away from another vicious swing and rolled towards his rogue weapon, crawling frantically away from the edge of the cliff.

Turpis lumbered behind him, blood streaking down his hairy legs. The meaty man placed his full weight on Abeo's ankle and listened with joy as he yelled out in agony. The injury had never fully recovered from the fall.

"Well, that was fun," Turpis panted, wiping the waterfall of sweat from his wrinkled forehead. "Time to die now. Turn over so I can watch the light go out of your eyes." He forced his boot under Abeo's stomach and rolled him over. As he did, he noticed Abeo holding a long brown rifle in his hands.

Abeo pointed the weapon at Turpis' terrified face. "Me first," he said laconically. He fired the rifle, and the bullet flew through the underside of the Turpis' jaw, exiting the top of his skull. His head burst from the force and cranial shrapnel littered the ground. Turpis' massive body wobbled like a decapitated dragon, and finally fell heavily onto the rocky floor.

Abeo breathed a deep sigh and struggled to pick himself off the hard ground. He looked up and saw Sanuye staring back at him with great admiration.

"Are you hurt, Skan?" he asked.

"I'm alright," Abeo wheezed.

"Well, this is a disaster," Foedus laughed manically. In all the commotion they had experienced, Abeo had completely forgotten the captain was still there. Foedus, down on his knees, clutched his wrist, the hatchet securely embedded into his forearm. Blood covered his entire hand, as if he had just dipped it in a bucket of red paint. His body, starved from exhaustion, was markedly frail; the ridges under his eyes had deepened into chasms. Abeo picked up the remaining rifle and pointed it at Foedus.

"So, it was all just a trap? You wanted me to try and take Veritas back so you could have both of us. Didn't take you to be that clever," Abeo jabbed.

"Had to try, you know?" Foedus laughed again, but it was a nervous laugh, unlike Abeo had ever heard before from his friend.

"No, I don't," Abeo replied.

"Of course you don't understand! You never did!" Foedus fumed, looking around wide-eyed like a player in checkmate, clinging to some escape that didn't exist. "I have a responsibility!" he yelled frantically; the volume in his voice increased as if someone had cranked a dial inside of his brain. "I have a job to do! And you just do whatever you want and expect there to be no repercussions! My life is on the line if I don't bring you two back!" He cackled again like a maniac, half sobbing, half laughing. "I had to try. My survival depended on it. You think you're better than me, but you would do the same. We all would." He swallowed hard and wiped his face with his uninjured hand, looking into Abeo's hazel eyes. "Do it," he commanded. "I'm dead already. No way to recover from this one, right?"

"I should," Abeo muttered. "I really should." He placed the rifle on his wounded shoulder and looked down the sight, aiming it at his longtime friend.

Foedus gave an elongated blink and leaned his head back, staring up at the beautiful sky. Neon ribbons wrapped eloquently around the piercing peaks above while glimmering stellar diamonds embedded themselves on an indigo tapestry. The sky was giving an encore performance.

Down below, blanketed under the cosmic cover, the Rubeus camp was astir. They were awoken by thundering booms emanating from up on the cliffs. After an extended period of silence, one more bang echoed through the valley, followed by ominous silence.

42

Petram awoke drenched in a pool of sweat. He lay uncomfortably on the ground, his arm wedged awkwardly under his thick frame. It took him a moment to recall what had just happened. Then, he rubbed the side of his face, cringed at the hypersensitivity, and remembered perfectly. The skin surrounding his right eye swelled, making it difficult for him to see. His face felt tender and warm.

"He didn't have to hit me that hard," he muttered to himself. A sharp pain pierced into the side of his jaw. Talking was going to be difficult.

Petram lifted his aching body off the firm ground and inhaled a deep and restorative breath. For the first time in what seemed like forever, he felt the soft caress of warm air blowing. For the life of him, he couldn't figure out what caused the fluctuations in temperature. Back home it was known that Stella brought with her light and warmth, but without any exposure to the orange orb, the warm air that periodically filled the valley seemed to have a mysterious origin. The Rubeus claimed the heat came from the wind and the water, though what they meant by this was unclear. *Cordatus would've understood,* he thought to himself.

Petram already missed his Praeceptoris. The old man's vacated companionship left a significant void in his life. At this moment, alone, wounded, and tired, he contemplated whether there was anything left for him in this world. Maybe he should have gone with Abeo. He could only hope that Christoph would allow him to travel home for some much-needed rest.

Wiping the dust and gravel off his broad shoulders, Petram headed towards the center of the camp. The fire had dwindled to nothing but embers; a foreboding stillness imbued the air. *Where were the others?*

Petram worked his way across the camp and went into Turpis' tent to see if either he or Prod were there. When he lifted the flap, an abysmal smell stung the inside of his nostrils and nearly forced him to vomit. He looked down and saw Prod's lifeless body staring aimlessly back at him. The white bandage around his shoulder was stained brown and yellow.

How could he be dead? he wondered. Foedus, a well-trained medic, had given him constant attention. True, the wound had been in a critical place; the infection could have had spread to the rest of his body. Still, at no point had any of them been concerned that Prod was dabbling with death.

Powering through the smell, Petram carefully lowered Prod's eyelids and immediately left the tent, inhaling a bulk of fresh air. He coughed violently and then ran to grab his canteen. Before he could get there, gastric juices forced themselves out of his mouth and onto the ground. His legs became gelatin, and he fell to the ground. Trembling, he punched the hard rock with his barren fist until his hands became a bloody mess. Walking over to the nearby stream, he dipped them into the cold liquid and felt the painful, yet oddly satisfying, sting of water entering his wounds. He sat by the creek and sobbed until the flood of emotions finally subsided.

After calming himself down, Petram reignited the fire and waited for the others to return. Time ticked on as it is prone to do. The fire crackled, its orange flames slithered up into the dark sky, and the warm breeze gently blew through his curly black hair. He waited and waited until he finally realized he had never read the letter from Cordatus.

Scrambling back to his tent, Petram grabbed the folded piece of parchment and made his way back to the light of the flame. It read:

My dear friend Petram,
This is, with great regret, the last time we shall have any correspondence. I want to leave you with my final lesson and parting words; both of which I

hope that you will graciously accept.

There was a time in my life when I believed I was destined to be alone forever. Having never been able to hold down a healthy relationship in my younger days, and having lost most of my family in one conflict or another, I retreated to the solace of the library. There, with the smell of old parchment and leather, and the soft hue of flickering candlelight, I found peace.

The pursuit of knowledge is a journey undesirable for the meek. It is an arduous adventure that requires vigorous commitment, combined with endless frustration and challenge, to fully conceive the scope of human thought. One must find a way to develop one's own identity from the pieces of the past. We can learn from old mistakes; we can find clues in the footsteps of yesteryear. We are the byproduct of countless years of contemplation, meditation, and consternation. Yet, we must individually decide what we want to be and how we want to plow into the future. It is our job as individuals to use our experiences as guidelines, not rigid rules, towards the development of self.

Now, as we sit here at this great crossroads in the evolution of society and civilization, we have to ask ourselves what the right course of action is. To many, the answer is simple: we have a social oath to fill—a treaty, even—with the society that breeds and molds us. Often, we forget about the liberties bequeathed to us. The menial ongoing of everyday life passes us by without any notice. We never ask: Who produced the food we buy at the markets? How is the market there in the first place? With what do we purchase these goods with? How have we determined the value of such things? For all its flaws, the Imperium has provided us with advantages that we relentlessly take for granted. Surely, we owe something to our ancestors for the sacrifices they made; the same ones that have put us in the position we're in. Yet, when I see the Rubeus, another much more important question comes to mind: nature.

You see, despite what we have known for millennia, despite what we can read in the endless knowledge held in the great libraries, there is something more primitive that we choose to ignore. There is an understanding that exists between them and us. We smile, and they do not cringe; they cry, and we do not ask why.

The people of the Imperium will assume one thing: that they are superior to all. Why do they think this? Because they've never had to think otherwise! Our knowledge is subject to our experience, and our experience is severely limited. Paradigm shifts are of great importance, but they are always met with the utmost resistance. We wish to be one way; we implant an image in our mind that, like wet cement, settles, dries, and hardens over time.

We are creatures subject to the limitations of our experiences. We don't connect with the future, yet everything we do inherently determines our destiny. The Imperium continues to play a most dangerous game, one that has no end. Their shameful actions will forever plague true reconciliation. How will it be possible for distant generations to properly atone for the mistakes of their forbearers? For how long will justified resentment remain just? Will it ever be truly possible to let go of the past? Will we ever outgrow the seeds of conflict that have been involuntarily planted below our feet? But no one asks these questions. No one bothers to worry about the consequences of their actions.

It is a fact of geometry that curved surfaces look flat at smaller scales. What should we say about this? Is the world flat or is it curved? Clearly, this greatly depends on our viewpoint. When we take a step back, we see the surface for what it truly is, but to see it that way, we must be willing to retreat from our comfortable vantage point. The Imperium may be flat to our eyes, but our world surely is not. Perhaps it is time we all took a step back and realize we don't share Unum with other beings, they share it with us.

You have been not only an incredible Discipulus, but a loyal and genuine friend, as well. I shall miss our conversations, our debates, and our love of a good vintage. Pass on my teachings and use them as a scaffold to sculpt your life, not as an instruction. Our time together must now cease, but in the real essence of the universe, we shall never be apart. I am now a part of you, as you have become a part of me.

Good luck on all your future endeavours. Stay vigilant, continue to question, inquire endlessly, but most importantly, bask in the beauty of life.

Forever your friend,
Cordatus

Cordatus was right. At this moment, Petram did not love the Rubeus as Abeo did. Nor did he have to. He questioned whether their lives were any less significant than his. His heritage told him that it was, but his intuition disagreed. Deep down, he knew that their existence somehow coincided with his. Their branches were connected in antiquity.

Petram folded the page and placed the parchment into his breast pocket. He then waited for the return of his companions. The bottle of whiskey magically descended towards its bottom, and the pile of ignasaxum continued to dwindle. He read and re-read the letter from Cordatus, hearing every inflection in the old man's voice as he did. Then, out of the darkness, a figure approached. It was Sanuye, followed by three other Rubeus warriors. They carried two bodies wrapped in black cloth. Behind them emerged Abeo, a rifle in his hand, and Foedus, who looked more ghost than man.

The Rubeus had been true to their word. Despite their disagreements, they returned the body of Cordatus. Through the process of elimination, Petram knew the second body had to be that of Turpis. What had happened, he could not even begin to guess.

"Nice work on the whole guarding thing," Foedus jabbed.

"I got suckered," Petram scoffed, pointing to the black eye that spread across his face.

"Figures," Foedus responded, eying Abeo.

Abeo ignored the captain, refusing to look at his oldest friend. "As promised, Cordatus' body. The other, as I'm sure you can imagine, is Turpis'." Abeo stated matter-of-factly.

"What happened? Where is Veritas?" Petram inquired.

"There will be time for all of that," responded Foedus. "For now, let us just part our ways in peace. Where's Prod?"

"He's dead," said Petram.

"Dead? How?" the captain asked.

"You tell me. You were the one caring for him."

"His wound was quite infected. Perhaps the infection entered his bloodstream; his body was never very ready for the cold." The captain's response seemed rehearsed, but Petram decided to leave it.

"So, what now?" Petram asked, looking at Abeo.

"Now, although we don't have to, we offer one last time for you to join us. When Christoph sees the mess that's been left here, nothing will end well for either of you. Come with us, come be in peace," Abeo plead.

"Where are you even going to go?" Petram asked.

"If you're not with us, then I cannot say," Abeo replied.

"Then I guess you cannot say," Foedus interrupted. "Petram, your will is your own."

"Indeed it is," Petram whispered. "I will stay with Foedus. He needs someone to speak on his behalf when Christoph arrives. Besides, as amazing as it is out here, I like the warmth. I like basking in the light of Lux. I want to go back home."

"I understand," Abeo responded quietly. He nodded at Petram and then motioned for the Rubeus to retreat to their camp.

Petram and Foedus watched as four white figures escorted the tall dark man away from their camp. Abeo was a man who had been enslaved by the woes of his mind. He had watched the darkness drown his thoughts like a surging wave of anguish. Yet, through the void, he became cleansed. The shadows washed away his sorrow and helped him emerge as a man free from his shackles.

And so, they disappeared from the light, never to be seen again.

43

Christoph arrived not long after the Abeo's departure. More than a hundred men accompanied the admiral. The majority were soldiers, but an assortment of different professionals, engineers, surveyors, physicians, scholars, and scribes, accompanied the Legion. Their coming brought with it such a sudden commotion, it was hard for Petram and Foedus to comprehend how their quiet campground had suddenly transformed before their eyes. They had been in isolation as just a small dwindling group for so long. Now, all around them, massive huts and barracks populated their obscure alcove. Men worked fervently to pile food stocks and build fires. In the blink of an eye, the Imperium had made its presence felt; they claimed the land in a flash.

Foedus and Petram sat patiently outside of Christoph's luxuriously built tent. Upon finding out the condition of things, the admiral had insisted on a private meeting with the two remaining Seekers. His arrival had initially brought with it excitement, but the news of three dead Seekers, and another two rogue, had made him irate.

"What do you mean they ran away?" Christoph berated them.

"I tried to stop them, but they got away. We were outmanned, there was only so much I could do," Foedus responded. Although there was validity to his story, he intentionally exaggerated his version in an attempt to save his skin.

Christoph walked off muttering to himself in frustration. "I'll talk to both of you later; there's too much to do right now." He shook his head angrily and then commenced commanding groups of soldiers, trying desperately to keep the bustle organized.

After everyone settled, Christoph beckoned his subjects for their official meeting. Petram's right foot stammered uncontrollably. He was nervous. The swelling around his eye had gotten worse; blue and yellow bruises stained his carmine skin.

Foedus, on the other hand, was dead quiet. His ghostly appearance had never been as prevalent as it was at this moment. His pale complexion glowed softly under the sparkling night sky.

"Enter," they heard Christoph's voice bellow from inside the tent. The two men gave each other apprehensive looks and walked in. Inside the tent, everything was perfectly arranged. From the stack of scrolled maps to the records and inventory logs alphabetically arranged; it was all protocolled.

"I'll give civilized society one thing, they sure know how to settle in a hurry," Foedus jabbed.

"I didn't ask you to speak, now did I?" Christoph responded, not looking up from the page he was scribbling on. "Three dead and two missing. So what am I to make of this mess?"

"Make of it whatever you want. I know you well enough to know you've already made up your mind about everything. Is there any reason for me to go into detail?" the captain replied with a tinge of derision.

Christoph looked up from his book, squinted his right eye, and stared back at Foedus. "Not much fight left in you is there? The dark does that to some people. I've seen it many times in my day. Not to myself, of course."

"Of course," Foedus mocked.

The admiral shot him another look but decided not to respond to this quip.

"So, Petram, perhaps you're more inclined to tell me what happened here?"

Petram swallowed hard and cleared his throat before responding weakly. "Well, I don't know all of the details, but I'm willing to give you my side of the story if you're willing to listen. I'm also prepared to speak on Foedus' behalf regarding his decisions. The Rubeus are very unpredictable. We were outnumbered on most accounts, taken by surprise on others."

"Yet two of my men have decided to side with them. How exactly does that happen?"

"That, uh, it's complicated," Petram replied.

"Complicated?" Christoph repeated skeptically.

"Yes, sir." Petram did not wish to get into the details of Veritas and Taree, or Abeo and his desire to abandon the Imperium. Implicating them more would only amplify Christoph's lust to retrieve the deserters.

"Not as extensive of a report as I had hoped for, but very well." He continued to scribble notes down, giving no indication of his feelings towards his subjects. "Where are these beings now?"

"They have a camp set up not far from here," Foedus responded. "We can show you, but they will most likely be hostile considering the circumstances."

"And what exactly are these circumstances, Captain Foedus?"

The captain looked nervously at Petram, then commenced on recounting the story to his superior. He mentioned the incident between Prod and Veritas and the ensuing chaos. He told him of Abeo's betrayal to his people, and how Abeo had ambushed Petram to break his Discipulus out of captivity. Finally, he mentioned the encounter on the cliff and the death of Turpis. His version, however, differed from reality. For the present audience, he felt it best to withhold the history between Turpis and Abeo and their ongoing conflict. Although he was already in a precarious position, Foedus did not wish to make his leadership look any frailer than it already appeared.

"So, Abeo and his new pals broke this kid out of your captivity, and then when you attempted to bring him to justice, he responded violently?" Christoph summarized.

"That's correct," Foedus replied.

"And how did you happen to catch Abeo sneaking away? Did you know he was going to try and break the kid out?" Christoph interrogated.

"I had my suspicions," Foedus replied, "but our encounter was complete chance. Turpis and I were out collecting food and water. We heard their approach and decided to take the opportunity to catch the betrayers."

"And yet not only did they get away, but you also lost a man in the process. How was it that you escaped their grasp? Why did they not just kill you?"

"I cannot say. I asked for no mercy, just that my body be returned to the remaining Seekers so that it could be brought home to the Imperium. Perhaps they had seen enough bloodshed."

A malicious smile spread across Christoph's weathered face. "Not yet they haven't."

"What exactly is your plan of action out here?" Petram asked, nervously awaiting the response.

"It's quite simple actually. We've come here mainly for the jewels and the resources, but the Imperium wants us to look for land we can settle in when the time comes. These people will be given the option of quietly stepping aside and letting us do our jobs, or else they will feel the full weight and strength of the Legion. If they run, we'll let them. If they get in the way, it might be a different story." Christoph opened a box sitting on his desk and removed from it a bundle of copper tokens.

"What are those for?" Petram inquired.

"You see, the Princep has given me explicit orders to squeeze all the riches I can from these lands. He wants to get to it before his father does. What he seems to have forgotten is that there is value in life. From everything I've heard, these creatures are physically capable beings. They have the necessary skills to mine the jewels; now, they can be put to work for the Imperium." He picked up a pile of tokens and shook them in his hand. "Our new friends will be given a simple task: find riches for the Imperium and receive a copper token; don't find riches for the Imperium, don't receive a copper token. Those without tokens may lose more than just their land. There isn't anything quite like cheap labor, is there?"

"You intend on enslaving them?" Petram asked, trying to mask his frustration.

"I'm employing them! They get to work for the vast empire, and, in return, we don't kill every one of them. It's simply the chain-of-command—nature's hierarchy working to perfection."

There was no response from the two Seekers. Foedus had returned to his solitary and quiet demeanour. Their fate had hung in the balance for so long, tension and anxiety had become a normal sensation.

"So, what to do with you two? That's my dilemma, isn't it?" The admiral's manic scribbling never seemed to cease. "What to do, what to do."

"Send us home." The words escaped Petram's mouth before he could catch them. He had never been so upfront with the admiral. Perhaps, in his despair, he had given up hope that things would end well for him. What did he have left to lose?

"Send you home? And have no Seekers out here? I think you forget that these soldiers are not accustomed to the darkness. We lost seven men on the way here from mere stupidity. We could really use your expertise. Send you home, eh? No, no I don't think that will work."

"I'm not staying," Foedus shot back. His stern glare firmly locked on Christoph.

"Boy, the dark sure has made your tongue sharp, hasn't it? Unfortunately, I believe that decision is in my hands, not yours."

"I don't care. Kill me or let me go home. I can't stay here any longer."

At this remark, Christoph put down his quill and looked back up at his long-time companion. "It's been an extensive journey for both of you. Although I can't say you've left things in tip-top condition, you've still made some significant discoveries. Probably the greatest ever by a Seeker. Your names will be alongside mine in the history books. You should be proud!"

Neither man responded to what they deemed were undeserved accolades.

"I'll grant you your leave, but only temporarily. Head home and rest. I'll send a couple of mules and some supplies for your journey home, but I want you both back out here soon. There's lots of work to be done. We've discovered a whole new world!"

Petram nodded and thanked the admiral.

"That will be all for now, gentlemen. You leave as soon as possible.

We'll settle in soon, but I want you back here in a hurry."

Foedus and Petram turned to leave the tent.

"Oh, Foedus, a word in private. One moment, I promise," Christoph said ominously.

The captain looked nervously at Petram, but turned around and walked back to the desk of his boss.

"What happened to the other kid? Proditor, I think his name was."

"He died of his wounds."

"No, that's not quite what happened, is it? You see one of my physicians studied his body. The man's quite a genius when it comes to finding the cause of death, has a real knack for cadavers. *He* tells me that the kid didn't die from his wounds. In fact, he tells me the wounds were healing nicely."

"Is that so?"

"It is indeed. Even more interesting, my guy tells me that the young man was poisoned to death. Imagine that!"

"Poison? How is that possible?"

"I was hoping you would tell me." Christoph glared portentously at Foedus.

"What are you implying?"

"I think you know very well what I'm implying. You see, the kid was sending me letters, keeping me updated and all that. He's the one who tipped me off about these beings before you were even willing to. That must have made you pretty frustrated when you found out, didn't it? One of your men going behind your back to rat you out for not doing your job."

"I wasn't aware of this," Foedus replied, clenching his teeth.

"I'm sure you weren't. I'm sure you didn't want to exact revenge on someone who betrayed you. Someone who you thought had the utmost respect for you, dangling that respect before you like a treat, only to throw it away. I'm sure that's not the case at all."

Foedus uttered nothing; his hands were clammy, but he hid any tell his exterior may have exposed. "We do what we have to," he stated calmly.

"Indeed we do," Christoph grinned. The two men locked eyes, both searching for a hint of partisanship behind their stern exteriors; instead, all they found were reciprocated steely glares. "Go home, get some rest. Eat something. You look like those disgusting beggars on the street. When you return, I'll let you try and mend the shattered pieces of your reputation."

Foedus nodded and said no more. He knew he would not return. This conversation was hypothetical at best. It was a dream, a facade that both parties engaged in. The arrow of time sifted the chunks of life into finer and finer grains; his shattered reputation was a natural outcome. Eventually, all order collapses into disorder; the thought finally resonated in his mind. Like the gradual processes that shaped the beautiful valleys, the monstrous mountains, the winding creeks and rivers, and the twinkling stars above, Foedus was just another moving piece in the machine of time and space, moving aimlessly and continuously towards a knowing unknown.

Not long after his conversation with Christoph, Foedus and Petram, the last of the Seekers of the Unknown, began their arduous journey back to a home where they no longer belonged.

44

Sanuye guided them through a labyrinth of jagged rock. Abeo shuffled his feet diligently, using as much guidance from the surrounding walls as possible. Even for him, the darkness was overwhelming. Veritas and Taree walked hand-in-hand in front of him. The young girl refused to let go of her lover.

"How much farther?" Abeo yelled from the back. His voice was as hollow as the cavern they traversed in. They had been walking non-stop for what seemed like ages. His breath became heavy and his legs weakened.

"Soon," Sanuye shot back. The warrior's pace refused to wane.

Abeo tiredly sighed. He wiped the sweat from his wrinkled forehead and begrudgingly pushed his sore legs against the hard incline. Sanuye was guiding them to his cousin's camp. Buried deep within the unknown, the white man assured his dark friends they would be safe there. In Sanuye's mind, the murky men of the Imperium would not dare venture farther inland, especially with the dark season approaching. He maintained the notion that, despite the mishaps that had already taken place, there was still peace and understanding to be had with the people of the Imperium.

Sanuye's naivety scared and saddened Abeo. He knew he would have to eventually tell his friend the grim reality undeservingly bestowed upon his people. For Sanuye, the friendship he and Abeo had built represented what could be. He simply could not believe that men like Turpis represented the majority. Even if they didn't individually share the communal beliefs, the average person would be hard-pressed to publically say otherwise. Go with the flow; conform to the norm. Easy choices are made because nature minimizes resistance.

"Is it true what he said?" Veritas turned and mumbled to Abeo.

"Who?"

"Turpis. Did you actually convince your wife and her sister to join the rebellion?"

Abeo sighed and paused. "I'm sure you've heard that I once had a son. He looked very much like you. When he was very young, only a toddler, he became violently ill. Cura and I took him to every healer in Crepusculum looking for a cure, but we found no remedy. Then, one day, Foedus told me he had heard that the Imperator's nephew had developed a similar illness and had been successfully treated by the royal healers."

Veritas lingered to walk beside Abeo. His brilliant blue eyes hovered in the darkness.

Abeo continued. "So, I took my son to Lux, I went right to the Palatium Imperium and beseeched the Imperator to save my son. At first, he laughed. He told me how preposterous it was that a Seeker be allowed the services of the royal healers. But I would not be deterred. Relentlessly, I begged for him to treat my son. Finally, the Imperator conceded. He granted me access to a healer by the name of Stultus who had remedied children with similar afflictions before. Truthfully, I was relieved."

"So what happened?" Veritas asked anxiously.

"I brought my boy to Stultus. He took one look at my son and shook his head. He told me that my child was an abomination, claiming that his pale skin and blue eyes were a curse from God. Stultus believed divine justice caused the illness. In the eyes of the Imperium, my boy deserved to die. It was the will of the heavens."

"So he just refused to treat him?"

"He did. And, because of Stultus' reputation, other healers in the Imperium became too afraid to even come near my son. My little boy died slowly in his bed because one ignominious moron with a notable reputation proclaimed he deserved to die. It was at this moment that I realized I didn't belong in the Imperium; I didn't want to belong. I couldn't justify partaking in a society that allowed an innocent child to die because of his father's social status and some erroneous spiritual belief. Maybe it's fitting that the same blue eyes that cursed my son blessed you out here."

Veritas said nothing. He put his hand on Abeo's shoulder; it was all that could be done. For the next while, the group continued on in silence. After extensive trekking through dark passages, the tunnel significantly narrowed.

Abeo crawled through a tight crevice and felt a sharp object dig into his back. Pushing up against the rock, his skin cells clung together, desperately trying not to break. Then, as the cave opened up, the sound of trickling water tickled the inside of his ears. Following Veritas carefully, he crawled through the final stony stricture and felt the immense relief of fresh air entering his lungs.

Looking across the opening, Abeo saw an immense plateau overlooking a sprawling mountain range. Water trickled down the adjacent cliff, meandering through the maze of miniature trenches that had been carved out from eons of erosion. As he looked upon the vista, Abeo saw diminutive bundles of yellow lights interspersed within the expanse. They were other villages, buried within the mountainous womb.

"Are we stopping here?" Abeo asked.

"Rest now. Climb after. Then down again," Sanuye replied as he bundled ignasaxum. He successfully concocted a fire, and the four of them lay down around it and attempted to get some overdue sleep.

***

When Abeo awoke, the others were still soundly resting. He had no idea how long he had been asleep for, but his body told him it had been a short and uncomfortable nap. Quietly, he got up and walked towards the cliff to take in the mesmerizing view one more time. The dancing neon lights had returned to their usual stage, ready to perform another spectacular show.

Looking to his right, Abeo noticed a narrow path and decided to follow it. Negotiating the terrain carefully, he climbed up the skinny trail, teetering nervously close to the daunting cliff. Near the top, the path flattened and revealed a small cliff exposing an even more astounding view. Looking for a place to sit, Abeo placed himself on a flat boulder and absorbed the panorama. Inhaling deeply, he relaxed the muscles in his body. He focused intently on the gentle movement of his chest, peered inside of his mind, and escaped the confines of his self. Breathing softly, he resonated harmoniously with his surroundings.

Searching through his memories, he looked for Cura's embrace. He thought about her chestnut hair and caramel skin; he conjured her calming voice in his mind, replaying it like a recording over and over. Although he knew that she was gone, he could still feel her existence. She lived in his memories; she flooded his brain with hardwired neural connections. She was, physically, a part of him. Her existence was defined by the relationships she had when she was alive. To him, that was all that mattered.

Abeo opened his eyes and returned from his internal exploration. Surveying the horizon, his gaze followed a circuitous trail scanning up and down the endless black perimeter of the rocky range. Something peculiar caught Abeo's eye but, before he could investigate further, his attention was hooked by the sound of approaching footsteps.

Emerging from the darkness, the silhouette of Sanuye materialized. His pale skin glowed eerily against the opaque veil from which he appeared. He moved his way up the steep trail and stood stoically in front of Abeo. He didn't say anything, he simply gazed back at his friend with his bright cherry eyes, knowing full well that something was bothering him.

"Beautiful light," Abeo proclaimed, waving his hands towards the sky.

"What wrong, Skan?" Sanuye asked.

Abeo motioned for him to sit down, and Sanuye obliged. "I have a great fear, my friend. Fear for the future of the Atanak."

Sanuye did not seem concerned by this claim. "Atanak have many great warriors. Atanak can protect. No worry, Skan."

Abeo sighed. He knew it was time that he revealed the truth to his friend. "There is something you need to know. The Imperium is far more powerful than you could possibly imagine. They have greater numbers, better weapons, more advanced technology, and a stronger desire for violence and bloodshed. They will come for the Atanak; they will destroy anyone who gets in their way."

"Atanak move well. We can escape the dark men."

"For a time, maybe. But eventually, they will find a way to capture every possible piece of land. Like a fungus spreading its reach, the Imperium will proliferate until everything they want is theirs."

The news continued to have little effect on Sanuye. He seemed to understand the words that Abeo said, but the true severity of the situation was lost on him.

"Wakan will protect us," he stated calmly.

Abeo shook his head, "I'm afraid not even Wakan can stop the coming storm."

"How many dark men will come?" asked Sanuye.

Abeo sat in silence, pointed to the sky, and looked at his friend. "More than the stars in the sky."

At this, the full weight of what Abeo was revealing fell upon Sanuye's mind. His eyes widened and, for the first time since the inception of their friendship, Abeo saw fear in his eyes.

"Why do the dark men want to hurt Atanak?"

"Because they are selfish; they will do anything that gives them greater riches and power. We are flawed creatures in this world, trying our best to make sense of the complicated nature of reality. Why should one being be more prestigious than another? Do we not all share this cosmos? Are we not all rooted in the same seed?" Abeo took a deep breath and tossed a loose stone over the cliff in frustration.

"Do not fear, Skan. Atanak here and now. Skan and Sanuye here and now. This is what matters, no?"

Abeo smiled at his friend and watched as Taree and Veritas emerged from behind him. Veritas sat down beside Abeo and put his arm around his Praeceptoris. "Not the worst view these eyes have ever seen," he said with a gentle grin.

Abeo sighed and stared at the Spiral Cloud illuminating the valley below. Maybe somewhere out there, buried in that cosmic swirl, was another world. Maybe there was another place that got it right; a place where people weren't exploited or enslaved; a place where the meaning of home was much more universal. Instead, Abeo was confined to his world, where his efforts to coexist were like a struggling vessel, perpetually beat back against the relentless current.

Abeo looked over at his friend and saw a somber man staring longingly at the beautiful expanse. He put his dark arm around Sanuye's white shoulders and his other around his young companions. Four people sat in harmonious silence and watched, for the first time, a blood-red sunrise.

Finally, Abeo was home.

About the Author

M.A.T. Reeson is an independent writer who lives in Edmonton, Canada. He is currently working towards a degree in clinical psychology and spends much of his free time writing. *Seekers of the Unknown* is his debut novel.

Thank you so much for reading one of our **Sci-Fi** novels.
If you enjoyed our book, please check out our recommended title for your next great read!

People of Metal by Robert Snyder

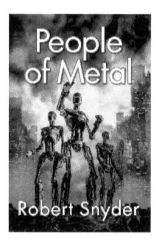

The well-intentioned leaders of China and the U.S. form a grand partnership to create human robots for every human vocation in every country in the world. The human robots proliferate, economic output soars, and the entire world prospers. It's a new Golden Age. But there are unintended consequences—consequences that will place biological humanity on a road to extinction. Ultimately, it will fall to the human robots themselves to rescue biological humanity and restore its civilization.

View other Black Rose Writing titles at www.blackrosewriting.com/books and use promo code **PRINT** to receive a **20% discount** when purchasing

CPSIA information can be obtained
at www.ICGtesting.com
Printed in the USA
LVHW041929221218
601131LV00002B/12/P